MW00475800

MURDER THROUGH AN OPEN DOOR

A PIPPIN LANE HAWTHORNE MYSTERY

MELISSA BOURBON

LAKE HOUSE PRESS

Published by Lake House Press

Cover Design by Mariah Sinclair | www.mariahsinclair.com

Print ISBN 978-0-9978661-7-9

PIPPIN LANE HAWTHORNE (BOOK MAGIC) MYSTERIES

The Secret on Rum Runner's Lane, a prequel
Murder in Devil's Cove, book 1
Murder at Sea Captain's Inn, book 2
Murder Through an Open Door, book 3
Murder and an Irish Curse, book 4

NEWSLETTER SIGN UP

Join my newsletter mailing list at https://melissabourbon.com/newsletter-sign-up/and receive a free exclusive copy of *The Bookish Kitchen*, a compilation of recipes from my different series.

For Caleb, Sophia, Jared, Sam, and Alex, with love.

And with gratitude and appreciation to every Book Warrior out there.

PRAISE FOR THE BOOK MAGIC MYSTERIES

#1 Amazon Bestseller!

"A combination of magic and mystery, "Murder In Devil's Cove" by Melissa Bourbon is a deftly crafted and impressively original novel by an author with a genuine flair for originality. While certain to be an unusual, immediate and enduringly popular addition to community library Mystery/Suspense collections, it should be noted for the personal reading lists of anyone who enjoys Women's Friendship Fiction, Cozy Animal Mysteries, or Supernatural Mysteries..."

–Midwest Book Review

"...Close reading as a super power[!] MURDER IN DEVIL'S COVE ha[s] all the makings of an original, unique story with a lovely tilt in advocacy towards literature fanatics. The heroine nature from Cassie's perspective was strong, and the female power got even better as Pippin grows up. Also, as a big fan of the Odyssey myself, I absolutely loved the role the epic played in guiding the narrative...Overall, I think this is a rewarding day read. The pages turn easily, and the characters are gripping enough for the reader to latch onto their motives and goals."

-29th Annual Writer's Digest Self-Published Book Awards

"The unraveling of the mystery involves Pippin's family

history (it goes all the way back to Roman times in Ireland), hidden clues, a long-lost keepsake, and a secret room. For mystery fans who enjoy amateur detectives who rely on mystical insights rather than Holmesian deductions, Murder in Devil's Cove will provide an entertaining read."

–Seattle Book Review

"A magical blend of books, mystery, and smart sleuthing. Melissa Bourbon's Murder in Devil's Cove offers mystery readers everything they crave and stands out in the crowded cozy genre. This captivating new series will leave readers spellbound."

~NYT and USA Today Bestselling Author, Ellery Adams

"This tightly woven mystery spins a web of intrigue where magic simmers, waiting for the perfect time to surface. I can't wait to read more about Pippin and what awaits her in the next Book Magic adventure."

~Dru Ann Love, Dru's Book Musings

Praise for Murder in Devil's Cove

This book had me at 'book magic' and wrapped me up in its unique plot from start to finish! . . . I really enjoyed the set-up, the plot, the characters and the setting; they all added intriguing layers to the story. . .

~Reading Is My SuperPower

I thought the author beautifully intertwined magic and mystery...Murder in Devil's Cove is an intriguing tale with forbidden books, a departed dad, family folklore, mysterious magic, renovation revelations, and one bewildered bibliomancer.

~The Avid Reader

This book totally sucked me in as the story tells the past as well as the present . . . a truly magical read for fans of cozies with a slight magical flair.

I totally loved it so I give it 5/5 stars.

~Books a Plenty Book Reviews

Filled with quirky characters and atmospheric descriptions of the quaint town of Devil's Cove, Bourbon hits all the right notes for a cozy: amateur sleuthing, several possible suspects, bookstores, and a touch of romance.

~Elena Taylor, Author

Blending a family curse and a hint of the paranormal with an intriguing mystery MURDER IN DEVIL'S COVE is a fantastic start to a new series.

~Cozy Up With Kathy

Praise for The Secret on Rum Runner's Lane

The Secret on Rum Runner's Lane by Melissa Bourbon is a fantastical book that I loved diving into. It was great from the first chapter to the ending.

~Baroness' Book Trove

This is the prequel to this new series and it had me hooked on the concept, the setting. and the characters.

~Storeybook Reviews

It may be a short story but it gives a thorough introduction of the characters as well as a picturesque view of Devil's

Cove. Sure to pique the interest of cozy lovers looking for a mini-mystery to draw them into a new series.

~*Books a Plenty Book Reviews*

. . . this was a quick read about characters that you immediately care about in a picturesque setting (two, actually).

~*I Read What You Write!*

THE SECRET ON RUM RUNNER'S LANE captures the uncertainty and underlying strength of women searching for their place in the world. It allows readers to get a glimpse of the past while seeing the glimmer of what's to come.

~*Cozy Up With Kathy*

The Secret on Rum Runner's Lane is a layered story with a well-developed backstory for a character whose decisions in that time period set the path for generations to come.

~*Reading Is My SuperPower*

The setting is enchanting with realistic characters you can root for. The mystery is perfectly solvable based on the clues hidden within the text. The paranormal aspect is an original idea.

~*Diane Reviews Books*

The author brings the story to life with her character development and vivid setting. I could feel Cassie's pain dealing with her family curse. I was totally transported into her world.

~*Socrates' Book Reviews...*

Praise for Murder at Sea Captain's Inn

*"**Melissa Bourbon has penned another outstanding adventure.**"* ~Kings River Life Magazine

*"**A born storyteller,** with a compelling and heart-warming style of writing which put me right at ease, author Melissa Bourbon has effortlessly and confidently developed Pippin into a tenacious and largely intuitive amateur sleuth, alongside her many other attributes, which include teaching sign language to a loyal and handsome 'Sailor' of the four-legged variety!* -Yvonne at Fiction Books

***Murder at Sea Captain's Inn** by Melissa Bourbon is an intriguing and well-written installment in what **has quickly become one of my fave series.** The elements of magical realism are what makes this series stand out from the rest, and this latest novel whets your appetite for even more."* -Reading is My Superpower

*"MURDER AT SEA CAPTAIN'S INN provides **an intriguing multilayered mystery.** The Lost Colony, the Lane family curse, family relationships, and mysterious connections converge creating an intensely captivating story. Readers' minds must be alert and nimble, sorting through the clues divined by literary classics and those craftily left by the author."* -Cozy Up With Kathy

"There are several layers to this mystery and the magical

*power of bibliomancy became one of the best parts of the story . . . **This is the first book I've read in the series and really loved it!"***

~Books To The Ceiling

"Full of plenty of clues while still keeping you guessing until the end. The use of bibliomancy is a nice touch as well as the adorable deaf dog Sailor."

~Books a Plenty Book Reviews

***"Ms. Bourbon writes in a way that makes the reader captivated and completely part of the story.** I love this story and the characters."*

~Baroness' Book Trove

Praise for Murder and an Irish Curse

*"I wholeheartedly recommend!...This book is rich with mythology and history with a bit of intriguing spell-casting and tarot, and the multi-generational characters add an exciting range of personalities from helpful to interfering, from sane to quirky, from open to secretive, from good to evil...**Top contender for my Best of 2022!"*** ~Kings River Life Magazine

***"To say it's a page turner is not doing it justice.** The writing is so well done that the reader feels as though they are actually entrenched with the characters experiencing all the twists and turns that kept me enthralled throughout."* ~Amazon Reader

"I can honestly say that I could not stop reading this once I started..." ~Amazon Reader

"I do not know where to begin with a review of this book except to say that this series remains one of the best I have ever read." ~a BookBub Reader

"This series quickly became a favorite, and this book's a prime example of why. The book is well-written with well-rounded characters, and a well-thought-out, original plot. The various relationships are well-done. ***I was drawn into this enchanting story from the beginning and kept hooked throughout."*** ~a BookBub Reader

"The book's nail-biting conclusion and the events leading up to it will have readers holding their breath! ...The author puts the reader in a perfectly rendered Outer Banks setting. ***She brings myth and legend to life and her imaginary characters come alive on the page. Kudos for an outstanding cozy!"*** ~a Goodreads Reader

"No ***matter how much I tried to slow myself down while reading this book, I just wasn't successful. I flew through this book.*** *I wanted to slow down because I could tell we were coming to an end and I wasn't ready."* ~Amazon Reader

*"**The author expertly weaves a tale with enough twists and turns that will keep you guessing until the very end** where the answer to the mystery is hiding in plain sight."* ~Amazon Reader

Praise for Murder Through an Open Door

*"**Page turning Spellbinder**...Beyond the richness of this tale is the strong weaving of Pippin's inner experience and the tenacity it takes to let love in."* ~Amazon Reader

*"**Without needing to think about it, 5/5 stars with ease!**...Now I'm left chomping at the bits for the next book in this series!"* ~Amazon Reader

*"**I can hardly wait for the next book in this must-read Book Magic series.**"* ~Amazon Reader

*"**Melissa Bourbon blockbuster fourth book in her Book Magic Mystery series is a must read** with a delightful writing style, complex ongoing mystery, wonderful characters, and a fascinating premise two-thousand years in the making..."* ~a BookBub Reader

*"**I love this series!** An intriguing mix of murder mystery, Irish*

myth, and family lore, with a touch of fantasy." ~Diane Kelly, mystery author

"I am happy to say that it was every bit as good as the first two, and has left me eagerly anticipating the next installment! " ~Cozy Mystery Review Crew

"Once I had finished the first chapter, I got chills up my spine and quickly set to work devouring this book. *Pippin is such an interesting character, and I absolutely loved the bibliomancy magic that the author weaves into these pages...5 out of 5 stars."* ~Bunny's Reviews

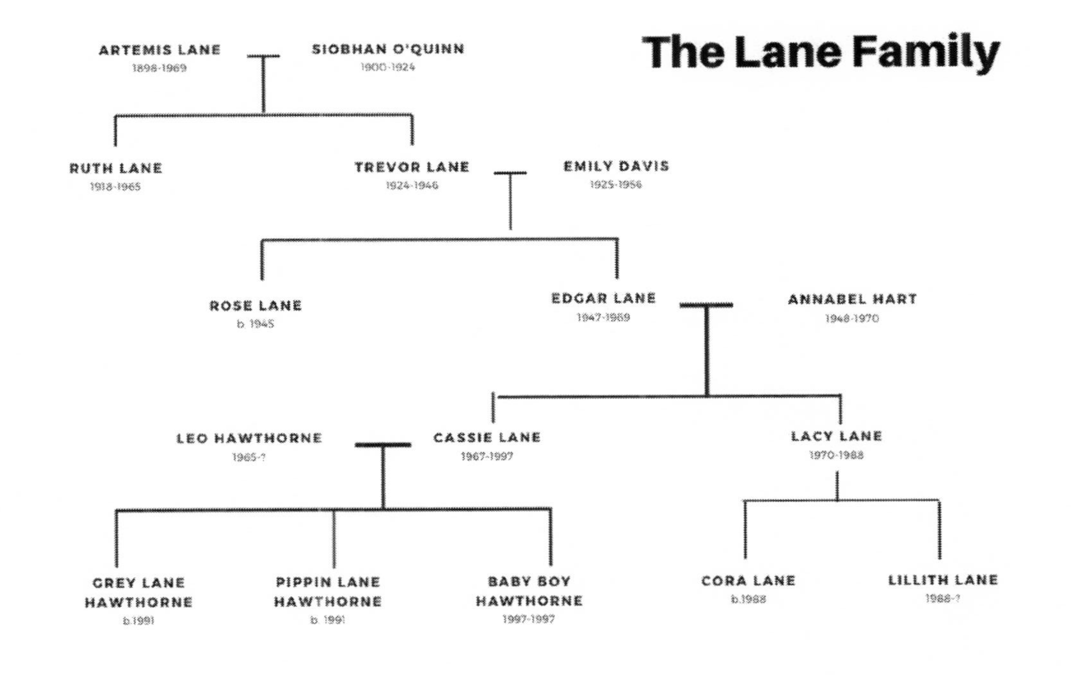
The Lane Family
ARTEMIS LANE
1898-1969
SIOBHAN O'QUINN
1900-1924
RUTH LANE
1918-1965
TREVOR LANE
1924-1946
EMILY DAVIS
1925-1956
ROSE LANE
b. 1945
EDGAR LANE
1947-1969
ANNABEL HART
1948-1970
LEO HAWTHORNE
1965-?
CASSIE LANE
1967-1997
LACY LANE
1970-1988
GREY LANE HAWTHORNE
b.1991
PIPPIN LANE HAWTHORNE
b. 1991
BABY BOY HAWTHORNE
1997-1997
CORA LANE
b.1988
LILLITH LANE
1988-?

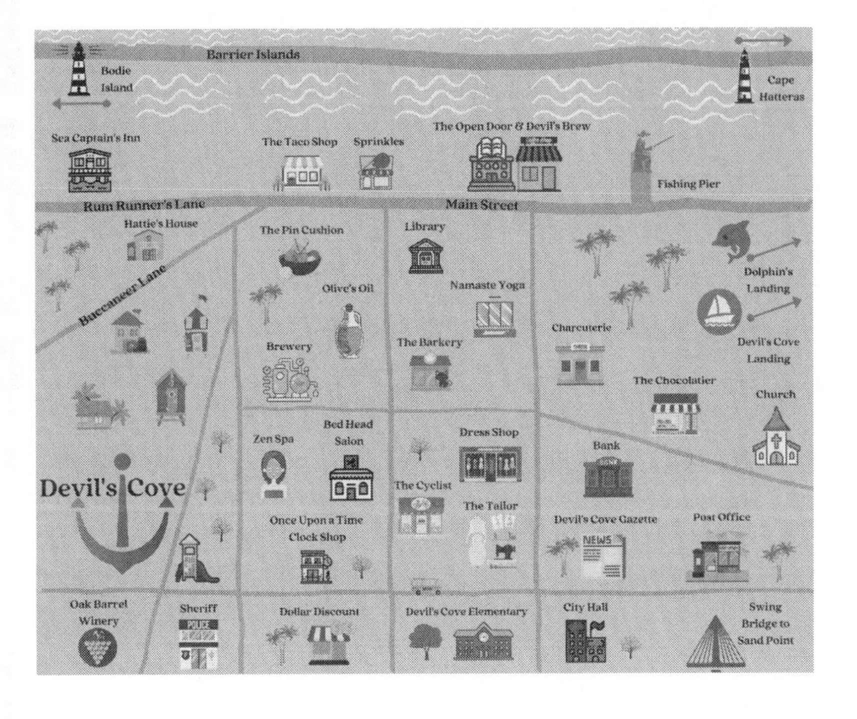
Barrier Islands
Bodie Island
Cape Hatteras
Sea Captain's Inn
The Taco Shop
Sprinkles
The Open Door & Devil's Brew
Fishing Pier
Rum Runner's Lane
Main Street
Hattie's House
The Pin Cushion
Library
Buccaneer Lane
Olive's Oil
Namaste Yoga
Dolphin's Landing
Devil's Cove Landing
Charcuterie
Brewery
The Barkery
The Chocolatier
Church
Zen Spa
Bed Head Salon
Dress Shop
Bank
Devil's Cove
The Cyclist
The Tailor
Once Upon a Time Clock Shop
Devil's Cove Gazette
NEWS
Post Office
Oak Barrel Winery
Sheriff
POLICE
Dollar Discount
Devil's Cove Elementary
City Hall
Swing Bridge to Sand Point

MURDER THROUGH AN OPEN DOOR

A Faery Song

Sung by the people of Faery over Diarmuid and Grania, in their bridal sleep under a Cromlech.

We who are old, old and gay,
O so old!
Thousands of years, thousands of years,
If all were told:

Give to these children, new from the world,
Silence and love;
And the long dew-dropping hours of the night,
And the stars above:

Give to these children, new from the world,
Rest far from men.
Is anything better, anything better?
Tell us it then:

Us who are old, old and gay,
O so old!
Thousands of years, thousands of years,
If all were told."
— **W.B. Yeats, The Rose**

PROLOGUE

You'll never convince me there is a hopeless situation or there is any finality in any success or any failure.
~Carlos Ghosn

GREY LANE HAWTHORNE was born seventy-three seconds before Pippin. As twins tended to be, they were connected by invisible threads. Lately, a few of those threads had broken. Grey had severed the first one by starting Hawthorne Custom Woodworking, leaving Sea Captain's Inn for Pippin to run alone. Pippin knew more tears in the fabric that held them together would come, but as much as she knew it would hurt, she knew they had to. Despite the challenges they'd faced, the last few months had shown her that they could support each other while still living their own lives.

"I'll still be right here on Devil's Cove," Grey had said when he'd told her he'd bought an old farmhouse with a barn and silo. He'd pointed to Sea Captain's Inn, the house they'd inherited that had once belonged to their parents. "Just not right *here*."

It had been an adjustment, but Pippin was getting used to living alone. "Only, you don't live alone," her friend, Ruby Monroe, had told her. "At any given time, you have a houseful of guests. This island is a vacation spot. I'd bet Devil's Brew, right down to the very last cookie in the bakery case, that you're *never* going post a No Vacancy sign."

The majority of visitors to the Outer Banks chose Roanoke because of its Lost Colony history. Or they headed all way to the southern end of Hatteras and take the ferry to Ocracoke. Or they took the more touristy route—Nags Head; Kill Devil Hills; Kitty Hawk. Pippin quickly realized, though, that Ruby was right. Even surrounded by other options for vacations, there were more than enough tourists interested in taking the road less traveled. And for their effort, they discovered the island's charm. They experienced the quaint downtown, the streets named after ships and captains and of times long past, and the amiable locals. They learned about maritime lore, tried wreck diving, and stared with awe upon the old houses along Rum Runner's Lane that face east. Devil's Cove was less popular than some of the other Outer Banks's locales, but it was still a destination spot.

Pippin looked at her brother sitting across from her at a bistro table on the back deck of Sea Captain's Inn. The view of Roanoke Sound spread out before them. The two-hundred mile stretch of barrier islands known as the Outer Banks created a buffer between the four sounds and the Atlantic Ocean. The faint sound of water lapping on her private stretch of beach seeped into her, like lotion being absorbed into her skin, calming her mind and soothing her heart. Sailor, her honey-colored rescue Vizsla, lay curled up at her feet.

Dry flecks of stain and paint from his woodworking marked Grey's skin. A bottle of beer dangled from one hand. As he stared out over the expanse of water, she could practically read his thoughts. "Greevie," she said, calling him by his childhood nickname, "The Lane family is not going to die out with us."

He turned his grey-green eyes to look at her and cast a wry smile. "The way we can read each other's thoughts, we should have become a circus act," he said.

He spoke the truth. Growing up, they'd finished each other's sentences and anticipated what the other was thinking. They'd had their own language and their own way of communicating. Some of that had dissipated as they'd grown older, but they were still bound together—two halves of a whole. "The Mighty Mind Reading Hawthornes," she said, spreading her hands out in the air in front of her as if they were revealing a circus marquee where they were the headliners.

They fell silent for a few minutes, small smiles on their faces. Behind them, in the west, the sun had begun making its descent. The day had turned to twilight. Before long, darkness would fall and only the distant lights from across the sound would be visible. "We have no idea how to stop it," Grey said.

Of course, he was referring to the ancient curse that had plagued their family for two thousand years. "We'll figure it out. We have no choice. It's that, or we die," she said, acknowledging the power of the curse that caused the Lane women to die in childbirth and the men to be swallowed by the sea.

He grimaced. “Or I stay off the water, like you want me to, and neither of us ever have children.”

“It’s possible,” she said, only she wasn’t sure if she really believed that. Leo, their father, wasn’t a Lane by birth, but he still died. Not swallowed by the sea, but still… It had been the same with Annabel Hart. She died giving birth to Pippin and Grey’s mother, Cassie, and her twin, Lacy—even though it was her husband Edgar who had carried the Lane blood.

“Anything’s possible,” he grumbled, “but are those the lives we want to live?”

Pippin bit her lower lip, staring into the growing darkness. The truth was, she did want to fall in love and have children. She wanted to cradle her newborn baby, to watch him or her learn to walk and talk and grow up. She wanted to be a grandmother. She wanted to live her life without worrying about the future. She wanted to have a family that wasn’t doomed to an unchangeable fate. “No, it’s not the life *I* want to live, and I know it’s not the one *you* want to live,” she said, “but we don’t have to. We can figure out how to break it.”

Grey took a long pull from his beer. “Peevie,” he said with a sigh, “if Dad couldn’t figure it out, how are we supposed to?”

Her exhalation was long and heavy. “He was close to figuring it out, though. And we have his notes to help us. He started with nothing. There’s something we’re missing though. We just have to figure out what it is.”

They fell into still silence again. The automatic porch light Grey had installed with the renovations turned off. Only lights from the barrier islands and the stars in the blue-black sky shone faintly. From the way Grey tilted his chin down and raised his eyes to her, Pippin knew exactly what he was thinking. *Isn't that what we've been trying to do?* He left the other question that loomed in both of their minds unspoken. *How, exactly, were they supposed to figure out what they were missing?*

CHAPTER 1

"There is no medicine like hope, no incentive so great, and no tonic so powerful as expectation of something better tomorrow."

~Orison Swett Marden

THE EVENING SKY was streaked with purples, reds, and blues by the time Pippin had finished tidying the living room and prepping the morning's breakfast. Running Sea Captain's Inn was often a twenty-four-hour job. She had phone calls roll over to an answering machine after six o'clock p.m. She' had learned that lesson after receiving calls at one o'clock, three o'clock, and even four-thirty in the morning. People kept strange hours, and sometimes didn't stop to consider that other people and businesses didn't follow the same irregular schedules.

Cleaning, laundry, and cooking topped the list of the ongoing tasks. On the menu was baked blueberry strata accompanied by fruit and sausage. Her grandmother's recipe box sat on a shelf in the kitchen, the cards with

Pippin's and Grey's favorites stained from use. Every day she prepared something new, so the guests never had the same breakfast twice. It made for a lot of planning, required efficient processes, and resulted in leftovers she often ate for dinner. This evening, she ate two eggs smothered with that morning's Shakshuka sauce. The garlicky tomato sauce was spiced with harissa and was topped with crumbled feta. She sat in the rocking chair on the wrap-around porch of Sea Captain's Inn facing west. She crossed the front panels of her sweater and let the cool temperature of late fall settle around her. As she finished her meal the sun set, ushering in the darkness.

Cars drove slowly down Rum Runner's Lane as people ambled down the sidewalks. The automatic porch light illuminated the area with her movement. She caught a glimpse of Morgan, the crow that had adopted Sea Captain's Inn, gliding past. Pippin knew the bird would circle around and perch atop the widows' walk. It was the crow's routine.

After finishing her meal, Pippin picked up the worn envelope she'd brought out to the porch with her. She turned it over and over and over in her hands. It was in response to the missive she had sent to her Great-Aunt Rose, asking about her mother's necklace and the ancient fragment of a scroll discovered hidden away in her father's secret study. She had to have read it at least a hundred times, looking for any bit of information that could help her figure out how to stop the two-thousand-year-old curse that plagued the Lane family.

The envelope was as worn as one of her grandmother's beloved recipe cards. She slipped the single sheet of stationery from the envelope. The paper had lost its crispness, the two creases of the trifold letter, once sharp, were now soft and indistinct.

My Dearest Peregrine,

What an odd coincidence that I should receive a letter from you today, after so many years and across so many miles. Just yesterday, I was cleaning out a cupboard and discovered your mother's copy of The Secret Garden. She loved that book so much, I think she must have read it a dozen times or more. Her name, with the curlicue "C," is inscribed on the flyleaf, and I spent moments just tracing it with my finger, remembering your mother's smile. I swear the flowers in the garden used to turn their faces to her, because she was brighter even than the sun.

But then the book fell to the floor, almost as though it were pushed from my hands, and when the pages fluttered still, I saw the words your mother was trying to give to me: "It was in that strange and sudden way that Mary found out that she had neither father nor mother left; that they had died and been carried away in the night."

It sent a chill down my spine, Peregrine. A harbinger of death. But whose? I do not know. I was just overwhelmed by a fear for you and for Grey.

Please be careful, my dear.

In your letter you mentioned that you found a fragment of a document among your mother's things. The letter from Morgan to her soldier, Titus. I wonder if it is related to the parchment that was tucked in your mother's book? It was just a scrap, and written in some old language. But the torn fragment was wrapped in a piece of notebook paper, and it looks like someone—perhaps your mother?—had made an effort to translate. It's just a handful of words: "Lir," "pact or contract," "descendants," "tribute? offering? sacrifice?"

Life has taught me that there is no such thing as coincidence. Finding your mother's book, finding the fragment of parchment, and then receiving your letter, out of the blue, the very next day? It means something. The family curse has been quiet for years, since your mother's death. But I feel that the magic is rumbling to life again.

With deepest love,
Your Aunt Rose

SHE LAY the worn page next to a newer, small package wrapped in brown paper on the bistro table. She let her fingertips dance across the hard exterior. She knew what it was. After reading the letter from Aunt Rose, Pippin had immediately written back to ask if she would send her Cassie's copy of *The Secret Garden*.

Days passed. Then weeks. Every day, Pippin checked the mailbox, her heart in her throat. Each day, her heart sank back into place, disappointed. With no word from Aunt Rose for so long, she had finally given up.

And then, today, it miraculously arrived. Pippin had put it in her office, waiting until the moment she could give it her undivided attention. Now was that moment.

It was wrapped in plain brown paper and addressed to Pippin in shaky script that betrayed Aunt Rose's age. Pippin and her twin brother Grey were twenty-nine, knocking on thirty's door. Aunt Rose was their late mother's aunt, which meant that she had to be close to ninety. Pippin peeled back the translucent tape on the small package. Her breath caught. There, cradled in the brown paper was an old copy of *The Secret Garden*. Green cloth covered the front and back boards, as well as the spine. On the front cover was a frame of climbing flowers. Inside the frame was a beautiful illustration of a little girl with curly blond hair wearing an orange coat and hat. She bent toward a garden wall, inserting a key into a mostly covered door. The title was captured in a gold scroll across the top of the cover, Frances Hodgson Burnett's name on a matching scroll beneath the illustration of the girl.

The book was old, but in good condition. Pippin carefully opened the front cover, turning to the copyright page. 1911, by Phillips Publishing Company. She immediately pulled out her cell phone and dialed Jamie McAdams, the proprietor of The Open Door Bookshop and an expert on old and rare books.

He answered on the third ring. "Hey there, Pip. Miss me already?"

She had seen him that afternoon when he'd stopped by to pick up his two daughters. Heidi and Mathilda had been coming around every afternoon to play with Sailor. Together, they were all learning sign language commands to communicate with the deaf dog. The truth was, she liked seeing Jamie on the regular, but giving in to any developing feelings was something she avoided at all cost. The Lane women were cursed. They died in childbirth. Likewise, the men were swallowed by the sea. Love was not in Pippin's future unless she and Grey could figure out how to break the curse. "Hey," she said, choosing not to answer his flirtatious question. Instead, she went straight to the reason for her call. "What year was *The Secret Garden* published?"

"Cut right to the chase, eh? Okay, let me think. 1910...no, 1911. At least in America. Maybe 1909 or 1910 in England. Right around there, anyway. Why?"

Pippin's breath caught. "It's a first edition."

"What is?"

Jamie knew about the letter from Aunt Rose. He knew everything about the pact Morgan Dubhshláine made with the Irish sea god, Lir. He knew about the resulting curse that pact had laden the Lane family with. And he knew how her mother and father, and now she and Grey, were trying to break it. "The book finally came," she said. "From Aunt Rose."

"And it's a first edition?"

Pippin could hear the excitement in his voice. His shop had new books, but primarily it was a used bookstore. He had a back room where he housed rare books, running a robust online business. Rare book collectors trusted Jamie's finds. "The copyright page says 1911. Twice," she said, noting the August 1911 date also enclosed in a box with the publisher's logo.

Aunt Rose's letter mentioned Cassie's name, with its curlicued C, written on the flyleaf. Pippin hadn't known what a flyleaf was, but Jamie had told her. Now she knew it was part of the endsheet. It technically could have something printed on it, but in this case the very first page was blank, except for two words written in pencil: Cassandra Lane. Just like Aunt Rose did, Pippin traced her finger over the letters of her mother's name.

"Pippin?" Jamie's voice came just as the crow suddenly appeared, soaring overhead then swooping down like a fighter plane, doing a barrel roll. Pippin jerked with a gasp, and the book fell. Then she felt her pulse ratchet up. It happened almost as Aunt Rose described in her letter—as if someone had pushed it.

"Pippin?" Jamie's voice again. "Are you okay?"

She blinked. Came back to the moment. "Yeah, yeah, I'm fine. I'll call you back," she said, and abruptly hung up.

Then she bent to retrieve the book, letting her gaze skim over the lines of the open pages. One sentence undulated. Slowly, the letters seemed to peel off the pages, as if they were nothing more than a sticker being pulled up. She read them aloud.

"At first people refuse to believe that a strange new thing can be done, then they begin to hope it can be done, then they see it can be done—then it is done and all the world wonders why it was not done centuries ago."

Pippin stared. An icy feeling tiptoed up her spine... because this was a clear message that she *could* break the curse that plagued her family and threatened, not only her future, but her life.

CHAPTER 2

"The world is full of magic things, patiently waiting for our senses to grow sharper."

~W.B. Yeats

HAZEL HOOD HAD APPEARED at Sea Captain's Inn two weeks prior, like Mary Poppins. The traveling innkeeper had a sixth sense that couldn't be explained, but Pippin hadn't needed an explanation. All she cared about was that Hazel had called at the very moment Pippin's head was ready to explode. "I travel all over the country, filling in when an innkeeper needs a vacation," Hazel had said. "I just finished up at a B&B in New Bern. That's not too far away from Devil's Cove. I heard about Sea Captain's Inn and thought I'd come meet you. In case you ever need a break."

New Bern was on the Neuse River; it was a few hours to get to Devil's Cove. Hazel Hood had made it in record time. The moment the woman had walked in, Pippin sensed her capableness. She had made herself at home and started helping out with an intuition that seemed born of more than just nature. Pippin was impressed with how she just seemed to know what needed to be done without being told. Hazel had a good ten—maybe fifteen—years on Pippin and was taller by an inch or two. She kept her blond hair short, and she had a casual style that would blend right in on the island. She carried a faux leather padfolio and a binder with her tried and true recipes. "I've been doing this a long time," she'd said. Pippin breathed a sigh of relief and had hired her on the spot. "I'm not going on vacation, but I need you now. Just until I catch up."

"I can stay until you get ahead," Hazel said, smiling. "I have no jobs currently lined up, so I'm flexible." She settled into the small quarters off the utility room and set to work.

Now, this morning, Hazel had beaten Pippin to the kitchen. She had preheated the oven and had the blueberry strata baking. Sausage links sizzled in the cast iron skillet on the stove. The starter was fruit served in individual green ceramic bowls.

It hadn't taken Pippin long to realize that she needed to implement a breakfast hour for her guests. She hadn't done that initially, and she'd ended up in the kitchen waiting on people for far too long. Now she served breakfast between eight and nine o'clock during the week, and up to nine-thirty on the weekends. After that, the kitchen was closed.

The guests all sat at the long, rustic kitchen table, or, if the weather was nice, on the back deck at the bistro tables. Either way, there was a view of the water and the sailboats, windsurfers, and kayakers that frequently floated by.

Grey had recently finished renovating the bunk rooms on the third floor, which were the last of the spaces to undergo a transformation. When they'd inherited the house, it had been old and decrepit, the abandonment of twenty years visible on the floors, in the walls, and marking every other part of the place. Grey had brought it back to life by gutting and rebuilding the insides and refurbishing the outside. Pippin had designed the interior and decorated with a keen eye to history blended with modern amenities. The living room had two plush sofas, a coffee table, and two chairs on either side, creating a comfortable seating area for guests. She also rented the space out to local groups for meetings and gatherings.

The reclaimed wood of the fireplace mantel was the pièce de résistance. It grounded the room with the rustic vibe that fed Pippin's soul. She had been slowly adding books to the built in shelves along the left wall. Some of her father's maritime art—ships in bottles—were displayed, along with books by local authors and about local history.

Stairs led to the second floor and the three main guest rooms. Sea Captain's Inn had nearly doubled its available occupancy with the bunk rooms on the third floor. Grey had divided the one large space into two separate rooms. One was smaller and had a plush full bed, a small writing desk, and a single armchair. The television was mounted on the wall across from the bed. The other had a queen bed—equally plush—a settee, a small table and chair, and an armoire for the TV. Luggage racks, lamps, rugs, and bathroom amenities completed the spaces. When the rooms were unveiled to Ruby and Daisy, Pippin's best friends on-island—or anywhere—they had stared in awe. "It's gorgeous," Ruby said. Daisy threw up her hands as if she had come to some monumental decision. "That's it. I'm moving in."

The inn had been in operation for just a few months, but already the guests came and went. Weekends were busier, but she was pretty well booked all the time, which meant Hazel Hood was a godsend.

The first of the current guests wandered in and found seats. Pippin and Hazel served the fruit starter, then the strata. Since the dining room with the long, communal table was in a shared space with the kitchen, they tried to keep the noise to a minimum. Pippin drummed her fingers on the countertop, mentally planning her day and waiting for the last couple to finish their coffee. They were checking out today, as was everyone else currently staying. Between eleven and three, Pippin and Hazel would be doing the laundry, cleaning the rooms, and getting everything ready for the incoming guests.

The second the dining table was clear of guests, Hazel flew into action, rinsing the dishes and loading them into the dishwasher. Pippin wrapped up the leftover strata and placed it in the refrigerator. She had gotten better at portion planning. She still frequently had leftovers, but not as much waste as she'd had the first few weeks the inn had been open.

"What's next?" Hazel asked once the kitchen was clean. She had been at the inn for several weeks, gently guiding Pippin occasionally with her expertise, all the while remaining deferential. "Did you finish the checklist?"

"Not yet. I've been working on the operating manual," Pippin said, "but it's not finished." It was another thing on her never-ending list of tasks.

"No problem. I'll restock the guest fridge," she said, and she strode off.

The rest of the day flew by. Eleven came and went. The guests left. While the linens were washing, Pippin and Hazel made up the beds with the second sets Pippin had purchased. They replaced the towels in the bathrooms, along with miniature soaps, shampoos, and body wash. The rugs were vacuumed. The floors were swept. The tubs and sinks and every other surface sparkled by the time they were done.

And then the entire guest check in process, from arrival to departure, started over again with the arrival of the new guests. June Rycliff, seventy-eight, and her fifty-five-year-old daughter, Heather Beadly, came first. They blew in like a gust of wind, happy and breezy and ready for their mother-daughter getaway. Hazel gave them a tour of the house, ending by situating them in the larger of the two third-floor bunk rooms.

Sue and Jefferson Macon, octogenarians who loved Devil's Cove and couldn't wait to try Sea Captain's Inn, arrived next. It was as if Pippin and Hazel were playing tag. Hazel came back to the registration desk—a freestanding counter off to one corner of the great room—just as Pippin and the spry couple left for their tour of the house. "This is lovely," Sue said when they stood in the doorway leading to their room. "Quite different from a hotel, isn't it, dear?"

Jefferson pinched his chin as he considered the space. "I might never want to leave," he said with a smile and a wink. Pippin left the pleasant couple to settle in and crossed paths with Hazel again, this time as she led Nancy and Peter Kernoodle to the largest room in the bed and breakfast. It was part of the two-room suite. The rooms could be booked separately or together, but this week, the smaller room remained unoccupied.

Finally, at four-thirty, Pippin had a moment to breathe. "You should take a break," Hazel told her. "I can cover things for a while."

That was all the encouragement it took. Pippin had no idea what she was going to do once Hazel left Sea Captain's Inn to move on to another job. For now, though, she was going to take advantage of her presence. She took Sailor for a leisurely walk along the beach, practicing their sign language commands. *Stop. Wait. Come.* Each sign became more familiar and easier to summon every time Pippin used them, and each time, Sailor responded to them better and better.

Pippin climbed the stairs to the back deck and went back inside through the door to the utility room. It was one way she could control the sand she tracked into the house. The guests were another matter. She couldn't brush the sand off them. She couldn't require they remove their shoes if they'd been on the beach. As a result, she swept twice a day.

Before stepping inside, she ran her hands up and down her pant legs, then stomped her feet to free any residual sand. She slipped her shoes off, leaving them next to the three-tiered shoe rack. She slipped on her inside slippers and pulled out her cellphone. She hadn't been able to show Jamie her mother's copy of *The Secret Garden* yet. After calling him about it the night before, she thought he might stop by to see the first edition, but he had a bookshop to run, and she had been too busy with the inn's guests to run over to The Open Door. Now she dialed his number and waited, disappointed when it went to voicemail. Showing him would have to wait. For now, she headed to her room with the old book. Her father's study had been in the back left corner of the house, just off the kitchen. It had been converted into her bedroom, but this wasn't her safe place.

She went straight to the built-in bookshelves and found the faux door that led up to The Burrow, Leo's secret room. *This* was her thinking place. She beckoned for Sailor to follow her, then shut the door behind them. Pippin climbed the staircase up, crossed the narrow landing, and stopped for a moment to breathe in and out, in and out. Her father's hidden room held secrets yet to be discovered. He'd kept his most treasured books here, along with all the research he'd been doing into the Lane family and the curse afflicting them. He'd tried to figure out how to break it, but he hadn't succeeded. Cassie had miraculously lived after giving birth to Pippin and Grey, but Cassie had become pregnant again and the curse had claimed both mother and child. The curse hadn't gotten Cassie the first time she gave birth, but it had gotten her in the end.

Leo spent every possible waking hour trying to save his children, but he died before solving the mystery, unintentionally leaving it to Pippin and Grey to solve. Pippin glanced around the small room. More built-ins, but these housed Leo's favorite books. He had all of Tolkien's writings. His love for the author had led to Pippin being named for Peregrin and Grey for Gandalf.

He had collected poetry by John Keats, William Butler Yeats and Robert Frost. He had volume after volume of Irish and Roman history. The shelves were filled with stories and information Pippin knew she would never be able to read. The sheer volume was overwhelming. Still, she had gone through every book looking for notes he might have left.

She looked at two stacks of books sitting on the floor next to the small writing desk. One was a collection Jamie had gathered for her, each having something to do with Gaelic history and the Tuatha dé Danann—the supernatural race of deities in Irish mythology. The Gaelic pantheon interacted with humans, just as the Greek and Roman gods did in pre-Christian times. Pippin had initially been skeptical about the truth of their existence but discovering and embracing her gift of bibliomancy had left no doubt in her mind. The magic of Tuatha dé Danann was real, and it had cursed her family.

Next to the books Jamie had brought was a stack from her father's collection. Each had markings or notes or annotations on the pages. So far, Pippin hadn't been able to decipher any of it, but with Grey's help, she hoped they would reveal what Leo had discovered. She would get to them, but first, she needed to look more closely at her mother's copy of *The Secret Garden*. Sailor settled on her dog bed and Pippin sat at Leo's desk. She set the book on its spine and closed her eyes. She always started with the same question, but for a moment, she wondered if she should ask something different. Something more specific. She drew a blank. "Okay then," she murmured. She opened her eyes and as she let the covers fall open, she said, "What do you have to say about me?"

The pages fluttered then settled. Immediately, the same line Aunt Rose had written about in her letter revealed itself.

> *"It was in that strange and sudden way that Mary found out that she had neither father nor mother left; that they had died and been carried away in the night."*

"My parents are gone. I know that," she muttered. She read the lines again, then let her gaze travel up, reading the lines above to see if they could give her any insight. Two, in particular, turned bolder against the aged yellow of the page.

> *"It is the child no one ever saw!" Exclaimed the man, turning to his companions. "She has actually been forgotten!...Poor little kid!" he said. "There is nobody left to come."*

"WHO HAS BEEN FORGOTTEN?" Pippin mused aloud, and then an idea struck her. Sasha. Ruby's niece. The girl had lost her mother to a car accident. Except that didn't quite work, because Sasha hadn't been forgotten, and Ruby *had* come for her.

Pippin tried again, closing the book. Balancing it on its spine and asking, "What do you have to tell me?" as she let the book fall open. The book fell open to a different page. A single line darkened. Undulated. Peeled from the page.

> *"I am sure there is Magic in everything, only we have not sense enough to get hold of it and make it do things for us."*

PIPPIN FELT a burst of energy surge from her insides. This...*this* was a direct message. One she didn't need to assign meaning to. One she didn't have to *struggle* to interpret. Her bibliomancy...her *magic*...she needed to make it work for her in ways she hadn't yet managed or discovered.

CHAPTER 3

"*Every tomorrow has two handles. We can take hold of it with the handle of anxiety or the handle of faith.*"
~Henry Ward Beecher

THE FREESTANDING RECEPTION desk was two-tiered. It was positioned to the left of the inn's entrance, kitty-corner to the great room, out of the way and just in front of Pippin's office. A guest book sat on the top tier, ready for the inn's guests to sign, with a space for a message next to the signature line. Sea Captain's Inn Guests engraved into the amber bamboo cover. The book was another personal touch—a way for visitors to the inn to feel connected to the place.

After the soft launch, Pippin had started a tradition of taking a photo with her guests—or at least with those who agreed. Grey and Kyron—Grey's business partner and Daisy's boyfriend—had refinished a piece of reclaimed wood, creating a rustic mantel, which hung above the fireplace. This had become Pippin's favorite backdrop for the keepsake photos. She'd had copies of her most recent guest's photos printed at the island's one copy shop and was affixing them into the guest book when she heard someone shouting her name from outside.

She and Hazel looked at each other, both striding to the front door and out onto the porch. Pippin laughed and slapped her hand over her mouth. There, in the middle of the street, was Hattie Juniper Pickle standing in front of a turquoise adult-sized tricycle. The three wheels were the same size as an ordinary bike. A wire basket was positioned in between the two back tires.

Hattie almost always had an unlit cigarette dangling from between two fingers. Now was no exception. Her knee-length leggings incorporated all the colors of the rainbow, swirled together like psychedelic sherbet. Her lime green Crocks matched her lime green t-shirt. The woman was a sight to behold.

Hattie had grown up in the house across the street and kitty-corner to Sea Captain's Inn. She had given Pippin her abbreviated life story the first time they'd met. She'd come back to live in her childhood home with her first husband—who was also her third husband. She'd lived somewhere else with the man she'd married in-between.

"Hattie Juniper Pickle, what in the world is that?" Pippin called happily.

The phone rang inside. "I'll grab that," Hazel said with a smile, nodding in Hattie's direction. "You have to go watch her ride that thing!"

Pippin didn't have to be told twice. Hazel went back inside, and Pippin skipped down the porch steps and jogged down the brick walkway. By the time she got to the street, Hattie's cigarette dangled from her lips instead of her fingers and she straddled the trike. "Pippin, meet Rizzo," she announced.

Pippin cocked a brow. "Rizzo?"

Hattie positioned one foot on a pedal and squinted at Pippin as if her cigarette was lit and smoke ribboned into her eyes. "Stockard Channing has always been my idol. I met her once. She's just as sweet as sweet potato pie. I debated between Rizzo and Stockard, but I do love me some John Travolta, too, so I went with Rizzo."

Pippin nodded her approval. "It's a good name."

She tapped her thumb against a little lever and a bell trilled. "It was a gift. Husband number two is trying to become husband number four." She pinched her left eye tighter and took the cigarette from her mouth. The facial tick had to be muscle memory from her smoking days. "'Course I'm not leaving this house, and he's out on Emerald Isle, so it's a nonstarter, but I'll still take Rizzo."

Pippin laughed. "Does husband number two *know* the bicycle...er, tricycle isn't going to work?"

Hattie backed the lipstick-stained filter end of the cigarette back between her lips and peered at Pippin. "You think I'm gonna lead a man on? Uh-uh. He knows there's no chance for a new union unless he moves in here with me. He refuses to live somewhere I already lived with another man—" She put her hand against her mouth and snarked, "Twice."

The next second, Hattie was on the trike and pedaling toward Main Street. Several cars passed her going to opposite direction. One person honked, waving an arm out the driver's window and yelling, "Way to go, Hattie!"

Pippin froze for a second, watching open-mouthed as Hattie swerved into traffic, her smooth three-wheeled ride turning dicey.

"Hattie!" Pippin took off running, but a few seconds later, the trike straightened. Hattie took her feet off the pedals and threw her legs straight out. The bell trilled and she let out a euphoric, "Whee!"

Pippin slowed and caught her breath. She tamped down the rush of anxiety that had flooded her at the idea of Hattie crashing.

Hattie took the ride back up Rum Runner's Lane slower so Pippin could walk alongside. A man was just sliding into the driver's side of a car parked right in front of the inn. Pippin didn't recognize him. Was it a potential guest, or another one of her father's old cronies coming out of the woodwork? She and Hattie were still a good hundred yards from the inn by the time the man started the car up. He sat with the brake lights on for a few seconds before finally putting the car in drive and pulling away, turning left at the corner a few houses down.

A minute later, another car that had been parallel parked on the right side of the street pulled out suddenly, cutting Hattie off. Luckily, Hattie had been pedaling at a snail's pace. It didn't stop her from slamming on her brakes and yelling, "Watch it, lady!"

The driver threw her arm out of the window and waved as if in apology before it turned and disappeared.

"Hattie, you need to be careful on that...on Rizzo. You need to be on the lookout for drivers because they might not see you."

"Will do!" Hattie hunched over the handlebars and pedaled hard, zooming forward after the car.

"Be careful!" Pippin hollered.

Hattie brandished her arm in the air, never breaking stride, her legs pumping rhythmically on Rizzo's pedals.

Pippin watched for another few minutes before heading back to the inn. "Someone just booked a room!" Hazel announced when Pippin walked in. "He just showed up on a whim, he said. I told him it wouldn't be ready until four and he said no problem. Said he'd go to town for a while."

A guest! Pippin exhaled the bit of anxiety she hadn't realized she'd been holding. So, the man wasn't one of her father's friends. She chided herself for thinking that everything was about her parents and the curse.

Hazel held a clipboard with a checklist and an uncapped pen. "The Brewery delivery came earlier. Gin White said to say *hey*. Oh, and the guy that just reserved the room? He asked for you. I told him you'd be back in a little while."

Instantly, Pippin felt a sense of foreboding. She had only seen him from a distance, but there hadn't been anything familiar about him. "What's his name?" she asked.

"Foley," Hazel said. "Connell Foley. Nervous type. Fidgety. But nice enough. He booked for a week!"

Connell Foley. She repeated the name but saying it over and over didn't make her remember it from somewhere. "Did he say why he wants to talk to me?" she asked, trying not to let her trepidation slip into her voice.

"Nope, although he was on the phone." Hazel put her hand to one side of her mouth as if she was imparting a secret. "His wife was upset she couldn't stay, too, because she liked the look of the inn. He told her to go on home, that he'd see her there. Afterward, he kinda shrugged at me, like he knew he was in the doghouse, you know? I told him the room was double occupancy, but he said, no, he was here to do one thing, and one thing only." She did the hand by the mouth secret voice thing again. "Whatever that one thing is, it has to do with you."

"Okay," Pippin said. She relieved Hazel at the registration desk, trying hard to tamp down the unease bubbling inside her, because she didn't know anyone named Connell Foley—which, in her mind, meant he *was* connected to the mystery that was now her life.

CHAPTER 4

"There are no strangers here; Only friends you haven't yet met."

~William Butler Yeats

THE NEXT MORNING, Pippin placed *The Little Princess* next to *The Secret Garden* on the bookshelf in her room. Twenty years ago, it had been her father's main study, the wall-to-wall built-ins housing nearly all of his books. Grandmother Faye had had the house cleared out, keeping only a few of her son's belongings. Sentimental, she was not. All that was left were the books Leo had hidden away in his secret room.

Most of the shelves in the built-in were still empty. Pippin didn't have volumes of books with which to fill them. She had the few books Heidi had selected for their book club of two, and she had her father's copies of *The Hobbit* and *The Lord of the Rings*. At some point, she would try to read them.

After the guest breakfast had been served then cleaned up, Pippin focused on the inn's website. It was up and running, of course, but she had to provide more information and photos to the man doing the website design. Although, truthfully, Jay Wagner, nephew of Chuck, who owned The Brewery, was more of a kid. Nineteen years old, at the most, and a lucrative career ahead of him if he continued on his path as a programmer. Pippin perched on the stool behind the registration desk, her laptop open, and scrolled through the photos she had taken of the guest rooms.

She jumped as a woman suddenly burst through the door with the force of a hurricane. She turned and pushed it closed, leaning her forehead against it for a second as if she had to catch her breath. Her blond hair fell in curly waves down her back. Finally, she turned. The front strands of her hair were pulled loosely back. She wore a pair of oval-framed red-lens sunglasses dropped low on the bridge of her nose. She peered over the top of the frames, her sage green eyes sweeping the room.

"Oh!" she exclaimed with a small jump when they landed on Pippin. "You startled me!"

Pippin took in the details of the woman. She was slight in stature, shorter than Pippin. Five-four or five-five was her guess. A few years older, but perhaps not. Her hair was beach tousled, but she was pale, a faint dusting of freckles over her nose.

Pippin swallowed. Grounded herself by gripping her hands on the wooden top of the reception desk. There was something familiar about her. A thread of worry tightened in her gut, that feeling that she was being watched surfacing. Everywhere Pippin went, she felt a pair of eyes on her. Had she seen this woman in town? On the beach? She forced a smile. "Didn't meant to startle you. Can I help you?"

The newcomer looked up and around, as if she wanted to soak in the aura of the place. "I just got to town—amazing little island, by the way. I asked around about a place to stay." She lowered her voice dramatically. "I'm not a fan of motels, you know. But then, who is? And then, bam!" Pippin jumped at the sudden vocal explosion. "The woman at the cheese shop—Collette something or other—said to try here." She threw out her arms, the black cording of a cinched cloth bag hanging from one hand, a collection of bangles stacked on her arms. "And here I am! Do you?"

"Do I…?" Pippin repeated.

"Have a room to rent?"

"Oh! Yes, I do," Pippin said, jumping into innkeeper action. She pulled up the reservation software on her tablet. "The last vacancy, actually. It's one of the bunk rooms."

The woman glided forward, her maxi skirt flowing like gentle waves around her legs as she moved. A sliver of her midriff showed between the bottom of her black crop top and the waistband of her skirt, layers of necklaces around her neck with brown leather cords tucked underneath her V-necked shirt. She had a vague modern witch thing going for her. Fleetingly, Pippin wondered what was in the woven bag. Hopefully not voodoo dolls or hex potions.

The woman put her glasses back in place, her eyes faintly visible through the lenses. "What's the bunkhouse?"

"Oh, it's very cool," Pippin said. "The bunk rooms are on the third floor. It used to be one large space, but we've turned it into two smaller rooms. The available room has a full bed."

She let her eyes roll up to the ceiling. "I've slept on rocks and pebbles, so that sounds heavenly."

"You travel around a lot, then?"

A veil of melancholy slipped over her. "Since I was seventeen."

Pippin read between the lines. Something had made the

woman leave home and a fissure had become a gulf. She understood exactly. When she had first discovered that Grey was refinishing an old boat and had every intention of taking it out on the water, the rift had been immediate and intense. Thankfully, neither one had let it grow into something insurmountable, but in the moment, fear had penetrated Pippin's soul and a gorge loomed. She knew there would be times when she or Grey would need their space. After a lifetime together, they had to forge their own paths. But Pippin would never let a crevice turn into a chasm. A chasm into the Grand Canyon. "It's only too late to mend fences if you stop trying," she said.

The woman stared. "You're an insightful one, aren't you?" She shrugged and laughed away her melancholy. She patted her bag, which now hung at her side. "My sister and I will reunite if it's in the cards."

Pippin's brows raised, intrigued. "Tarot?"

The woman slid her glasses down the bridge of her nose again, looking over the rims. "Do you do tarot?"

Pippin pressed her hand to her chest. "Me? No." She looked around, as if shy about admitting it and gave a little lift of one of her shoulders. "I've always been curious, though."

A slow smile spread on the woman's face. She pointed her finger at Pippin. Her head moved in a kind of half nod, half shake as she said, "I detected that about you."

Whatever unease Pippin had initially felt when this woman blew into the inn dissipated. She felt like an old friend. Like someone Pippin had met during another lifetime. With a relieved smile, she opened up a new registration page. "Shall we get you checked in?"

"Lil Hart."

She typed in the name, got credit card information, and finished the check-in process. "Do you have any luggage?"

Lil fluttered her hand in a way that was already becoming familiar. "I'll get it later. Just show me to my room," she said, adding with a flourish, "Lead on, Madam Innkeeper."

They climbed the stairs, passing the access door to the widow's walk, then up the second flight to the third-floor bunk rooms. Each room had a dormer, and even though the one now reserved by Lil was smaller, it was well-appointed.

"Are they named? The rooms, I mean," Lil asked.

"Not yet." One of the details Pippin planned to do for each room, but hadn't yet accomplished, was to add name placards outside each door. Initially, she'd thought to name each room something related to seafaring. That went with the history of the inn, after all. What she had recently been tossing around, instead, was the idea of bookish names. She smiled to herself when she thought of Heidi's reaction. The girl would be thrilled at Pippin's commitment to books.

"It'll happen, I have no doubt," Lil said. Inside the room, she tossed her bag onto the fluffy down comforter, threw her arms wide, and spun around. The part of her that didn't remind Pippin of a modern-day witch brought up thoughts of wood nymphs. "This is perfect!" she exclaimed before stopping suddenly. She flung herself across the bed, and closed her eyes, and just like a storm that stops suddenly, Lil seemed to sink into sleep.

CHAPTER 5

"*Language is an archaeological vehicle... the language we speak is a whole palimpsest of human effort and history.*"
~Russell Hoban

PIPPIN STRADDLED her bicycle and road south down Rum Runner's Lane until it turned into Main Street. She headed past the taco shop, past the ice cream shop. She rode until she was smack in the middle of the street between the town's library and The Open Door Bookshop.

Then she stopped.

With one foot on the ground for balance, she faced the library. The memory of standing in this very spot with her mother when she had been just a little girl had begun to fade. For Pippin, the library had always been forbidden. Her mother had kept her away from it, crossing the street at an angle so they never walked on the sidewalk directly next to the old, converted house or the bookstore on Main Street. Her friend Daisy, the local librarian, had helped Pippin see the library in a new way...as a place for lost souls. A safe place for people who had nowhere else to go.

But Pippin's meeting with the man with the clear eyes... the man she knew only as Hugh...had taken place in the library. He'd tainted the space again, and she hadn't been back since.

The sign hanging over the porch swung lightly in the breeze. She shivered. The ocean was a great moderator of the island's southeastern climate. It cooled in the summer and warmed in the winter. Still, the Outer Banks had four distinct seasons. Fall had settled in, and Pippin braced herself against the winter chill brought by the Atlantic.

She turned to look at the opposite side of the street. Two businesses sat side by side, housed in the same vintage brick building. On the right was Devil's Brew, the local coffee shop owned and operated by Ruby Monroe. And on the left was the bookshop, co-owned by Cyrus McAdams and his grandson, Jamie. The sign conveyed everything one needed to know about the store.

The Open Door Bookshop
Purveyor of New, Used, and Antiquarian Books

THE MASSIVE POTS flanking the doorway were filled with winter flowers, and the blue and white and silver decorations in the store's window conveyed the peaceful idea of winter. Silver stars hung from the ceiling, tufts of white represented snow the island rarely saw, and books you wanted to read while snuggled under a blanket, a steaming mug beside you, were displayed, tempting passersby inside to the enticing warmth of the shop.

Pippin debated, weighing her needs and options. She had research to do. None of the books stacked in The Burrow had given her any direction, and she would never find peace until the two-thousand-year-old curse that had plagued her family, and which had brought death to her small island, was broken.

She waffled. On the one hand, Daisy Santiago kept the library's collection as fresh and up to date as possible. Anything a patron couldn't find could be ordered from another Dare County library, and the microfiche went back as far as the town did.

Jamie McAdams, on the other hand, had old texts and documents and rare finds one couldn't come across anywhere else. He ran a robust eBookstore, selling to rare book collectors everywhere. Jamie knew more than she did about the Lane family and their Irish roots. He probably knew more than Pippin's own father had...and Leo had known a lot. A. Lot. The Burrow was filled with all of Leo's most precious and valuable books. It also held a fragment from an old parchment which Pippin thought was correspondence between Morgan Dubhshláine to a Roman soldier named Titus. These were her oldest ancestors. One —or both—of them were responsible for the curse Pippin and Grey had tried to break by offering the ancient hilt of Titus's sword to the Gaelic sea god, Lir. It had almost cost Grey his life and the curse had remained intact.

Pippin couldn't give up the fight. If it took every last second of her life, she would finish her father's work. She would free Grey and herself, and any future descendants, from the iron shackles Morgan Dubhshláine and Titus had unwittingly bound to them.

She decided on the bookshop. As she dismounted her coral Electra cruiser, a car slowed as it drove down Main Street. Pippin looked up in time to see the driver turn to look at her. A moment later, the car turned and headed west on one of the downtown streets. Pippin's heart slid up to her throat. Camille Gallagher—the wife of one of the men responsible for her father's death—had been driving.

Was it Camille's heavy gaze Pippin so often felt? Was she doing her husband's dirty work in his stead?

She dismissed the idea. Camille hadn't known anything about what her husband and father-in-law had been up to. She was a victim just like Pippin and Grey were. She shoved her anxiety away and wheeled her bike to the curb just down from the bookshop. She strung a bicycle lock through the spokes and secured it to the built-in public bike rack. She took her purse, a new black crossover bag with colorful dogs embroidered all over—a gift from Daisy—slung it over her shoulder, and backtracked.

Before she started any research, she wanted sustenance. Maybe she even needed it. She went into Devil's Brew. Temperate island weather meant coffee and tea were always welcome, but the brisk winter day made it especially nice.

Ruby spotted Pippin the second she stepped inside and waved her over to the table where she sat, a laptop opened in front of her. "You look white as a sheet," she commented as Pippen walked up.

Pippin heaved a sigh. "I just saw Camille Gallagher and it...spooked me," she said, keeping her voice low. Small town island living meant you never knew who was listening.

"She's in here a few times a week. I will say, she doesn't look too good," Ruby said. "I only have Sasha, and it is hard work taking care of her. She's got two kids she's raising alone now. I feel bad for her."

So did Pippin. Jimmy and Salty were heading for prison, and Camille was now a single mother. If there was a way Pippin could help, she would, but the blankness on Camille's face staring at her from the car sent a chill up her spine. Help from the woman who'd put her husband behind bars was probably the last thing Camille wanted.

Pippin slid into the chair opposite Ruby. Despite all the trauma she had gone through recently, she still looked like a warrior from Wakanda. Women paid hundreds of dollars to get a mass of spiral curls like Ruby's. Her hair was dark, with highlighted bits framing her face and emphasizing her high cheekbones. Her skin was the luminescent color of sable and seemed to glow from the inside out. When Ruby's cousin died in a car accident, Ruby became Sasha's legal guardian. It was a challenge, but she had stepped into the maternal role with grace and aplomb. "Today's ordering and bookkeeping," she said, then she raised her arm, waving at the rail thin teenage boy behind the counter. "Wycliff, bring me another green tea and—" She looked at Pippin, brows raised.

"A caramel latte," Pippin said.

"A caramel latte," Ruby repeated to Wycliff. "Anything to eat?" she asked.

"No. The latte's good, thanks," Pippin said pulling a five-dollar bill from her bag.

"Don't even worry about it," Ruby said, but Pippin kept the bill in her hand. "You don't need to subsidize my coffee habit. Now, how's Sasha?"

"She still has nightmares sometimes. She misses her mama," Ruby whispered, "and she *still* won't talk." Sasha was supposed to start kindergarten, but Ruby didn't think she could do it. "She won't verbalize at all," she said now.

A bouncy head of dark hair appeared next to Ruby like a

Jack-in-the-Box. Pippin slapped her open palm against her chest with an extra dramatic flair when she saw Sasha. "Oh my gosh! You scared me!"

The six-year-old gave a closed-mouth smile, the somber expression she'd had a few months ago carved permanently onto her face. Her skin was a few shades lighter than Ruby's and lacked the brightness. Sasha scurried around Ruby's chair until she stood next to Pippin, a stuffed penguin tucked under her arm. She carried the stuffed animal around with her everywhere. "Her mom gave it to her a few weeks before she died," Ruby had said when Pippin asked about it.

Sasha opened her mouth, as if to speak, but instead she just looked around, her eyes wide. The gap where her two front teeth had been a few weeks ago, was just visible between her parted lips.

"Are you looking for Sailor?" Pippin asked.

Sasha nodded, closing her lips and offering a slight smile.

"She's at home. You can come over later to play with her, though," Pippin said. "In fact, why don't you and Aunt Ruby both come for dinner?"

Sasha looked up at Ruby for permission, her brown eyes big and expectant.

Ruby's expression was hesitant. "Are you sure? Don't you have guests?"

Pippin fluttered her hand. "Sure, but we don't serve them dinner."

Sasha tugged on Ruby's sleeve. That's all it took. "Okay, sweetheart," she said to Sasha, then she looked at Pippin and added, "but I'm bringing something."

When Ruby offered to bring food someplace, that

usually meant a sweet treat of some sort. Who was Pippin to deny her that pleasure? "Ginger cookies," she requested.

Ruby's red lips curved up. "You got it." Wycliff arrived with a steaming mug of tea for Ruby and an oversized cup and saucer for Pippin. He'd taken the time to create a little latte art, pouring a Christmas tree into the foamy top.

Sasha puffed out her cheeks and stared at Pippin. "What is it?" Ruby asked her.

Sasha answered by raising her eyebrows and pointing toward the archway that led to the bookshop.

"You want a new book?" Ruby frowned. "But we still have the ones we got from Daisy at the library."

Sasha pursed her lips and shook her head. She jabbed her finger in the direction of The Open Door again. After another second, Ruby's face cleared. "Oh. You want Mathilda to come?"

Sasha's face lit up, the smile reaching her eyes for the first time.

"I'll check with Jamie," Pippin answered, not sure if he had the girls tonight, or if his ex-wife, Miranda, did. "Either way, though, Sailor will be waiting for you."

Sasha pressed the tips of her thumb, index, and middle fingers together, then flicked them apart. The American Sign Language sign for okay. Figuring out how to communicate with Sailor had started to bring her out of her sadness. Now she was on a mission to learn a new sign every week, which at least gave Ruby a way to communicate with her, as well.

Sasha flapped her arms like a bird, raising her brows in another unasked question.

"Have I seen Morgan?" Pippin said, guessing that Sasha was referring to the black crow.

Sasha clasped her hands together and nodded.

"Every day. She perches on the weathervane, on one of the window frames, or on the porch," Pippin said. Sasha clapped her hands and bounced on her toes, and Pippin added, "She'll probably be around tonight," because the bird had basically taken up residence at the inn.

Pippin finished her coffee and conversation, then left them, heading through the archway that connected Devil's Brew with the bookshop.

CHAPTER 6

"No one is actually dead until the ripples they cause in the world die away."

~Terry Pratchett

PIPPIN ENTERED The Open Door through the archway that led from Devil's Brew to the bookshop. She walked between the free-standing shelves of used books on her left and new books on her right. Straight ahead was a service counter with its old-fashioned cash register. The wall behind the counter was exposed brick, just like the one in the coffee shop. On it were shelves lined with bookish gifts like mugs, games, and stationary. Anything a book lover might want could be found right here.

Beneath the gifts were shelves stacked with books that had been special ordered. Each book or group of books was wrapped with a sheet of white paper and a rubber band and was labeled with the customer's name.

Pippin still marveled at how every inch of the store was

filled with books or with something book related. There were sections for nonfiction featuring poetry, religion, science, and self-help, among other topics. The fiction sections seemed never-ending. Mysteries, romance, young adult, sci-fi. There was something for every kind of reader.

She let the pads of her fingers dance over the spines of the books as she walked past. They created a veritable rainbow of muted colors. The volumes held story upon story upon story, characters upon characters upon characters, each as unique as the billions of people in the world.

For Pippin, though, that was only half of what the books offered. For the Lane women, books held much more than the stories written on the pages. They came alive. The words lifted off the pages. They revealed things from the past. They foretold the future. They held stories that no one else could read.

Day by day, Pippin was learning to love both the stories written on the pages, and those hidden deeper, embedded into the ink and paper.

She took a moment to watch the customers perusing the shelves and shelves of books. One held a stack of four, pressed close to her body, carrying them as if she were in high school and they were her schoolbooks. Another righted an overturned stepping stool—one of the several Jamie kept throughout the store to help reach the taller shelves, pushing it out of the way. Two women whispered quietly in the corner, their voices hushed as if this were a library rather than a bookshop. She took a closer look, recognizing them as guests from her inn—mother and daughter, June Rycliff and her middle-aged daughter Heather Beadly. They must have felt the weight of her eyes on them because they stopped their whispers and turned to her. Smiles spread across both their faces. "Pippin!" June exclaimed, gesturing wide with one hand. "This place is a gem, isn't it?"

"It sure is. Have you found anything?"

Heather held up three used paperbacks. "Found these," she said. "I can read a book in a day, so one isn't near enough. Now all I need is an afternoon on the beach."

"One at a time for me," June said with a laugh, flashing the paperback in her hand. They went to the register to check out, then waved as they left.

Pippin browsed, allowing herself time to breathe and center herself. Understanding her divination had given her a new relationship with books, one she was trying to cultivate on multiple levels. Jamie's daughter, Heidi, had her reading for their mini book club. Pippin picked books off her father's shelves in The Burrow for her bibliomancy as a way to stay connected to him. Her mother had tried to protect her from what she saw as a curse. Bibliomancy had brought only pain and unwanted knowledge for Cassie. As a result, she kept Pippin away from books. The result was that Pippin read slowly and with effort, combatting the letters that flipped and turned, but slowly, she was getting better, and the words and understanding came faster the more she read.

She jumped when Erin McAdams appeared from between two shelves, her arms laden with a stack of books. Like mother, like son, Pippin thought. It had to be the consequence of working in a bookstore. You were always reshelving misplaced volumes and adding new inventory to what already existed. "Pippin, my dear. Grand to see you here," she said, an Irish lilt in her voice.

"Mrs. McAdams," Pippin said as she hurried forward as the pile of books teetered, looking like it might tip the beanpole of a woman right over. “Can I help you with those?”

Her green eyes sparkled. Jamie’s eyes. “Erin, please, and good heavens, no. God knows I might be thin, but I’m strong as strong as Ériu,” she said with a wink.

The word struck a familiar chord, but Pippin couldn’t place it. “Ériu?"

“My namesake from Tuatha dé Danann, the mighty race of supernatural beings. Ériu was considered the goddess of Ireland itself,” she said. She pulled the first book from the stack and shelved it, continuing as she talked. “I could tell you about a time when I was just a wee bitty of a thing, but I beat my da at an arm-wrestling match. Now I know you’re going to say, but he must have let you win, and you’d be right.” She laughed heartily. “But even then, I was strong in spirit, and that’s what you need to make it through life. Jamie’s girls? They have the fighting Irish spirit—despite their mother.”

Her bit of Irish brogue made everything she said sound rhythmic and lyrical. “Heidi definitely has spirit and she has me reading more than I ever thought I would,” Pippin said.

“That girl, she has books on the brain. She lives up to her name—of noble kin, and Mathilda is strong in battle. A metaphor, of course. Even at her age, you can see her fighting spirit. And then there’s Jamie. I wanted to give him a proper Irish name like Aidan. His father, he wanted Janus.” She rolled her eyes up to the ceiling for a beat. “Janus, who was the Roman god of beginnings, of gates and transitions, of time and doorways, passages, and endings. Of war and peace. Of beginnings and endings. That’s far too much of a burden for one child, even a dear boy like my Jamie. We compromised on Jamie, the supplanter. The substitute. Ha. As if my Jamie could be a substitute for anyone or anything.

He named The Open Door after Janus, he did. Despite his father's shortcomings, it was a way to honor him. Jamie is a glowing ember. A giant flame. Always happy out leaping about the place. A name has meaning, and Jamie lives up to his."

Names. So much came down to a person's name. "Names have meaning," Aunt Rose had once said. Pippin had visited her great-aunt only once, in the wake of their mother's death, so the visit was wrought with melancholic memories. The lighthouse, the bookstore, the cemetery where her grandparents, Edgar and Annabel, were buried, alongside Edgar's father, Trevor, Edgar's Aunt Rose, and his grandfather, Artemis.

"You both are the namesakes of wonderful fictional characters," Aunt Rose had told Pippin and Grey. "That was your father's doing. Your mother, she would have steered clear of literary names. Names have meaning, you see. Your mother's name had a direct correlation to who she was."

Cyrus had been the one to tell Pippin the meaning behind her mother's name. In Greek mythology, Cassandra was a Trojan princess. Apollo gave her the gift of prophecy, but he later cursed her, making it so no one would believe what she foretold.

Pippin and Grey had spent hours and hours trying to understand the reasoning behind their mother's name. Why had their grandparents chosen a name for their daughter whose meaning included the fact that her prophecies would *not* be believed?

Now, out of nowhere, Pippin had a thought. By default, a bibliomancer was someone to be looked upon skeptically. After all, as Grey had told her numerous times, Pippin was the one to assign meaning to the passages that jumped out at her when she practiced her divination. That left a lot of room for human error. Maybe Aunt Rose and Erin were both wrong. Maybe a name was just a name. After all, Grey meant grey-haired and Pippin had been named for Peregrin, which meant traveler. But Leo and Cassie had named them more for the characteristics of their namesakes. Gandalf was wise and loyal. It was only recently that Pippin realized how opposite Gandalf and Pippin were in *Lord of the Rings*. Gandalf did everything he could to protect his friends. He pushed them to be better versions of themselves, to stand up for what they believed in and what was right, whereas Pippin Took had a knack for finding trouble.

"*You* spoke to Sauron," Grey said once during a sibling squabble.

She'd looked at her twin with utter confusion. "What are you talking about?"

"Sauron. He's only the worst bad guy in the history of all JRR Tolkien's work," Grey had said. "He ruled over Mordor and wanted to rule all of Middle-earth—"

"I know who Sauron is," she said. Leo had told them bedtime stories from The Hobbit and the Lord of the Rings books.

"So, you know that *you*—well, Pippin Took—accidentally spoke to him?" He'd put air quotes around the word 'accidentally'.

"Oh yeah? Well because of Pippin, he and Merry escaped from the orcs," she'd shot back. "Plus, Gandalf is vain."

"He's brilliant!" Grey had shouted, and back and forth they'd gone until their father had interrupted.

"Gandalf does have vanity, but Grey is right. He's much more than that. He was introverted, like both of you. He's an observer, a powerful speaker, and he shines when sharing his wisdom. *'All we have to decide is what to do with the time that is given us.'* That's Gandalf in a nutshell. He chooses to spend his time fighting against Sauron. He's intuitive and thinking. '*Gandalf thought of most things; and though he could not do everything, he could do a great deal for friends in a tight corner.'* Gandalf knew Bilbo and Frodo both possessed the One Ring. He observed their behavior and made apt deductions. He's a strategist, but more than anything, he is wise. He's able to identify other people's strengths. He encourages Aragorn and King Theoden to lead their troops into battle. He pushes Frodo to destroy the One Ring. Gandalf is one of the greatest of characters of all time. A true masterpiece."

Pippin had deflated. "But you named me after a silly Hobbit," she had said, having little understanding of what a Hobbit actually *was*.

"My sweet girl," Leo had said, "Peregrin Took is possibly my favorite character from Tolkien's books. He is the youngest hobbit. Adventurous and curious and tenacious, all at once. He exemplifies resilience. He became a knight. A Knight of Gondor, and he proved to be loyal and courageous. He is a true friend."

Looking back, Pippin realized how her father spoke about Gandalf and Peregrin in the present tense, as if they were real people, still living. They'd always been real to him. She had a sudden jolt of a memory. Her father had crouched in front of her, her little hands in his. "Pippin, my sweet girl, Peregrin Took has the unique ability to remain positive in the face of danger and pessimism. He's mischievous, and that makes him so important. '*We Hobbits ought to stick together, and we will. I shall go, unless they chain me up.*' You, Pippin, have that same doggedness. That same determination. No matter what you seek, you will never give up."

"Never give up," Pippin murmured.

"Pippin, love?"

Pippin snapped back to the moment, refocusing her gaze on Erin.

Erin had set down the stack of books she held, looking intently at Pippin. "Are you all right, my dear?"

The passage from *The Secret Garden* came back to her.

"It was in that strange and sudden way that Mary found out that she had neither father nor mother left; that they had died and been carried away in the night."

She looked at Erin. "My parents. They're not here to do the work," she said softly, clarity about the lines finally coming to her. Cassandra and Leo were gone, but Pippin and Grey were still here. Still capable. Grey had been skeptical about her divinity, but after their encounter in the Atlantic's water at Nags Head, those doubts had vanished. Others might not have believed Cassandra's prophesies, but Pippin did.

"What work is that, love?"

"Jamie...he's not here?" she asked, instead of answering. She wanted to talk to him. To tell him about the message from her mother's book.

"No, love. He's having a bit of a free gaff."

Pippin's face went blank at the Irish slang. "The girls, they're off with Miranda. Not that they want to be, mind you, but she had something special she wanted them for. I suspect whatever it is has everything to do with Miranda and nothing with the girls. Jamie's taking a bit of time for himself. At home with nothing to do."

Pippin couldn't imagine Jamie literally doing nothing. At

the very least, he'd be reading, which to him, was the farthest thing from nothing. "He's a great dad. He deserves a free gaff," she said, using Erin's phrase.

Erin flashed a conspiratorial smile. "That he does. That boy hasn't had it easy, you know. First with his da taking off like he did. Then with my cancer. He's a good boy. Jamie's da, he was a chancer." Pippin gave Erin another blank look and Erin went on. "He was, as the American's say, a risk taker. Always on the lookout for the next big thing. He wanted something for nothing. Thank God Jamie inherited his good sense from Cyrus. How that apple fell so far from the tree is still a mystery. Cyrus is a good man. He's been there for Jamie."

Cyrus was there for her, too, just as he'd been there for her parents,

The Secret Garden had to be able to tell her more. She asked Erin if she had a new copy, wondering if it would give her different messages. Erin disappeared, returning a moment later with a compact hardcover version of the Burnett novel. As Pippin took it, a loud racket came from Jamie's rare books room. It reverberated like an aftershock of an Earthquake. The sound thrummed through Pippin's body.

Erin grabbed the store keys from the counter, and they took off running at the same moment. Erin fumbled the keys, her hands shaking as she tried to push it into the lock. She stepped aside so Pippin could unlock the door. Everything was quiet again and for a moment Pippin thought she had imagined the sound, except Erin had heard it too.

The lock turned and Pippin yanked on the handle and threw open the door.

Miss Havisham, the bookshop's long-haired cat, ambled

out, not a care in the world. "How did you get in there, muffin?" Erin asked, her gaze following the cat.

The question was answered the next second. Because there, through the open door and splayed on the floor of the rare book room, was a man's body.

CHAPTER 7

"I love old books. They tell you stories about their use. You can see where the fingerprints touched the pages as they held the book open. You can see how long they lingered on each page by the finger stains."

~Jack Bowman

ERIN CROSSED herself and muttered something under her breath. A prayer, Pippin thought, because the body lay there, unmoving. Unseeing eyes stared up at the ceiling. Scattered near him, in a clump, were several books.

"Call Jamie," she told Erin as she dug her own cellphone from her bag. Less than fifteen seconds later, she was telling the woman on the other end of the 911 call that a man had collapsed, and they needed an ambulance.

"Is he breathing?"

Pippin quickly put the call on Speaker, dropped to her knees, and put the phone on the floor. She gagged at the pool of blood under the man's head, his gray hair matted with it. "Oh my—" She thrust herself backward, stifling the cry hovering in her throat.

"Ma'am? Is he breathing?"

She put her hand on her chest as if she could still her thrumming heartbeat. "There's b-blood."

The woman's voice came through the phone but sounded far away. "It's okay, ma'am. The paramedics are on their way. Can you check for a pulse?"

In the distance, she heard the wail of a siren. Thank God. Hurry, hurry, she willed.

She forced herself back to her knees and pressed two fingers against the man's skin, feeling for the rhythmic beating of the carotid artery. Searching for signs of life. "There's no pulse," she said, and then louder, "There's no pulse."

The siren blared closer.

Erin spun around with her cellphone still glued to her ear. Pippin could see the distress hovering just under the surface. "No pulse," she hissed into her phone.

"What in God's name is going on in here?" Pippin recognized Cyrus McAdams's deep voice. It came from the threshold between the rare book room and the bookshop.

The siren shrieked, now on Main Street. Pippin spun around to face Jamie's grandfather. "Cyrus! He's...he's..."

The silver-haired man hurried forward, but before he reached her, chaos broke out. Miss Havisham yowled an ear-splitting moan as the paramedics rushed in.

Cyrus bent and touched Pippin's sleeve. She stood and they moved out of the way as the medics took over. It only took a moment before they stepped back. There was nothing they could do. The man was dead.

~

Pippin committed the scene to memory. The way the body lay. The unopened books and where they were. She stilled her shaking hands long enough to open a new note on her cellphone and type in the titles. A few were familiar, but three were obscure books with just as obscure titles. They had to do with Irish history, Gaelic and Celtic languages, and Tuatha dé Danann.

The Devil's Cove sheriff's department converged on the bookshop. Two black SUVs parked out front, Devil's Cove Sheriff's Dept. written on the sides in blue with white accents. As usual, Lieutenant Roy Jacobs led the way, a handful of deputies trailing in his wake. He took in the scene, spoke with the medical examiner on the phone, who was en route from Nags Head, and gave orders to his deputies before making his way to Pippin, Erin, and Cyrus.

The man was stocky, had dark circles framing the base of his eyes, and his gray hair was on the verge of disappearing altogether. He wore a navy-blue uniform, the creases of his pant legs crisp and sharp. Rectangular gold bars gleamed from the corners of his shirt collar, showing his rank. "What happened?" he asked, the question directed to both Pippin and Erin. They spoke, finishing each other's sentences as they told the story. "We heard a noise," Erin said.

Pippin followed that with, "It was Miss Havisham—"

"Miss who?"

"Heidi and Tillie's cat, Miss Havisham. Named for a—" Erin broke off. "Never mind. It doesn't matter. She knocked over an entire shelf of books." She pointed to the heaps of books underneath an overturned bookshelf. "We heard the noise, so we ran—and when we threw open the door, Miss Havisham came out and we found a...a..."

"A dead body," Pippin finished.

Erin prattled on, speaking her thoughts. "We heard the sound, fierce it was like the rumbling of an earthquake, 'course those are felt beyont the likes of the Carolinas. Ah, sure look it, it was like thunder, and it was shocking."

Jacobs waggled his head, his eyes wide as if Erin was speaking in a foreign language. It was true, her accent had grown heavier with the stress. "Did you see him go in there?" he asked Erin, referring to the dead man.

"Well no. That door, it's always locked."

"But the cat was in there, as well as the man."

"I do recall seeing him in the shop," she said, her brow furrowing, "but that was yesterday."

"Yesterday? Not today?"

Erin shook her head emphatically. "Definitely not today. I remember because there was a ruckus with a kid spilling his chocolate milk, and another pulling books off the shelf, and the mother was frazzled, and that man—" She pointed to the body, "— he was gone when I was done with the cleanup."

Jamie appeared in the threshold and Erin shrieked. "Jamie, my love! Oh, thank heavens." She grabbed his arm and dragged him in.

In one quick sweep with his eyes, Pippin saw Jamie take in every detail of the room. He covered his chin with his hand. Beneath it, his jaw tightened.

Jacobs cleared his throat. "You're sure he was gone when you were done helping the other customers?"

"Very sure, officer," Erin said. "Absolutely."

Jacobs looked at Pippin. "And you, Ms. Hawthorne?"

Pippin folded her arms as if they were a barrier to the chill coursing through her body. "We were talking. We heard a thud—"

"Like an earthquake?" Jacobs asked.

"I've never been in an earthquake, but maybe?"

"Go on," Jacobs said.

"We could tell it came from the book room, so we ran in. The cat ran out. The man was just lying there. I called 911. But it was...it was too late."

Erin hung her head and tried to steady her trembling hands. "Poor man. What a way to go. Alone while thieving."

"What makes you think he was thieving?" Jacobs asked, cocking his head.

Erin flung her arms out and made a sound as if the answer was obvious. "What else would he be doing in here?"

"There's a wallet, Lieutenant," one of the deputies interrupted. He held it in nitrile-gloved hands, flipping it open and holding it out for Jacobs to see. "Connell Foley. Aged sixty-eight." Jacobs turned back to Pippin, Erin, Cyrus, and Jamie. "Connell Foley. Does that name ring a bell?"

Pippin's head felt fuzzy with shock. Connell Foley. "He checked in at the inn yesterday," she said quietly, knowing how bad that sounded. His was the second dead body she had found, both guests at Sea Captain's Inn.

They all stared at her, then Jacobs said, "You didn't mention you knew him."

A thread of indignation wound through her. "I don't. I didn't. My assistant checked him in. I wasn't there. He showed up needing a room. We had one, but it wasn't ready. He told her he was going to go downtown to wait."

Jacobs took notes, looking up when he was ready for the next question. "What time did he come back?"

"I didn't see him come back," she said. She didn't mention that he'd told Hazel he wanted to speak with her.

"And you didn't see him leave this morning?"

Pippin shook her head, wishing she had checked on him

last night. What time her guests came and went was none of her business. "No," she said. "He didn't come to breakfast. I didn't see him leave."

Jacobs fell silent for a solid thirty seconds. Finally, he turned to Jamie and Cyrus. "What about you? Do you know him? Has he been in here before?"

Cyrus cupped his chin, similar to how Jamie had. His index finger tapped thoughtfully against his jaw. "I do not know the man," he said.

"Connell Foley," Jamie said, repeating the man's name. "Is there a business card?"

The deputy searched the wallet. He pulled out a stack of credit cards, sorting through them until he came to a cream-colored card. "Says Heritage Rare Book Dealers," the deputy said.

Jacobs looked hard at Jamie. "Rare books. Do you know him?" he asked, but Jamie shook his head. "No, but—"

"But—?" Jacobs prodded.

Jamie held up a finger and said, "Wait a second." He left the back room, returning a few seconds later with a slip of paper in hand. "One of my employees took a message yesterday morning. This man asked me to call him back." He handed the paper over to Jacobs.

"Connell Foley," Jacobs read, his voice conveying how very interesting the message was. "You never called him back?"

Jamie shook his head. "No. Noah told him I'd be back in a few days. I'd planned to call him tomorrow."

Pippin remembered what Erin had said. Jamie was having a day at home where he could disconnect from the bookstore for a while. So much for the free gaff.

Jacobs held up the paper. "The note says he was looking for a first edition of *Captain Blood* and something else." He pointed to one of the books near the body. "That's *Captain Blood* right there?"

"Yes," Jamie said. "No idea what the other book he wanted was, though."

"Tell me about these books," Jacobs said, pointing to the volumes scattered on the floor.

Jamie's temples pulsed. Pippin could see the strain in him. "*Treasure Island*. If it had been a first edition, it would be worth about ten thousand dollars. But that one is *not* a first edition."

Jacobs balked. "Ten K? For a bloody book?"

Jamie scrubbed his face before answering. "The first printing was in 1883. I have one—" He pointed in the general direction of a bookshelf. "It's a first edition. All first issue points are present, it's in a custom fold-out case, and that particular copy comes with a letter from an English bookseller, dated 1901, stating that the book is a first edition."

"And you keep valuable books right here in plain sight?"

"Not in plain sight. I had a lot of the books in an old storage closet upstairs, but I moved them down recently. This space has better climate control. I actually took today off to take care of some maintenance for the store. New locks. And the humidity here is pretty brutal on books. I picked up a dehumidifier, and I'm working on creating a safe room for the really valuable editions." He pointed to a bag just inside the door to the book room. It was from the local hardware store. The heavy-duty plastic packaging for a new deadbolt stuck halfway out of the bag.

"A little too late to stop this guy, but better late than never. Help me out here, professor," Jacobs said. "What are first issue points?"

"Not professor," Jamie said, his voice sharp.

"But you were. At Carolina, if I'm not mistaken."

Carolina was what locals called the University of North Carolina at Chapel Hill. Pippin had no idea Jamie had taught there. Or why he didn't want to be reminded about it.

"I was," Jamie said.

"And then at UNC Wilmington?"

She stared at Jamie as he nodded. A professor at two different universities. Two doctorates. And here she had barely made it through high school.

"I'm here now," Jamie said. "Just a businessman in Devil's Cove."

"With a room full of very valuable books. You might consider installing a security system."

Jamie pointed toward the corner. "I've *been* updating it. The new cameras were installed a few weeks ago."

"So, they work?" Jacobs asked.

Jamie met Jacobs gaze. "Unfortunately, no. Not yet."

Jacobs tutted. "Unfortunate indeed. Was the door locked?"

"Absolutely."

Jacobs bent down to inspect the locks. "Yet the guy managed to get in here, so you better get those new locks installed, pronto."

"Oh!" Erin suddenly clapped her hand over her mouth, muffling her cry.

"What is it, mam?" Jamie asked.

"The keys." Erin dropped her hand and patted her sides. Her pockets. She swung around and pointed to the counter in the main store, then she swung back around and looked at Connell Foley. "He asked me a question about the antiquarian books—because of the name of the store: The Open Door: Purveyor of New, Used, and Antiquarian Books. I pointed to the room. Oh, I pointed to the room, didn't I, then another customer came in." She covered her mouth again, her hand trembling. "I didn't think he was a dosser."

Jacobs raised his eyebrows and dipped his chin. "A *what*?"

"She didn't think he was a thief," Jamie said, translating his mother's Irish slang.

Jacobs summoned one of his deputies. "Any keys on the body?"

Another of Jacobs' deputies crouched at the side of Connell Foley's body and searched around him. She looked up and shook her head. "No."

"They're in the door," Erin said, pointing to the keys hanging from the lock. "They were on the counter, just where I leave them."

Jacobs thought, then said, "He got in here somehow, so either he used the keys and put 'em back before you noticed, or the door was unlocked the whole time."

The color drained from Erin's face. "I'm sure it was locked. Oh Jamie, I'm so sorry, love—" She stopped suddenly. "Wait. He's been there since yesterday?"

"That's my guess," Jacobs said. "Anybody else in the store besides the mother and the kids with the milk?"

"Oh Lord, yes. There are people milling about all the time."

"During the height of the summer season, we get hundreds of people through here a day," Jamie said. "Fewer in the fall, but with Christmas coming, it picks up again."

"Anyone familiar?"

Erin thought about it, her eyes looking up to the ceiling. "My mind's a bit muddled. I need to have a think about it, but no, I don't think so."

Jacobs frowned. "So, no way to find out if anyone saw our Mr. Foley here use the keys or just waltz in here. Okay, let's go back to the books for a minute. What are the first issue points you mentioned?"

Jamie's wire-framed glasses had slipped. He pushed them back into place. "They help establish a book's value. A first edition book is the earliest printed copy of that book. Obviously, that means they hold the most value."

Jacobs flicked his bushy eyebrows up. "Right. Ten thousand dollars. I got that."

"The issue points are basically established identification criteria. They guarantee that a book is, in fact, a first edition."

"So, what, like copyright date?" Jacobs asked.

"Yes, but it's more than that. There may be codes on the copyright page indicating if it's a first printing. The type of binding can help date a book. A particular dust jacket. And then there's discerning if a book has typographical mistakes in it. If they do, many would have been caught and changed during subsequent printings. That makes the original state, *with* the errors, far more valuable. Those mistakes represent the earliest version of the book in question." Jamie pointed to the copy of *Kidnapped*, by Robert Louis Stevenson, laying by Connell Foley's body. "That one is worth about $7500, and *Captain Blood* over there? By Sabatini? It's not as well-known so it's valued at about $2500."

Jacobs shot a short breath from his nose. "For a bloody book," he muttered, repeating his earlier sentiment.

Jacobs wrapped up his questions and gave an admonishment. "I'll be back in touch. In the meantime, steer clear until we're done in here."

And with that, the lieutenant kicked them all out of the room. Pippin took a last lingering look before Jacobs shut the door on her.

"What is it?" Jamie asked, his hand on the small of her back as he guided her away from the rare book room.

"I'm not sure," she said. But she kept coming back to the books situated around the body. She knew they could tell her something.

CHAPTER 8

"*I don't believe in coincidence.*"
~Juliette Binoche

After the shock of discovering the dead body started to dissipate, Pippin's first thought was of Heidi and Mathilda. How would Jamie tell them a man had died right there in their bookshop? And sweet Sasha, who'd had enough trauma in her life. She didn't need to have this in her consciousness, too. Looking at Jamie, she knew he'd handle it in the best possible way. He'd do anything to protect them.

While she waited for Jacobs and the medics to finish, Pippin made two phone calls. The first was to Hazel to say she would be late coming back to the inn. "Not a problem," Hazel had said. "Everyone is out sightseeing. It's quiet as a graveyard over here."

Pippin grimaced at the all too accurate expression. Of course, Hazel had no idea about the dead body the authorities were in the process of removing from Jamie's rare book room, but the words slid into Pippin's mind and took root. A man had taken his last breath...exhaled his last breath... right here. She closed her eyes and sat quietly, wondering if she might be able to still feel his presence, but no. Aside from the authorities, the place was as quiet as Hazel had said the inn was. Jamie had closed the store early, and Ruby had pulled the pocket doors between the café and the bookshop closed.

Pippin's second call was to Grey. She filled him in on the last several hours and an hour later, he had joined her at The Open Door. Lieutenant Jacobs and his people had finally finished processing the scene and were now gone. Now, back in the rare book room, Grey, Jamie, and Pippin stared at the spot on the hardwood floor where Connell Foley had lain. To Jamie and Pippin, it was as if Jacobs had used chalk to draw the outline of the body.

"They're thinking heart attack?" Grey asked.

"Or stroke," Jamie said. "Whatever happened, he collapsed and hit his head on the way down."

"Was he stealing?" Grey asked, pointing to a short stack of books sitting on top of a heavy wood table.

Pippin nodded. One of Lieutenant Jacobs' people had picked up the books from where they'd lain on the floor, leaving them for Jamie.

Grey strode over and grabbed them. A fine layer of dust coated his dark hair. While Pippin was the spitting image of her mother, sharing a fare and freckly complexion, emerald-green eyes, and strawberry tinted locks, Grey favored Leo with his chestnut hair and gray-green eyes. He looked at the first one. "Tuatha dé Danann."

It was not a rare book at all, but a compendium of the mythological Irish gods. Why did this rare book dealer have books on Irish gods?

"It's not from here," Jamie said, peering at the title.

Grey flipped through the pages. "Coincidence that this guy had *this* book given the pact between Morgan Dubhshláine and Titus?"

Pippin's gut answered that question with an emphatic *NO.* "He wanted to talk to me," she reluctantly admitted.

Grey and Jamie both turned to face her. Grey spoke first. "I thought you said you didn't know him."

"I didn't. He told Hazel he wanted to see me when he registered at the inn, but I have no idea who he was or what he wanted."

Grey's face was grim. "Someone Dad knew, or another treasure hunter?"

"Good question." And one for which Pippin didn't have an answer. She pointed at the other books he held. "Those could tell us something." He handed over the copies of *Treasure Island* and *Captain Blood*, as well as another nonfiction book.

"Is this one from your store?" she asked Jamie, holding up *The Kingdom of the Barbarians.*

"Neither of the nonfictions are from here. This one looks cool, though," he said after taking it from her and riffling through the pages. "I don't know much about the Alani and their looting. They have a complicated history."

"I know next to nothing about them," Pippin said.

Jamie screwed up his face, as if he could pull the information from some deep forgotten crevice of his brain. "I believe they were semi-nomadic. Mercenaries and merchants," he said.

"What do they have to do with the Irish?" Grey asked.

Jamie didn't have an answer to that. "Good question."

"Can I take these home for a while?" Pippin asked Jamie.

Jamie believed in her bibliomancy one hundred percent. He answered immediately. "Absolutely."

"I'll keep them in The Burrow. Safe and sound," she said.

"They aren't valuable," he said.

"What are you thinking, Peevie?" Grey asked.

"The guy was a guest at the inn, he wanted to talk to me, *and* he has books on Ireland and Rome. Like you said, it can't be a coincidence."

"I agree. I think we have to figure out if he was connected to your father at all." Jamie nodded at the books. "They may give you some answers."

Pippin registered his use of 'we' rather than 'you'. The Lanes weren't his family, but he was invested in helping her figure out the truth. "I think they will," she said. The more she thought about it, the more confident she was that they would.

After a few more minutes and a quick goodbye, Grey headed to the front door of the shop. Pippin walked with him, ready to head back to the inn, but her grumbling stomach reminded her about dinner. With the discovery of Connell Foley, she had forgotten all about the dinner with Ruby and Sasha. "Come for dinner?" she asked Grey. "Ruby and Sasha are coming. And maybe Jamie."

Grey lifted one surprised eyebrow. "I thought you were steering clear of relationships."

"It's for his girls. And for Sasha," she said quickly. Perhaps too quickly.

The corner of Grey's mouth quirked. "If you say so."

She backhanded his arm. "Until we break the curse, I *am* steering clear of relationships. And you should, too."

"Stay away from the water. Stay away from women. Peevie, you ask too much."

"So don't stay away from women. Just be careful."

"You, too, little sister," he said with a wink.

"Dinner?" she called after him as he walked out.

"Don't wait for me, but I'll come by later."

Heading back inside, Pippin found Jamie and told him about her promise to Sasha. "So, would the three of you like to come over for dinner?"

Grey had planted a seed. Her heart thumped extra hard as she extended the invitation. Or maybe he'd just watered it. Either way, she willed it to become steady again. Jamie was a friend. Ruby was going to be there. Mathilda and Sasha were friends. Heidi adored Sailor. It was an ordinary dinner with ordinary friends.

Wasn't it?

She chided herself. Of course it was.

"Hello?" Jamie snapped his fingers in front of her. "Pip, you okay?"

She blinked away her runaway thoughts. "Yeah. Fine." She smiled; thankful he couldn't see into her mind. "So, dinner?"

"If you're up for it," he said.

"I am," she said.

"Then we'll be there after Miranda drops the girls off. I'll bring you the books."

A few minutes later, Pippin was on her townie bike cruising back to Sea Captain's Inn. As Main Street turned into Rum Runner's Lane, she felt a surge of uneasiness and the prickling weight of someone's stare. She stopped and turned in time to catch a glimpse of Camille Gallagher disappearing behind one of the old brick buildings.

CHAPTER 9

"Perhaps there is a language which is not made of words and everything in the world understands it. Perhaps there is a soul hidden in everything and it can always speak, without even making a sound, to another soul."

~Frances Hodgson Burnett, *The Secret Garden*

RUBY, Jamie, and Pippin sat out on the back deck after dinner. The three girls sprawled at their feet, playing with Sailor. Heidi practiced her sign language with the dog, while Mathilda did all the talking for Sasha, asking her questions, then trying to guess the answer. Sasha nodded or shook her head or used her own version of sign language to communicate with Mathilda. It wasn't very efficient, but it worked for them.

"Girls?" The three of them looked up at Pippin. "Do you want to take Sailor for a short walk on the beach?"

"Oh yes!" Mathilda said, jumping up and clapping. She looked at Sasha. "Do you want to?"

Sasha nodded, and once again, Pippin saw her faint smile reach her eyes.

"I'll get the harness," Heidi said.

Sailor didn't hear the words that had been said, but she understood the buzz of activity. The second Heidi returned from the utility room with the harness and leash, the dog's backside wriggled from side to side and her tail wagged twice as fast. Heidi slid the harness onto Sailor and pulled the strap under her chest. "Don't go too far," Pippin said.

"Right." Jamie waited until his daughters met his eyes. "Not past the next neighbor's dock, and stay away from the water," he said.

Mathilda threw her chest out and held her chin high as she saluted him. "Aye aye, captain."

Jamie's lips quirked with amusement and he saluted right back.

The three girls formed a line, with Sailor in the lead, and marched down the stairs.

"Sasha?" Ruby called.

The little girl stopped and turned around with her eyes wide. "Stay with Heidi and Mathilda, okay?"

Sasha pressed her lips together and nodded, then scurried to catch up with the McAdams girls.

They all watched the three girls walk across the sandy beach. Heidi held on to the leash. Without Pippin there to make Sailor heel, the dog stayed several lengths ahead of the girls. Mathilda and Sasha fell back slightly, and Mathilda slid her arm through Sasha's. Ruby started. "She doesn't have her penguin," she said. Her eyes went wide, and her lips spread into a victorious smile. "She doesn't have her penguin!"

Grey suddenly appeared at the French door. "Who doesn't have her penguin?" he asked.

Pippin looked at her brother, taking the time to note the changes in him. He'd always been sort of ruggedly handsome, but now he sported the beginnings of a beard. His hair grew in loose curls. He looked a bit rumpled with his baggy jeans and long sleeve t-shirt. The upward curve of laugh lines around his eyes didn't hide the dark shadows underneath. "Sasha," Pippin said.

As Jamie stood and rearranged the chairs, pulling an extra one over to their bistro table, Grey took a step back and stooped to pick up an object from the kitchen floor. "Is *this* the penguin?" he asked.

"One and the same," Ruby said. Her eyes glistened. Joy, Pippin thought. Joy that maybe, just maybe, Sasha was starting to heal.

Grey backtracked a few steps and set the penguin on the kitchen counter, grabbed a bottle opener and a few bottles of beer from the refrigerator, then came out to the deck. He handed Jamie a beer, then held out his hand and notched his chin up in greeting.

"It's been a minute, Grey," Ruby said. The bookshop and coffee shop were connected, but earlier she had closed off Devil's Brew to keep her customers out of the Jamie's store and missed Grey's visit. "How are things?"

"Ah, you know, toiling away. The sailboat's coming along." He held his open palm out toward Pippin. "And before you say anything, don't worry, Peevie, I have no plans to take it out on the water. But it keeps me busy."

"What about all those custom furniture orders?" Pippin asked, swallowing the anxiety that flared the second Grey had mentioned the boat. "Don't *those* keep you busy?"

"There are twenty-four hours in a day," Grey said, lightly running his thumb and forefinger over the sides of his stubbled mustache. "I can only build furniture for about twelve of them."

"And the boat?" Ruby asked.

Grey shrugged. "That's elbow grease. It's labor intensive and kind of therapeutic. It gets me out of my head."

"It's a labor of love, I think," Ruby said, shooting Pippin a knowing look.

Grey gave a half smile. "It is definitely that."

Jamie stood and held up the half-full bottle of Malbec they'd opened at dinner. Ruby shook her head and covered the top of her glass with her hand. "I'm driving, *and* I have to work in the morning."

Pippin felt the fuzziness at the edge of her thinking, but it felt good to be with these special people. Her friend. Her brother. Jamie. She held her glass up to him. For some inexplicable reason, her head tilted to the side, and she drew her lips to the side in a coquettish smile. "I'll take her share, professor."

She almost slapped her hand over her mouth after the moniker came out. She watched him to see if he would balk as he had when Lieutenant Jacobs had called him that. He didn't. Instead, he looked intently at her, a gleam in his amber rimmed eyes, and gave her a coy grin of his own. "Absolutely," he said. As he came around next to her and filled her glass, he leaned in close, his mouth at her ear. "Anything else, Pip?"

Pippin's mind whorled from the low rumble of his voice. It seemed to seep into her and spread its warmth through her insides. Somehow, she managed a nonchalant "Nope. All good."

His free hand grazed her arm as he stood straight again. She swallowed, her earlier playfulness forgotten, and nervously stared out at the eastern horizon, at the barrier islands and the Atlantic beyond. Was the wine clouding her perception, or was Jamie flirting with her? With that dimple-laden smile, she couldn't be sure. He had a natural flirtatiousness about him.

She thought about their interactions. A few times she had thought there was a sizzle of something between them, but she'd pushed the idea away. She trained herself to never give in to her feelings. It didn't matter that she was enamored with Jamie.

Oh God. She did a mental head slap. It was true. She *was* enamored with him, wasn't she?

In her peripheral vision, she saw Grey sit down and open his beer. He caught her stare and his forehead furrowed, just a touch. He gave a slight nod, silently communicating, *Are you okay?*

The slight lift of her mouth on one side gave him her answer. It said, *Don't worry, I'm fine.*

Jamie's expression was inscrutable. Maybe she had imagined the entire thing. Maybe the spark between them had been in her wine-fogged imagination.

Grey handed the bottle opener to Jamie, who was back in his chair. As he popped the lid from his bottle, Grey raised his. "Here's to labors of love," he said.

"To labors of love," they each said as they clinked glass against glass, bottle against bottle, and glass against bottle.

Heidi's and Mathilda's voices drifted up to them over the sound of water lapping against the island's shoreline. They sang a song, interspersed with laughter. Pippin peered over the deck railing. The three girls held hands, sang an old children's song, and spun around in a circle. Pippin had a sudden flashback of Daisy and her doing the same thing. The voices from her memory merged with the voices of

Jamie's girls. "Ring around the rosies, pockets full of posies, ashes, ashes, we all fall down!"

Heidi and Mathilda and Sasha collapsed onto the sand in a pile of giggles. Sailor joined in, laying down right on top of them.

The sound of happy children created a soothing background to the adult conversation, which turned to Connell Foley.

"God, I was dying to come over to see what all the commotion was about," Ruby said. "Death in the bookshop. Doesn't that sound like an Agatha Christie novel? Except, of course, it wasn't murder. But still..."

It did, now that she mentioned it, but Jamie didn't look too pleased about it. "I could have done without a death in *my* bookshop, thank you very much," he said.

"Are the books he was stealing super rare?" Ruby asked.

"Early editions would be, but not the copies he had. What I can't figure out is why he called and gave his name if he planned to come the very next day," Jamie said.

Pippin swirled the wine in her glass. The more she thought about it, the more something about the event bothered her. Finding another dead body gave her plenty of unease, but it was more than that. It was something about the books Connell Foley had been stealing. Something she couldn't yet put her finger on. Although her brain felt a little soft around the edges, her words came out just fine. "Maybe it was crime of opportunity. He saw the keys on the counter and figured, why not? Maybe he had the heart attack or stroke before he'd gotten around to actually trying to steal anything valuable."

They fell into a moment of silence for Connell Foley. Unsuccessful thief or not, the man had died yesterday.

By the time the girls trudged back up the steps from the

beach, Grey and Jamie were taking the last sips from their beers. Pippin leaned toward Jamie. "Have you told them?" she asked quietly.

"I told them a man got sick in the shop today and the paramedics had to come for him."

However he phrased it, he'd clearly downplayed the entire incident. They hadn't spoken about it at dinner, and the girls hadn't mentioned it. Maybe he wouldn't have to tell them anything. Ignorance was bliss, right? That maxim had proven true for Pippin. Maybe life wasn't perfect before she had learned about the curse, but now that she knew about it, she couldn't ignore it. There was no more ignorant bliss.

Heidi and Mathilda's voices tumbled over each other as they unhooked Sailor's harness. The dog slipped inside and headed straight for her bowl, noisily lapping up water. And then suddenly, the frantic sounds of hyperventilating came at them. Sasha's face was screwed up in panic. Ruby flew from her chair and dropped in front of her. "What's wrong, baby?" Ruby asked, clutching her niece's arms.

Sasha made sounds, but no words. "P-p-p...n-n-n..." And then the sounds stopped, and she cried. Huge droplets spilled from her eyes, and she shook her head from side to side frantically. "P-p-p...n-n-n," she cried.

It sounded like she was trying to say Pippin, but that couldn't be. Sasha worked herself up into a wail, her cries cutting through the darkness.

Heidi and Mathilda stood side by side, looking helpless. Mathilda looked at Jamie. "What's wrong with Sasha, Daddy?" she asked, her voice small.

Jamie slipped out of his chair and crouched down next to his girls, whispering something to them. At the same time, Grey disappeared into the kitchen. A second later, he was back and went to his knees next to Ruby. He held out the stuffed penguin. "It's okay, Sasha. Here he is. Here's your penguin."

Sasha lurched toward Grey, wrapping the penguin up in a bear hug before falling into Grey's arms. She buried her head into the back of the stuffed animal, and slowly, her racking body stilled. "It's okay, sweetie," Grey said, his hand on her back. "It's gonna be okay."

Ruby laid her hand on Sasha's arm and met Grey's eyes. "Thank you," she mouthed. After a solid minute and once Sasha was calm, she picked up the wine glasses and the beer bottles, taking it all into the kitchen, needing something to do. A moment later, she was back with her purse and car keys in hand. "Come on, baby. Let's go home," she said softly.

"I'll carry her to the car," Grey said. He stood, Sasha and the penguin both cradled in his arms. He gave Pippin a light kiss on her cheek and said, "Talk later, Peevie."

"Thanks for dinner. I left the cookies for you," Ruby said to Pippin before following Grey out the door.

On the front porch, Jamie helped Mathilda into her colorful hand knitted sweater. The pinks and oranges and purples matched her striped tights. Pippin gave an unconscious glance across the street at Hattie Juniper Pickle's house. Mathilda and Hattie were about six decades apart, but they had the same fashion sense.

"Do we have to go?" Mathilda asked, looking up at him. She was his mini-me, her brown eyes amber rimmed, and her hair dark.

"We do, squirt," he said, ruffling her hair. "It's way past bedtime."

Mathilda gave a loud sigh. "*Okaaay*. Bye, Miss Pippin," she said with the put-upon sigh of a six-year-old.

"Bye, Mathilda," Pippin said, bending to brush a kiss across her cheek.

Mathilda clapped her hand to her cheek as if she could hold the kiss there. "Now one for Daddy!"

"Mathilda," Jamie said, his tone half scolding. His daughter stared up at him with her big innocent eyes.

Heidi balked. She was eleven, and the idea of her dad kissing anyone was mortifying. "Oh. My. God. Tillie, you're so stu—"

"Don't say it," Jamie warned.

Heidi clamped her mouth shut.

Mathilda titled her head back and looked from her dad to Pippin and back. "That's what grownups do when they like each other, isn't it? They kiss! She likes you, Daddy, and you *really* like her, so now you need to kiss!" She cupped one hand to the side of her mouth, adding with a hushed giggle, "On the *lips*."

Heidi hung her head, complete mortification at her little sister clear on her face. She grabbed Mathilda's hand. She dragged her out the door and down the steps, and toward Jamie's sporty silver Audi.

Jamie didn't budge. As the girls climbed into the back-seat of the car, he turned to Pippin with a slight grin. "She's not wrong. I *do* really like you, Pippin."

Pippin's heart thrummed in her ears. For such a little thing, Mathilda definitely read them both. Pippin *wanted* to kiss Jamie. She hadn't thought about it so explicitly, but now that she had, she couldn't un-think it. She felt an energy surging from him. He wanted to kiss her.

"Mathilda's perceptive," he said.

"Yeah," she said.

"Will you let me take you out? On a date?" he asked.

If she did, she'd be breaking her steadfast rule of never getting into a relationship. "But the curse..." she started.

He caught her gaze and didn't let go. "We're going to break it."

We. Not just her, or even her and Grey, but Jamie, too. "I—"

He shoved his hands in his pant pockets and rocked back on his heels, and then, as if he could read the fear on her mind, he said, "Think about it."

She slowly exhaled the air she'd been holding in her lungs. "I will," she said

He gave her that dimpled quirk of a smile and then did just what Mathilda had asked. Or almost. He leaned in and let his lips brush her cheek, rather than her lips, the touch as soft as a breeze blowing across her skin.

The crow circled over the inn and cawed. Pippin stayed rooted to the spot on the porch and watched as Jamie walked to his car. She watched as his taillights disappeared. She clung to his words. *We're going to break it.*

She wanted to break the curse with all her heart, but it had always been so she could have a relationship with some unknown man. So she could bear children and be a mother to some fictional children. It had always been about a hypothetical future.

Now, for the first time, Pippin's need to break the pact Morgan Dubhshláine had made with Lir was gut-deep, because tonight had brought her feelings for Jamie McAdams to the surface, and like Pandora's Box, once they were out, she'd never be able to tuck them back inside.

CHAPTER 10

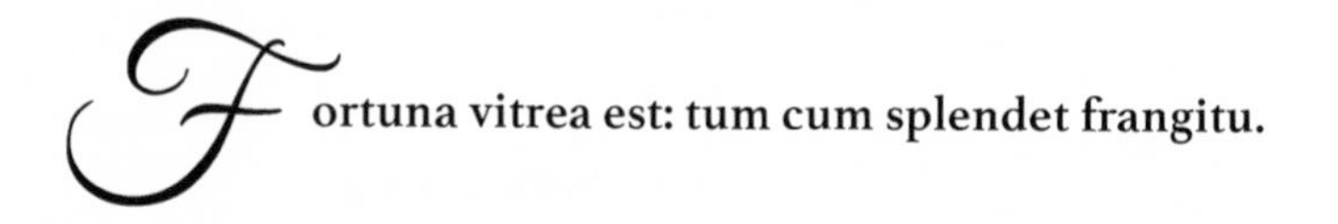

Fortuna vitrea est: tum cum splendet frangitu.

Fortune is like glass: the brighter the glitter, the more easily broken.

~Publilius Syrus, 1st cent. AD, Roman author of maxims

Later that night, alone in her room and waiting for sleep to come, the discovery of Connell Foley's body replayed in her mind like a reel, over and over and over. She heard Jamie's voice in her head as he explained the first issue points to Lieutenant Jacobs. There were sometimes codes on the copyright page, he'd said.

Pippin was a novice bibliomancer. The divination was still new to her. So far, her bibliomancy had helped her learn something about the past, or it had foretold something about the future. Sometimes the message was obscure, but at other times the message had been clear—like with *The Secret Garden*. The book had told her that her parents were gone. That she and Grey were alone. It had told her to embrace her magic.

That word—*codes*—it had become cemented in her mind, solidifying until it wouldn't budge. A code was a message used to communicate something secret. Bibliomancy read between those lines to reveal the hidden truth. She sat up in bed, wide awake despite the wine and the late hour, her thoughts going back to the idea that Cassie may have left some code in *The Secret Garden*.

The second she thought it, she scoffed to herself. Of course, there couldn't be a message from her mother. Cassie knew her fate would be the same as every other Lane woman. So why would there be a message from a mother—who never intended to *be* a mother—to a daughter who never should have existed?

There wouldn't. It was that simple.

But still...

She couldn't quite let the idea go. The fact that she had her mother's book—a first edition, no less—had to *mean* something. There had to be a reason.

She flicked on her bedside lamp, scurried up to The Burrow to retrieve the old copy of *The Secret Garden*, handling it carefully now that she knew it was valuable. Nowhere near the value of the books Jamie had talked about, but still...

The fact that Aunt Rose has blithely slipped it into an envelope and stuck it in the mail sent a rush of goose pimples over her flesh. It could have been so easily lost!

Pippin scooted back and folded her legs under her but changed her mind before she started. She swapped out the book, choosing *The Little Princess* instead, because her mother had that book when she had been here on the island. She'd had that book when she met Leo. If Cassie had tried to leave a message, wouldn't it be in the book she'd had when she'd fallen in love?

She straightened her sheets and the quilt, brushing them flat, before getting down to business. She riffled the pages then balanced the book on its spine. She inhaled a deep breath before forcefully blowing it out. She asked her question and let the book fall open. "Do you have a message for me from Cassie."

The pages settled and a line turned bold and lifted up.

> *"Perhaps there is a language which is not made of words and everything in the world understands it. Perhaps there is a soul hidden in everything and it can always speak, without even making a sound, to another soul."*

PIPPIN READ and reread the two sentences. A soul hidden in everything, she mused. As in an inanimate object? Subconsciously, her hand found her pendant—the one that had belonged to her mother and that Leo had hidden away for Pippin and only Pippin. The pad of her thumb brushed over the top, feeling the soft raised edges of the fleur de lis. The Lane family—her mother's side, was Irish. So why did this pendant bear a symbol that was distinctly associated with the French?

A soul hidden away. Speaking without making a sound. What did the fleur de lis actually mean? She reached for her laptop, also on her bedside table. She woke it up, opened a browser window, and typed *fleur de lis* into the search bar. The history of the symbol materialized like magic, a list of websites with information at her fingertips.

She clicked on the first one. The fleur de lis, she read, was most often thought to be a lily, but some identified it as a lotus flower, or an iris. Pippin scanned the website. It was far too text heavy for her to read easily and quickly, and certainly too much at two in the morning with slightly bleary eyes.

She looked for keywords, piecing together that it had religious meaning. The three petals represented the holy trinity, the lily being an emblem of the Virgin Mary. Another meaning came straight from the lily itself, which was thought to represent life, enlightenment, and excellence.

She kept scanning, all the while the pendant still trapped between her thumb and index finger. Her mother's necklace, left for Pippin.

Then she saw the words. *The fleur de lis represents the strength and power of a mother's unconditional and deep love for her child.*

This was the soul of the necklace. A feeling of warmth settled over her. The pendant spoke to Pippin, all without making a sound.

Her gaze was caught by the next section on the website: the spiritual meaning of fleur de lis. It went on to describe it as a sigil. Pippin had to stop to look up the word. *An inscribed or painted symbol considered to have magical powers connected to spirits.*

The pendant became warm to Pippin's touch. A sigil connecting her to Cassie's spirit.

Something else about the definition tickled the back of her mind. *An inscribed or painted symbol.* She undid the clasp of the chain and let the necklace slip from her neck for the first time since she finding it in the hiding place Leo had designed for it. The front had the very faint fleur de lis. The back had two trees on either side of something bumpy Pippin hadn't been able to discern. The pendant itself was an uneven circle, rough and imperfect.

The silver hadn't exactly tarnished in the time she had been wearing it, but parts of it had actually worn off. She froze. Thought. That didn't make sense. Silver didn't *wear* off. Even with her bedside lamp on, the room was too dark to see well. She grabbed her phone again and turned on the flashlight, directing the beam of light at the pendant cradled in her palm. The silver was definitely thin around the edges. Underneath...was that...the tiniest bit of gold?

She ran her finger around the outer edge of the pendant, then used her fingernail against the place the silver gave way to gold. It didn't scrape away the silver, but it left behind a thin line. A scratch. The necklace wasn't solid silver. It was silver plated.

She couldn't conceive of a reason a *gold* pendant would be plated with *silver*. Gold was the more valuable precious metal. As she mused, she absently pressed the sharp edge of her nail against the fleur de lis. She froze as it sunk into the design. Her nail became embedded in the very thin shape. Her heart jumped. That was not supposed to happen. Pippin's mind flew went back to the first part of the line *The Little Princess* had just given her.

> *Perhaps there is a language which is not made of words and everything in the world understands it.*

THERE *WAS* A LANGUAGE THAT EVERYONE, everywhere understood. Money. Like numbers themselves, it was the only universal language. She thought about Salty Gallagher. He'd said he wanted the necklace to remember Cassie by. But he'd also admitted to being a treasure hunter. He'd told her there were others like him, people who were after a treasure somehow connected to the Lane family.

She closed her hand around the pendant. Remembered a recent conversation with Hugh—the man with the clear eyes—in the library. He'd talked of treasure. Of old letters. Weapons and armor. He'd talked of...this. *This* was what they were after. She'd had the thought before but hadn't been able to explain *why* the necklace would be valuable to anyone but her. Now, despite still not knowing *why*, she knew it was true.

Whoever had plated the original pendant with silver had tried to disguise it further by adding the fleur de lis. But they'd given that symbol meaning. The fleur de lis was a sigil connecting the pendant to the ancestors in the Lane family, dating back to Morgan and her Roman soldier Titus.

Her breath caught. Morgan's Roman soldier Titus. Pippin drew the necklace from her hand and dug her fingernail deeper into the faintly embossed lily. The tiniest bit scraped away. She grabbed a pair of cuticle scissors from her bedside drawer and worked at the design until most of the flower was gone. A dull gold smudge was left underneath. Her breath caught. She grabbed up her phone again. On the floor in her dog bed, Sailor's breathing remained slow and steady. The complete opposite of Pippin's pounding heart. She dialed. Four and a half rings later, Grey's groggy voice said, "This better be good, Peevie. It's two o'clock in the morning."

"Oh, it's good," she said.

That was all it took. She and Grey were inextricably connected in a way other people weren't. She could hear the rustling of bedding as Grey readjusted himself. "Okay," he said, his voice a little less raspy than it had been a few seconds ago. "What is it?"

"Mom's necklace," she said, her breath feeling ragged in her dry throat.

"What about it?"

"Grey, I think it's an ancient Roman coin."

CHAPTER 11

"*Coin collecting is the only hobby that you can spend all your money and still have some left."*

~Unknown

"*Words are the coins making up the currency of sentences, and there are always too many small coins.*"

~Jules Renard

Pippin tossed and turned the remainder of the night. She awoke early and took Sailor on a long beach walk. The island's shoreline didn't have the crashing waves of the Atlantic, but it did have sand and lapping water from the four sounds that surrounded the piece of land. The public access was a half mile north of Sea Captain's Inn, so the beach didn't get much foot traffic. That meant it was nearly private. Since moving back to her childhood home, Pippin had come to love the restorative peacefulness of the early mornings on this strip of sand.

Between eight and nine o'clock, she and Hazel served breakfast to the guests. A few minutes into the breakfast hour, she dealt with the first complaint of the day. She was quickly realizing that while most people were lovely and amiable, there were always a few who would test the patience of even the most even-tempered innkeeper.

Lil Hart sat at the far end of the table. She shuffled a large deck of cards, pulling out several at a time, laying them down, muttering under her breath, then sweeping them up again and shuffling them back into the deck.

Hazel refreshed the hot water for her tea while Pippin dealt with the Kernoodles. Nancy Kernoodle started out breakfast by sending back their coffee after using the almond milk Pippin had put on their table instead of cream. "I must have misunderstood," Pippin said. "Under dietary requests on your reservation form, it said you preferred almond milk."

Nancy pursed her lips, vertical lines sprouting upward from them. "Our daughter's been telling us how bad almond milk is for the environment."

"It takes one hundred and thirty pints of water for one glass of the stuff," Peter said, "and it doesn't even taste that good."

Pippin gave them an accommodating smile, resisting the urge to tell them that the almond milk they were now sending back wasted all that water for nothing since it would have to be thrown out. "No problem," she said. "I'll bring you creamer."

"I prefer my eggs over easy," Nancy Kernoodle said after the egg bites had been served atop a bed of fresh spinach.

Pippin's brow furrowed. She absently touched the coin pendant, deciding it was best to wear it until she and Grey met with Jamie at ten o'clock. She didn't want it out of her sight. "The egg bites are steamed. They can't be made over easy," she explained to Mrs. Kernoodle.

The woman harrumphed, and not ten minutes later, as they stood to go, she said, "By the way, the bed is too soft."

"No! It's too hard. My back is killing me," Peter Kernoodle said. He placed his splayed palm on his lower back to drive home the point.

Pippin's smile became tight. The mattresses were all top quality. If the Kernoodles had aching backs, which Pippin sort of doubted, she thought it was probably because their mattress at home was overdue for replacement and their bodies were in shock from sleeping on one that had actual support. "I'm so sorry to hear that it was—" Too soft, or too hard? "—not to your liking," she said.

"Some people just like to complain," Hazel whispered as the Kernoodles left the dining table.

"I'm so glad they're gone. I don't think I can muster up another smile for them right now," Pippin said.

Hazel fluttered her hand. "Oh, golly gosh, I get it. I've dealt with plenty of people like the Kernoodles. There's no pleasing them, so there's no sense trying."

Sue and Jefferson Macon had come and gone early. Lil had glided out with no indication of her plans for the day. And June Rycliff and Heather Beadly, mother and daughter, finished their leisurely breakfast at nine-fifteen. Pippin had fielded questions from them about Zen Spa, Charcuterie, the cheese shop in town, and The Chocolatier. "We have a fun day ahead!" Heather exclaimed. The glee she exuded was the direct opposite of the curmudgeonly demeanor of the Kernoodles. Pippin much preferred Heather's joyfulness. "Have a great time," she said, seeing them off a few minutes later.

Ten minutes later, Pippin stood at the front door. "I'll be back as soon as I can," she said to Hazel.

Hazel's gaze dropped to Pippin's fingers gripped around the pendant at her neck. The extended glance gave her an uneasy feeling. She had to learn more about what she thought was a Roman coin and figure out what to do about it.

"Take your time," Hazel said with a smile, waving her off.

Pippin had called Jamie after she'd walked Sailor, telling him she had made a discovery. She had been vague about the details, suddenly acutely aware that all the people around her at Sea Captain's Inn were strangers. Even Hazel had blown in on the wind. The idea that Hazel wanted Pippin gone so she could search the house flitted through her mind. It had happened before, after all.

But no. She pushed the thought away, refusing to give it credence. She could be cautious without turning paranoid.

She wheeled her bike from the shed and headed down Rum Runner's Lane. Biking to town almost always made more sense. It took far less time than driving in her car, parking, then walking back to the bookshop. She only drove when she went grocery shopping or needed to carry more than her bike could handle.

Less than fifteen minutes later, and fewer than twenty-four hours after finding Connell Foley's body, Pippin was back in the rare book room at The Open Door Bookshop. She looked around with a discerning eye. There wasn't a scrap of evidence that there'd been a death in the room the day before. Jamie had even cleaned the blood stain from the hardwood floor. Eerie.

Grey came in next. He held two disposable cups of coffee from Devil's Brew. Pippin took one of them gratefully. She needed extra bolstering today. "Doing okay?" he asked.

"Kind of freaked out, to be honest." She held the necklace out, the chain taut on her neck. "I did some research. Grey, this thing could be worth a lot of money. I mean, we knew it was, after Salty, but I'm talking *really* valuable."

"Do you think mom and dad knew what it was worth?" he asked. "Maybe that's why dad hid it?"

They'd only be able to guess at the answer to that question. Her expression said, "Who knows?" but at the same time, "I think it's possible. Probable even."

Grey shook his head. His face mirrored hers, wrought with sorrow and shock for their parents and whatever mystery they'd lived through...and died for.

He held out his hand. "Can I see it?" he asked. He watched silently while Pippin unclasped the chain, refastened it, and held it out between them. The pendant dangled at the end. Grey looked at it, following the back-and-forth movement of it as if he was being hypnotized. He reached for it, and like Pippin had, he turned on his phone's flashlight.

At the same time, Jamie entered the room from the store and closed the door behind him. "What are we looking at?" he asked.

Pippin told Jamie what she had told Grey over the phone. "There was some sort of compound—super thin and made to resemble the fleur de lis. The whole thing is silver plated. I scraped it away and—" She tapped the coin in Grey's hand. "It looks like a head, doesn't it? Like Julius Caesar or something?"

Grey handed it over for Jamie to take a closer look. Jamie turned it this way and that, holding it up to see it from every angle. "It does. Maybe not Julius Cesar, but Roman for sure."

“Is it worth a fortune? Is that why my dad hid it?” Pippin asked.

Jamie handed it back, then folded his arms over his chest. He paced the rare book room, past shelves of carefully curated books, each of which had been held by a myriad of hands, read by who knew how many pairs of eyes, loved by people from eras gone by. “Could be,” he said, quickly followed by, “I have an old friend who’s a numismatist,” Jamie said. “I can get in touch. Find out what we’re looking at.”

Pippin raised her brows at him. “A numi-what?”

“A numismatist. It’s someone who studies currency—coins, tokens, paper money.”

“A professional coin collector?” Grey asked.

“Kind of,” Jamie said.

“Okay,” Pippin said, “but I’m not letting it out of my sight.”

“Of course not. I’ll take a few photos and send her those.” Jamie gave Pippin a serious look, tilting his chin down for emphasis. His gaze strayed to the spot on the floor where Connell Foley had lain, a reminder of the other losses they’d witnessed. “And then,” he said without looking at her, “you should lock it away.”

CHAPTER 12

"Flow with whatever may happen and let your mind be free. Stay centered by accepting whatever you are doing. This is the ultimate."

~Zhuangzi

CONNELL FOLEY'S wife arrived before lunch. Pippin, Grey, and Jamie came out of the back room just as she walked in, a wad of tissue on one hand. Though they both had dark hair and eyes, she was the opposite of her husband in height and weight. She went straight for the check-out counter where Erin was rubber banding specially ordered books together. Erin took one look at the distraught woman and read between the lines. She rushed out from behind the counter. "Oh, my dear, are you his wife? Are you poor Mr. Foley's wife?"

She had gotten over the fact that Connell Foley was a dosser who'd stolen her keys and broken into Jamie's rare book room. This woman had lost her husband, and that was that.

"My Connell, yes. His Bernadette is here. " She looked around. "Where is he? In there?" she asked, pointing to the open door behind Pippin, Grey, and Jamie.

"Is he...here?" Erin repeated slowly as she shot an alarmed glance at Jamie.

The woman nodded, her chest heaving with the effort of a breath through her stuffed nose. She held up the fisted tissue in her hand, staring at it as if she didn't understand why she held it.

Jamie stepped up. "Can I get you a cup of coffee?" he asked her.

"Tea," she said, and let him lead her through the archway connecting the bookshop to Devil's Brew and to an empty table. Pippin and Grey followed. Pippin glanced around. The coffee shop was half full, with a spattering of people in line or sipping coffee at tables. Some looked like tourists. The Kernoodles sat at the couch. A woman with her kids, and another family of five were at different tables. The mother was on her phone while her boys sipped what looked like hot cocoa. The other family had a tourist map spread out on the table between them. "Cape Hatteras!" the man said, clearly trying to pump up his children about visiting the old lighthouse.

Mrs. Foley's gaze skittered around nervously, bouncing from table to table. The woman was lost in her own world. For a moment, the color drained from her face and realization of what had happened to her husband seemed clearly written in her expression, but she brought her attention back to the tissue in her hand and her face went blank again.

From the counter, Ruby took one look at the woman and, like Erin, knew exactly who she was. Three minutes later, a cup of peppermint tea sat in front of her, a ribbon of steam rising from it.

"Have you spoken to the police?" Pippin asked once the woman calmed down.

She nodded, snuffling some more before she said, "Yes, but I don't understand. They said someone... but, that can't be right."

"I'm very sorry about your loss," Jamie said.

Mrs. Foley's eyes went wide, then glassy. She averted her gaze and let her eyes bounce around the café. They mother gathered up her thing and ushered her kids out. The Kernoodles extricated themselves from the couch, catching the door before it closed all the way. Bernadette Foley's eyes followed the movement. It was as if she was desperate to avoid looking at Pippin or Grey or Jamie. Anything to postpone further conversation about her husband.

"Ma'am—" Pippin started to say to bring the widow back, but she stopped, startled, as the woman who'd just left Devil's Brew paused outside the plate glass window while her kids slipped on their lightweight jackets. She turned to glance back inside, her eyes pulled to Pippin as if drawn by a magnet. Camille Gallagher.

Even from where she sat, Pippin could see Camille's face turn pallid. Camille scurried into flurried action, grabbing her kids by the hands and dragging them down the sidewalk and out of view.

In a flash, Pippin was up and racing across the coffee shop. She flew out the door calling, "Camille!" A few people ambled about, but Camille had vanished. Pippin looked up and down the street, searching. There was no sign of her. Finally, she gave up and went back into Devil's Brew.

As she returned to the table, she waved away Jamie and

Grey's curious glances. Bernadette was speaking. "People don't take others up on their offer to help, but they should. I'm good with my grandchildren. I could babysit—"

"What's she talking about?" Pippin whispered to Jamie.

"Something about wanting to babysit those kids," he whispered, tilting his head toward the door Camille and her sons had just gone through. "She bounces around from topic to topic."

"Denial."

"Yeah."

A moment of heavy silence fell like a blanket fluttering down to smother them. And then Mrs. Foley screwed up her face, and when she opened her eyes again and let her face settle back to normal, the complete change was evident. In the blink of an eye, she had gone from a woman talking about babysitting and her grandchildren to one who was almost vacuous. "What loss?" she asked, as if there hadn't been a huge gap of time between Jamie offering his condolences and now.

Jamie looked at her, puzzled. "Your husband?"

Mrs. Foley started to wave her hand, but stopped, her eyes glassy and staring into space over Pippin's shoulder again. Pippin spun around, half expecting to see Camille again. For a moment, she thought she did see the woman driving by, staring at the café from the driver's seat.

Mrs. Foley emitted a low mewl, bringing Pippin back. Whatever this weird thing with Camille was, she would deal with it later. She turned to see Mrs. Foley squeeze her fist tighter around the mass of tissue she still clutched. Panic slid onto her face as if she couldn't figure out how the tissue got there, or what she was supposed to do with it. Erin seemed to know what she needed. She darted off and reappeared seconds later with a small trashcan. Mrs. Foley tossed her tissue wad into it, then sat back. She looked at Jamie. Her mouth curved up in a smile. It could have been painted on for the lack of emotion it held. "You're lovely, aren't you? Who are you?"

He placed his hand on his chest. "I'm Jamie McAdams—"

She snapped her fingers. "I know! You're that Hollywood actor—"

"No, I own the bookshop—"

"Michael...Mat...Matthew! The Texan—"

Jamie shook his head. "Mrs. Foley, I own the bookshop where your husband—"

He stopped when Mrs. Foley's face started to fold in on itself like a melting sugar mold. Pippin took a seat across from her. "My name is Pippin Hawthorne. I run Sea Captain's Inn—"

"Oh! Yes! Connell has a room there. I wanted to stay there with him, too, but he's been here on business, you see."

"How did you get here?" Pippin asked, thinking that she needed to call Lieutenant Jacobs to come take over with the grieving widow.

"Goodness, what a question. I drove, of course."

Pippin rolled her finger in the air, indicating her, Grey, and Jamie. "We, uh, found your husband—"

"You found him!" Mrs. Foley's blank face suddenly looked lit up from within. "Oh, thank heaven! Where is he? I've called and called, but he hasn't answered. He does that... gets wrapped up in his books. He loses all track of time, but I do worry about him."

Pippin couldn't hide her puzzlement. When Mrs. Foley had come in, she had seemed to understand that her husband was dead, hadn't she? "Mrs. Foley," Pippin said. "Are you okay? Can I get you anything?"

"A cup of tea would be lovely. Connell loves his afternoon tea. Unless he forgets to have it, of course."

Pippin shot a bemused glance at Jamie and Grey before giving the cup of peppermint tea a gentle push closer to Mrs. Foley. "Here you go."

Mrs. Foley gave a baffled look at the tea. "Oh. Lovely."

Grey crouched down in front of Mrs. Foley and took her hand. His eyes locked onto hers as if the connection could snap her back to reality. "We found your husband, ma'am. Did you talk to the police?"

An invisible curtain fell over her eyes rendering them vacant again. "I dreamed something terrible happened. That Connell left me for his books. He's always hunting for something new." She chuckled. "Something old, I mean, of course, but something new. A new old book. And others were after it, too. They all wanted the book."

"You dreamed that something happened to your husband?" Pippin asked gently.

"He sank to the bottom of the ocean. He was sure it was there, and then he held up his hand! Eureka!" She grinned for a long second before her lips turned downward into a frown. "He had the book. He had it, but it was too late because he didn't have it anymore and oh she was angry. So angry." She shook her head, the movements so fierce, as if she could shake the nightmare away.

"Who was angry?" Pippin asked.

Mrs. Foley shook her head violently, as if she could fling away the horrible image of her husband at the bottom of the ocean. Her eyes turned glassy as she stared past them all, out the front window at some blurry point in the distance, and her voice became low and hoarse and laden with doom. "The angel of death."

Pippin's eyes pricked with emotion, for the pain this woman, now a widow, had experienced, and the shock she was in—because while she had a loose grip on reality, she knew the truth. She knew her husband was gone. Pippin blinked hard. Grey lifted his brows, willing her to be strong, and Jamie squeezed her hand, holding it for a few seconds.

"Mrs. Foley, I'm not sure—" Jamie began, but she fluttered her hands, stopping him.

"He's staying at an inn around here somewhere. A bed and breakfast." She stood suddenly, slipping the strap of her purse on her arm. "I'll meet him there."

It was as if she had completely forgotten that they'd already talked about Sea Captain's Inn. "Of course. Absolutely. My brother and I, we own the inn," she said, gesturing toward Grey.

Mrs. Foley looked down at the mug of tea. "Oh, how lovely," she said, as if she was seeing it for the first time. The billowing steam had dissipated. She didn't seem to care. She took a sip, then another. "Thank you," she said, her voice hardly more than a whisper, the rim of the cup still pressed to her lips. "Yes, thank you."

THE IDEA that Connell Foley was somehow connected to the Lane family had taken up residence in Pippin's mind, refusing to let go. The book on the Irish gods had been the first root to take hold, but like kudzu, the "mile a minute" vine of the South, new offshoots were taking hold. Why had the rare books dealer contacted Jamie? Why did he have

Captain Blood, Treasure Island, and *Kidnapped* in his hands when he fell?

Then there was the fact that he'd rented a room at Sea Captain's Inn and had asked for her.

None of it felt right.

By five o'clock, everyone on the island had heard about the death at the bookshop. It was happy hour at the inn, and all the guests were in the great room sipping on Merlot and Pinot Grigio. And all eyes were on Bernadette Foley as Pippin led her up the stairs. Before they reached the landing, Pippin glanced back and locked eyes with Hazel for a moment, silently communicating that she would be a few minutes. Hazel gave a quick nod in return, along with an expression that said, *Don't worry*. Then Pippin's gaze landed on Lil. She had her wine glass to her lips, her red-lens glasses low on the bridge of her nose, looking over the frames at Bernadette. The intensity of Lil's stare struck Pippin. A thin strand of disquiet threaded through her, winding around the mass of kudzu vines already there. It was nearly impossible to destroy kudzu vines. They were an invasive species that covered everything in sight. Bit by bit, Pippin was going to have to pick away at the invasive stems inside of her until she freed herself of them.

Lil blinked and looked away, as if she'd suddenly broken free from a trance. Pippin shook away her uneasiness and led Bernadette to her husband's rented room. The woman stopped in the threshold. Her gaze skittered from the neatly made bed to the closed suitcase on the luggage rack to the single pair of shoes sitting on the floor next to the antique writing desk. Her shoulders lifted, then released with a jagged exhalation. She grabbed ahold of the wide doorway molding. "I thought he'd be here. I'll just wait for him?" Her voice lifted at the end, forming the sentence into a question that didn't need to be answered.

"Mrs. Foley?"

Pippin voicing her name seemed to propel the woman into the room. "Thirty-six years," she said. "We've been married thirty-six years this past March."

That sounded like a lifetime. Pippin didn't know the pain of losing a spouse, but she knew the pain of losing a parent, and empathy pooled inside of her. "That's a long time," she said. It was longer than Pippin and Grey had been alive. "I'm glad you had those years together."

Mrs. Foley turned to face Pippin. "We'll have thirty-six more—" Her voice faltered.

Pippin took her arm and guided her to the bed. "Mrs. Foley, if there's anything I can do..."

She trailed off, leaving the offer open for Bernadette to fill in the blank. The woman moved from the bed to the desk. She sat on the rail-backed chair and looked blankly at Pippin. "Do you think nightmares can be true?" she asked, her eyes wide, her voice almost childlike.

This poor woman. Her mind skittered all over the place. "What do you mean?"

"My Connell, he's at the bottom of the ocean, holding that elusive book. Eureka!" It was the same dream she had recounted at Devil's Brew. Pippin's breath caught in her throat as Bernadette continued. "But oh, for a minute she is so, so angry. She says he took everything from her. Connell? Connell took everything from you?"

Her skin was sallow, her eyes pinched, as if she was reliving her nightmare this very moment. "Who's so angry?" Pippin asked.

"The angel of death. She helps me, though. She helps my Connell, too. She doesn't take him. I can't help him, but she does. And then she walks me out of the nightmare—out of the water—and into the light." She looked at Pippin with an uncomfortable intensity. For a moment, Bernadette Foley seemed in possession of her thoughts. "I saw her again. I don't want her to take me." Her voice rose an octave. "Do you think nightmares are true? I don't want her to take me!"

"I...don't know," Pippin said.

"I think they can, and she'll be back for me," she said, and then, in a flash, a curtain fell over Bernadette's eyes, turning them from lucid to blank.

Disappointment cascaded in waves over Pippin. She wanted to ease the torment of Bernadette's nightmare's but she knew she couldn't force the topic. The woman's mind was like an ocean tide, lucidity ebbing and flowing. Pippin strode to the small armoire that housed a television, a binder with tourist information about Devil's Cove, the history of the inn, and several complimentary bottles of water. She grabbed one and offered it to Bernadette. Instead of drinking it, she absently spun it in her hands. Pippin didn't know what the protocol was when a guest at the inn lost all sense of reality. "Can I call a doctor for you, Mrs. Foley? Or call someone else? A friend? Family?"

She looked up, fear in her eyes, "No need. She's coming for me. Ruthie will come."

"Ruthie?"

"I'm so tired. I'll just lay down for a bit, while I wait for Connell," she said.

Pippin hesitated. She didn't know who Ruthie was, and she hated to leave the woman alone, but Bernadette seemed done talking. As Bernadette's eyelids fluttered, Pippin finally headed to the door. "I'll leave you to rest then," Pippin said. "The phone is right here." She pointed to the landline that connected guests to front desk. "Call if you need anything."

No reply. Pippin was at the threshold when Bernadette said, "He's a good man. People change, but he's always been a good man."

Pippin stopped. Turned around. "Has he changed?"

Bernadette's eyes were glazed, and she stared blankly, not focusing on anything, speaking as if to herself. "People always change, don't they?"

CHAPTER 13

"Hope is the denial of reality."
~Margaret Weis

PIPPIN PASSED by the guests sipping their Oak Barrel wine, and went straight to the front porch, took out her cell phone, and dialed the sheriff's department looking for Lieutenant Jacobs.

He came onto the line, cutting right to the chase. "What can I do for you, Ms. Hawthorne?"

"It's about Mrs. Foley," she said. "Connell Foley's wife?

"What about her?"

"She came into the bookshop earlier when I was there. And now she's upstairs in the room her husband was staying in. But here's the thing, Lieutenant. She doesn't seem to realize her husband is dead."

"What's that?" he asked, and she imagined him poking his finger in his ear to see if he'd heard correctly.

"She's up there waiting for him to show up."

"Like he's going to waltz right through the door?"

"Exactly. I asked if she needed a doctor, but she said no. But I think when she realizes the truth, I'm afraid she's going to completely break down."

"I'll send the doc over to check on her. Worst she can do is refuse to be seen when he shows up. Doc Wilkenson is a good egg, though. He'll give it a good shot."

Lieutenant Jacobs was true to his word. Dr. Wilkenson arrived forty-five minutes later. Pippin kept the door unlocked during the day, but he knocked anyway. He looked every bit the small-town British TV doctor, complete with black travel medical bag. All that was missing was a feisty office assistant and a mangy dog.

He had fine silvery hair with a steep receding hairline. His ears, large and protruding, rivaled Yoda's. He had an affable curmudgeonliness about him, from the horizontal lines carved across his forehead to the way his brows angled in at the nose and shot up at an angle. His scowl had a lightness to it. He was like Doc Martin, secretly content but outwardly grumpy. "I am here to see the woman who lost her husband," he stated as he stepped into the foyer.

Pippin held the door open and stepped back. He gave a little bow of his head as he entered. From the registration desk, Hazel straightened up and batted her eyes. "Hello there," she said with a waggle of her brows.

"Right, right. Hello there. Here to see the woman who lost her husband," he repeated.

Now Hazel's lips quirked with amusement. "Yes, you said that already."

Pippin held out her arm. Instead of locking hands with her for a shake, he turned slightly and offered his elbow. Pippin dropped her hand and bumped her elbow against his. "I'm Pippin."

"And I'm Hazel," Hazel interjected, her eyes glued to the doctor, that little smile still painted on her lips.

"Yes, yes. Fine. I'm here to see the woman who lost her husband."

Okay then. So, Lieutenant Jacobs thought the good doctor was a good egg because they were the same type of person, both gruff and straight to the point. Pippin might go so far as to say that Dr. Wilkenson lacked ordinary social graces. No bedside manner. "She hasn't come out of her room," Pippin said.

"This way?" he asked, taking off toward the stairs before she could respond.

Pippin rushed to catch up with him. "Take a left at the top," she said.

At Bernadette Foley's door, she raised her knuckles to knock, but Dr. Wilkenson stopped her. "Allow me."

Pippin took a step back and watched while Dr. Wilkenson knocked on the door with three unhurried raps. "Ma'am, I'm Dr. Wilkenson. I'm here to check on you."

He waited a solid thirty seconds before trying again, with a *rap, rap, rap*. "Ma'am. I need you to open the door."

Another thirty seconds passed, but the good doctor wasn't giving up. He knocked again. Just before his knuckles made contact the third time, the door flew open. "What do you want?"

Dr. Wilkenson wasn't fazed by her irritation. "I am here to check on you, ma'am."

Bernadette looked past the doctor, landing on Pippin. "I don't need a doctor," she said, her voice like a child refusing to admit she's sick.

"I was worried—"

"No need to be. I need rest while I wait for Connell,

that's all." She turned to Dr. Wilkenson. "Thank you, but I don't need a doctor."

And then she closed the door. The lock clicked as it turned from inside.

Dr. Wilkenson wasn't so easily deterred. He knocked again. "Ma'am. I'd like just a moment of your time," he said through the door.

There was silence for a few seconds, and then Bernadette cracked open the door.

"Just a moment of your time," the doctor said again, his voice soothing now.

Bernadette opened the door wide enough for the doctor to step inside, then she quickly closed it again.

Pippin stayed in the hallway for a minute in case Dr. Wilkenson needed her. When she heard the low murmur of their voices through the door, she left the doctor to his patient and went downstairs to the registration desk. Ten minutes later, Dr. Wilkenson was back downstairs. "Is she okay?" Pippin asked, coming out from behind the desk to meet him at the foyer.

"She said someone is coming, but she does not have a grasp on reality so that may or may not be true," he said. "Keep an eye on her. Make sure she eats," he said. He dipped his chin as he said, "Ma'am," and then he was gone.

"Can't say I've ever met anyone quite like him," Pippin said to Hazel, but Hazel's gaze was still on the front door. She looked...smitten. "Hazel?" she said

Hazel blinked. "He's kind of cute, isn't he?" A slight blush spread on her cheeks. "Golly gosh," she said under her breath to herself, fanning herself.

Pippin looked at the front door as if she could see Dr. Wilkenson beyond it. About as cute as an old trout, she thought, but she said, "Yeah. Adorable."

"I get it. He's probably not for everyone, but I bet I could put a smile on his face." She winked saucily. "In fact, I know I could."

Despite the circumstances, Pippin laughed. "I bet you could, Hazel Hood. I just bet you could."

PIPPIN'S THOUGHTS tumbled over one another throughout the rest of happy hour. After the last of her guests had gone on to their evening plans, she made sure the front door was locked. The good thing about running an inn that only served breakfast was that other than dealing with guest needs—or an emergency—her nights were her own. The guests could reach her through her cell phone, and any after-hours calls from rooms to the front desk were forwarded, as well. She heaved a sigh. Finally, she had time to think.

It was still light out and she longed to be outside. To clear her head. She leashed Sailor and roamed the downtown area of Devil's Cove. She walked up and down every street—past the salon, the bicycle shop, past the dollar discount store, the elementary school, city hall, and the office for the Devil's Cove Gazette. Eventually, her feet brought her to the blue clapboard house, the hand-carved sign announcing it as the LIBRARY swinging from the eaves. The old building was open until eight PM. In the gloaming, the warm lights from inside gave the place a soul, like a beating heart.

She wasn't going to let old fears and memories keep her from the library forever. She and Sailor bypassed the wheelchair accessible ramp and climbed the few steps to the porch. The musty smell of books commingling with the staleness of old carpet had felt foreboding the first time she'd stepped foot inside. Now it was as familiar as the woman behind the circulation desk.

Daisy Santiago was a wisp of a woman. She had the darkest hair Pippin had ever seen. It wasn't quite as black as obsidian, but it was close, but there was the faintest hint of brown, too. She wore it in a pixie cut with long strands framing her face. Olive complexion. Always bold and colorful jewelry. Eyelashes for miles. And glasses with frames that matched her always colorful outfits. She was one of a kind—and Pippin's oldest friend. They didn't really remember each other from their toddler days, but Daisy had old photos of them playing together. Now, twenty-five years later, they'd rekindled that old friendship.

"Hey stranger!" Daisy bellowed, belying her slight stature. If she had an inside voice, she didn't use it often. She came out from behind the curved desk and bear-hugged Pippin. She bent until she was nose-to-nose with Sailor, scratching her behind the ears. Looking up at Pippin, she said, "Where have you been? I feel like I haven't seen you in a year!"

It *had* been a few weeks, at least. Just seeing Daisy gave Pippin a jolt of energy. Her vivacity was contagious. "The inn," she said.

Daisy stood again. "So, busy, right? I should have come around to check on you, but..." She held up her left hand and wiggled her fingers. The ring on her finger caught the light from the sun streaming through the skylight in the library roof.

Pippin grabbed Daisy's hand and stared at the diamond on her ring finger. "You're engaged!"

Daisy squealed, jumping up and down in her ballet flats. "Better! We're married!"

Pippin's gaze traveled from Daisy's ring to her face. "You and Kyron got...married?"

If Daisy heard the faint concern in Pippin's voice, she didn't let on. She had known Kyron less than a year. He seemed the perfect complement to her. The yin to her yang. But still...

"I know it was fast, but when you know, you know. We've been planning it for a month, then we got our parents together and went to Elkton!"

"Elkton...?"

"Maryland! It used to be the quickie wedding capital of the East Coast. It's at the three corners where Delaware, Pennsylvania, and Maryland meet. Do you know, there used to be at least *fifteen* wedding chapels there. Not anymore, of course, but still..."

"Why there?" Pippin asked.

"Philadelphia Story? It's where Katherine Hepburn and Cary Grant eloped to." She practically swooned. "*So* romantic. We went to the Little Wedding Chapel on Main Street."

Daisy's happiness was just as contagious as her energy. Pippin wrapped her up in a hug. "That's so great. I'm so happy for you," she said, the words swaddled in a swathe of sorrow for the happiness she was afraid she would never have.

Daisy pulled away. "Are you okay, Pips?"

Pippin turned her head and swiped at her eyes. She gave a quick laugh. "I'm fine," she said. "Just really happy for you."

Daisy squeezed her hand and Pippin smiled.

Daisy left Harold Manatee, the assistant librarian, to close up for the day, and pulled Pippin and Sailor up the stairs. The periodicals were housed on the second floor, as well as several private study rooms, a conference room, and the nonfiction titles. She led Pippin into one of the private study rooms that overlooked Main Street. Pippin held up the leash. "It's okay for her to be in here?"

Daisy waved away the question. "Absolutely!" She hitched at the waist and rubbed her hand under Sailor's chin. "There's my good girl," she gushed.

From the window, Pippin could see The Open Door Bookshop, Devil's Brew, and the fishing pier. For the next twenty minutes, Daisy filled her in on every detail of their long weekend in Elkton.

"It sounds amazing," Pippin said, and it did. She worked to keep the tiny hint of melancholy she felt out of her voice. Daisy and Kyron had what she never would. Never *could*. They'd found love and were making a future together. Jamie shot to her mind. If there was anyone she might want that with, it was him. Those John Lennon glasses. The slight curl in his hair. Those dimples. And, most of all, his brains. It was a powerful combination.

She shoved the thought away, but Daisy had seen something in her face. "Pippin..." she said, the way she said her name posing the question, *What's going on?*

Pippin opened her mouth to speak as she glanced out the window. To say that nothing was going on. That everything was fine. But the words turned to dust. Because there, across the street and staring right at her, was Hugh—the man with the clear eyes.

CHAPTER 14

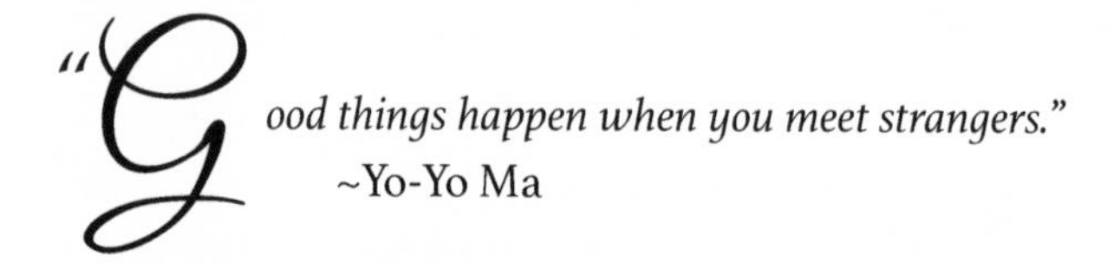

“Good things happen when you meet strangers.”
~Yo-Yo Ma

PIPPIN SPUTTERED. She took off for the door, her feet kicking out from underneath her when Sailor’s leash pulled taut. The weight of the dog, lying on the floor, was an anchor holding Pippin back.

Daisy craned her neck to look out the window and see what Pippin had seen. “What—?” she started, but the question evaporated, and she gasped. “It’s him!”

Daisy had been with Pippin when she had met Hugh in the library. When he’d revealed their ancestral connection. “I have to talk to him,” Pippin said in a panicky voice.

Daisy grabbed the leash from Pippin. “Go! I have her!”

Pippin flew down the stairs. Raced past Harold. Plowed through the door.

Her long skirt whipped around her legs as she rushed down the porch steps. She did a hard left at the sidewalk...

and stopped short. Instead of vanishing, Hugh was walking toward her. No, strolling toward her, as if he had not a care in the world. His hair had taken on a silver hue. That, along with his crystalline eyes, felt incongruous with his black slacks and crispy white button down—the only thing Pippin had ever seen him wear. The way the fading sunlight hit him created an eerie incandescence that slipped around him like an aura. An involuntary shiver swept over Pippin's skin.

"Ah, dear Pippin. It is good to see you," he said, his slow Southern voice dripping with nonchalance.

His nearly translucent eyes chilled her just as much now as they had during their previous encounters. "I didn't know you were back on the island," she said.

He raised his oddly peppery brows. "But I never left."

If he hadn't left, he'd been keeping himself hidden pretty well. She wondered where, exactly, he was living. "Okay then, why are you still here? What do you want?"

His mouth lifted on one side in a sardonic smile. "I don't want anything, Pippin."

"You're here so you must," she said.

"*You* came out to see *me*," he said.

It was true, but he'd *wanted* her to see him. She knew that with certainty. Months ago, when they'd met in the library, Hugh had revealed that Titus was a common ancestor between them. Pippin's connection to Titus came from Morgan's lineage. It was her descendants who'd eventually come to America.

Titus had loved Morgan, but he'd also loved another woman in Rome. A woman he'd left pregnant. *That* was Hugh's lineage.

They were bound, whether Pippin liked it or not. His intense gaze bore into her. A jolt of anxiety shot through her. It was that same feeling that had come over her before... the feeling that he could see inside of her. That he *knew* what she was thinking.

"I don't mean here, right this second. I mean on the island. Why are you in Devil's Cove?"

That infernal smile stayed firmly in place. "Because you are here, of course. We are yoked together, you and I," he said with his cavernous voice.

Maybe he *could* read her mind. "I don't think I like the sound of that."

He leveled his gaze at her. "You don't trust me yet."

Yet? She didn't think she ever would. "Should I?"

His otherworldly eyes pinched together under his beakish nose. Under the shadows cast by the late afternoon sun crossing his face, he looked a thousand times more sinister than he had the previous times she had met him, and that was saying a lot. "Our shared ancestors go back two millennia."

"But the Lane side has nothing to do with you," she said. *That's* why she didn't trust him. He had inserted himself into her history. What she didn't know was why.

He tsk'd as if he was scolding petulant child. "Pippin. I have nothing to hide from you. Ask me anything. I am an open book."

She bristled at the expression, staring at him. While he knew about the curse on her family, she hadn't explicitly told him about her divination. But he'd known that Cassie had left Oregon behind and ended up here, on the Outer Banks. The last time they'd met, he told her he was a student of humanity, so of course he knew about her bibliomancy.

As the light faded, the old-fashioned streetlights went on. The evening breeze picked up, stirring Pippin's skirt and chilling her legs. She moved, crossing the street and standing against the building to block the gusty night air. She positioned herself in a spot where Daisy would still be able to see her—see them—from the library window. Hugh followed. She asked the first question that came to mind. "Did you actually know my parents?"

"Alas, no. But I have heard much about them. Committed and loving people from what I gather."

"And who exactly did you *gather* that from?"

"That isn't important."

"Of course, it is," she snapped. "Who's talking about Cassie and Leo? Who's after...after..."

He cocked a peppered brow at her. "After...?"

It felt as if he was toying with her, only pretending to ask her questions—questions to which he actually already knew the answers. If felt as if he could read her mind or see inside her soul. She shivered. Willed any thought or image of the Roman coin from her mind in case he really could. "After whatever the Lane lore says."

"Some do believe that Titus gave something to Morgan. That story has been passed on through oral history, and the parts that survived have been committed to paper."

Committed to paper in a manner only the Lane women could read. *My Descendants*. Pippin remembered the Yeats poem from a book of poetry her father had. Looking at it in the context of what Hugh was saying, it felt like Morgan speaking to her future descendants. They possessed something. *Yes, the necklace*. They knew something. *Yes, that the curse was real*. They had to *do* something. *Yes, break it*.

She stood there silent, waiting for him to offer something else. Hugh paused for a weighty few seconds before responding. "I have come to believe your father discovered something more *valuable* than whatever trinket Titus bestowed upon Morgan."

She caught her hand going to her throat, stopping it before it got that far. "Valuable? Like, what?" she asked.

He tilted his head. Considered her, as if he was trying to gauge if she knew more than she was saying. "That's the mystery, isn't it?"

"*How* have you come to believe this?" she asked.

His gaze was steady on her. "I understand you found the body of a dead man in the bookshop."

Hugh had a tendency of not answering her questions directly. Having a conversation with him was like taking a scenic road trip. Her radar flared at the mention of Connell Foley. "Yes, a rare books dealer."

"Connell Foley. I knew him."

Pippin pressed her back against the wall, taking a moment to process. How could Hugh have known the dead man?

He slipped his hand into his pocket, withdrawing a piece of paper. On it was a single name written in neat straight up and down print.

Seamus O'Dulany

SHE LOOKED at the name on the paper, then up at him, but without her even registering the movement, Hugh had started walking. He headed away from town, going north on Main Street. "Who is Seamus O'Dulany?" she called after him.

He walked on, never breaking stride, not turning around.

"Hey!" she hollered. Held up the slip of paper. "What am I supposed to do with this?"

A woman's raspy voice by her side made Pippin jump. "I seen that guy before."

Pippin tamped down the sharp beating of her heart. "Who, him?" she asked, pointing to toward Hugh's retreating figure.

"He's a ghost. Here one minute, gone the next. He goes to the pier at night." The woman snapped her fingers to emphasize the point.

She was bundled in layers of clothing. Her face was shadowed under a hood, but Pippin could see the thin lips and the leathery skin, courtesy of the sun and the elements. She kept one eye on Hugh's shrinking figure, the other on the old woman. "What's he do at the pier?"

"Stares out like he's lost in another world. Like he can see past the barrier islands straight to the Atlantic."

So, it wasn't just Pippin who felt the man saw more than what was visible to the naked eye. The woman started walking in the opposite direction Hugh had gone. "Can I help you with anything?" Pippin asked, wondering where the woman lived...if she had a home. Or if the pier *was* her home.

She kept walking though. Without turning around, she threw up one arm and wagged her index finger toward the sky. Her way of saying she was just fine.

Pippin let her go. Wondering about where the woman lived made her pose the same question to herself about Hugh. Where was he staying? There were a few other bed and breakfasts in town. There were also some short-term rental homes. Any hotels were across the swing bridge in Sand Point or beyond. Somehow, she couldn't see Hugh in any of these scenarios. They all felt too pedestrian for the man.

A crow cawed as it glided overhead, disappearing into the fading light. Pippin made a split-second decision. Her thumbs flew over the keyboard of her cellphone as she texted Daisy, asking her to watch Sailor for a while longer. And then she was off. By now Hugh was several blocks away and just barely in her sights. Instead of heading straight from Main Street to Rum Runner's Lane, he veered left and took Buccaneer, heading into the residential part of town. Pippin raced across the street, following in his footsteps, running until she was just a block and a half behind him.

On a normal evening stroll, she would have stopped to chat with neighbors who sat on their porches, or she would have leisurely admired the bright old houses in the historic district, and their colorful flower gardens. Not tonight.

A rustling sound nearby entered her consciousness, and then a voice said, "Nice evening for a walk, isn't it?"

Pippin jerked and stifled a screech as another woman appeared. "Yes. Uh, sorry. I have to..." She hurried along, peering at Hugh's figure growing smaller as the distance between them grew longer.

"It's Pippin, isn't it?" the woman's voice followed Pippin.

Pippin took her eyes off of Hugh for a split second to take a closer look at the woman. Black dress and a black cape. Dark hair and dark eyes. An aged face and spotted hands. She was slight, but stood tall, her shoulders back. Recognition sparked. This was Hattie's longtime friend, Wenna. The first time they'd met—well, the *only* time they'd met—was when Wenna had been visiting and the two friends had been sitting in rocking chairs on Hattie's porch. Just like she had then, Wenna reminded Pippin of an old crone, her face carrying the wrinkles of three lifetimes. Despite that, her voice was strong. She thought all of this in a mere second, responding with a quick, "Yes."

She looked down the street, trying to spot Hugh again. She narrowed her eyes, hoping to catch a glimpse of his shadow. But he was gone. Like the woman earlier had observed, he vanished like a ghost.

She stopped now and turned to Wenna. "You're Hattie's friend."

"Good memory, my dear," she said warmly. Her gaze followed Pippin's. "Are you looking for someone?"

In the distance, she saw nothing but dark houses and the low lights of the street lamps. "I was, but he's gone now."

Pippin glanced at the slip of paper Hugh had given her. She had been clutching it in one hand, but now she flattened it out and tucked it into the pocket of her skirt.

Wenna watched her, her head cocked slightly to one side. "Which way are you going now, my dear?" she asked.

"Back to town," Pippin said. "To the library."

Wenna glanced at the darkening sky. "It's not closed?"

"It is now, but I left my dog there with my friend—"

"I see, so you could catch up with another friend."

"I wouldn't call him a friend," she corrected, "but yes. I need to go back and get Sailor."

"I'll walk with you to the corner," Wenna said. "If that's all right with you."

"Of course." Pippin thought about holding her arm out for the old woman to hold onto, but Wenna's cape billowed behind her as she practically glided along. It was as if her feet didn't even touch the ground. She moved like a dancer, and Pippin felt clumsy and heavy-footed next to her.

"I'm off to visit Hattie," Wenna said.

Pippin hoped Daisy and Ruby would have that. That

when they were old biddies, the three of them would sit together on the inn's porch, rocking to and fro, reminiscing about the good old days before the curse had been broken. "It's good to see you again."

"Indeed, it is," Wenna said as they reached the corner. "This is where I leave you."

"Are you...I can walk the rest of the way with you. To Hattie's," she said peering into the dark sky.

"No, my dear. I am perfectly fine. You go get your dog. I will see you again." She said it matter-of-factly, as if there was no question on the matter.

Before Pippin could object, Wenna was on her way, heading up Rum Runner's Lane toward Hattie's colorful house. She walked quickly and with determination. The further she went from Pippin, the fainter her figure became. Once she had nearly disappeared into the darkness, Pippin turned and headed back down Main Street. The library was locked up tight. No sign of Daisy or Sailor, or even Harold. It was only then that Pippin thought to look at her phone. There it was; a text from Daisy. *Sorry I couldn't keep Sailor. Kyron picked me up. I left her with Jamie.*

Pippin sent her a thumbs up emoji before backtracking diagonally across the street to The Open Door. The bookshop was closed, too, but Pippin could see Jamie standing behind the register. He looked up when she knocked, smiling when he saw it was her. When he came to unlock the door for her, Sailor was by his side. Pippin caught Sailor's attention and gave a huge smile and excited jazz hands to say, "Hello!" She crouched and pressed her nose to Sailor's, her hands on either side of her face. It had become their special greeting, and Sailor's tail whipped excitedly. "Hey, girl," Pippin said, letting her go and standing up. "Thanks for watching her," she said to Jamie. "I didn't plan on being gone that long."

Jamie locked the door behind her. He had stacks of bills in different denominations lined up on the counter. "Cashing out for the day," he said, but he didn't resume the task. His smile faded. "Daisy said you saw ol' clear eyes."

"I saw him from the library window." A shiver threaded up her spine. "He was staring right at me."

One of Jamie's eyes pinched with concern. "Do you think he's watching you?"

That thought had crossed her mind. "He definitely knew I was there, and seemed to expect me to come meet him," she said, not directly answering Jamie's question.

"What did he say?"

She answered by retrieving the paper from her pocket and handing it to him.

"Seamus O'Dulany? Who's that?"

"I have no idea."

"Do you think he knows about the coins?" he asked.

She shrugged in a way that communicated she had no idea. "He said he thought my dad discovered something else —besides the sword hilt—but he didn't know what it was." She'd thought he was fishing for information, as if Pippin could tell him what else Leo knew. "He knows about Titus and Morgan, about the stolen sword hilt, about Cassie leaving Oregon and coming here, about Leo's research. So how can he *not* know about the coin?" she mused.

Jamie dipped his chin in agreement. "So, is he friend or foe?" he asked.

That was an unanswerable question. A small part of her thought Hugh *was* trying to help her. The name Seamus O'Dulany, for example, might lead her to some vital discovery that would help her break the curse.

Then again, he had to have an ulterior motive. Their shared ancestor was on Titus's side, so Hugh wasn't subject to the curse. He had nothing to fear from the sea. But that didn't mean he didn't want whatever treasure might be out there. "He could be either. I have no way to know," she said, shrugging her shoulders.

Jamie considered this. "Maybe he's just a treasure-hunter. Nothing more."

Pippin dismissed the idea with a quick shake of her head. "No. Jamie, he's after something. Something only I can lead him to. He said he had nothing to hide, and that he was an open book." Pippin repeated what he'd said in her head. *Ask me anything. I'm an open book.* "I didn't ask him the right question," she said suddenly.

Jamie picked up the paper Hugh had given Pippin. "Seems like the right question might be about this. Who is Seamus O'Dulany?"

CHAPTER 15

Walls have ears.
Doors have eyes.
Trees have voices.
Beasts tell lies.
Beware the rain.
Beware the snow.
Beware the man
You think you know.
-Songs of Sapphique
~Catherine Fisher, *Incarceron*

PIPPIN HAD GONE to bed thinking about Seamus O'Dulany, and had woken up thinking about Connell Foley. The same questions she had had about him from the beginning were circling her mind. *Why had he booked a room at the inn? What had he wanted to talk with her about?*

She served brunch with Hazel, then went about her morning tasks. She sorted through upcoming reservations on her tablet at the check-in counter, but her mind kept drifting to Bernadette. She hadn't seen or heard a peep from her since Doc Wilkenson's visit. And then there was Hugh, and Seamus O'Dulany. She waggled her head as if she could dislodge whatever bit of helpful information was tucked away out of sight. Whatever bothered her about the whole thing was just out of reach. "Who else was in the bookshop with him?"

Hazel looked up from the coffee table where she was straightening a stack of magazines. "What?"

Pippin started. She hadn't realized she'd spoken aloud. "Oh, nothing," she said, chastising herself for being so distracted. "Just thinking. Out loud, apparently."

Hazel's forehead crinkled with concern. She left the coffee table and magazines behind and came over to Pippin. "Are you still thinking about the man who died?"

Pippin hadn't meant to spark a conversation about any of this. She gave a reluctant nod. "Just ignore me," she said, trying to drop the subject.

The front door opening stopped Hazel from pressing her train of thought. They both turned to see a stocky man framed in the doorway. He quickly scanned the room. When he saw them, he broke into a wide smile. "Pippin!" His voice boomed, echoing in the big, open room.

As he walked closer, the crow's feet shooting from the corners of his eyes and the strands of grey threaded through his dark brown hair became more evident. Up close, he looked ten years older than he did from farther away. "Mr. Riordin," Pippin said, offering him a smile.

Jed Riordin had been one of her father's friends from the marina. His boat had been docked a few slips down from Leo's, but he'd proclaimed himself as nothing more than an amateur fisherman, not in the same league as Leo.

Two vertical lines carved into the space between his eyes. "Call me Jed. We're like old friends, aren't we?"

Pippin didn't agree with *that* statement. She had met the man twice, once when he'd popped in unannounced to ask about her father's belongings, and the other time at the grand opening party for Sea Captain's Inn. The second time, she had scarcely had time to acknowledge him, she'd been so busy. He was on the membership roster of Synkéntrosi. Synkéntrosi was a Greek word meaning 'gathering'. In the context of Devil's Cove, it was a discussion group that had started as a couple of men getting together to talk about big ideas. That was back when Leo was a young man. It had grown since then to include twenty or thirty men who met monthly. Jamie and Cyrus were part of it, as was Quincy Ratherford of the Devil's Cove Gazette, and other island residents. Max Lawrence had been part of it. He'd protected the necklace for two decades. Now he was dead.

The fact was, outside of her small group, Pippin didn't know who she could trust. "It's good to see you again, Jed," she said, making an effort to be friendly.

He slapped an open hand against the desk's counter, making a startlingly loud walloping sound. "By God, you did do something great with this place, didn't you? Your dad would be mighty proud of you. It's going well, I assume?"

"It is. Great, in fact," Pippin said, not mentioning the fact that two of her recent guests had died while staying at the inn. At least Connell Foley hadn't died on the premises, although that didn't change the fact that he had been a guest and was still dead. Whatever curse was upon the Lane family, it seemed to have spread to the inn itself.

"Great, great. Glad to hear it." He swiveled his head, letting his gaze travel the great room. As it came back to

Pippin, he leaned in and lowered his voice. "Listen, can I pull you away for a second?"

Being alone with another person whose motives she didn't trust was the last thing she wanted to do, but she gave a tight smile. "Sure." She glanced at Hazel. "I'll be back in a minute," she said, then led Jed Riordin out to the front porch. Instead of stopping there, however, he turned and headed down one side of the double stairway leading to ground level. Pippin had no choice but to follow. He stepped over the flowerbed and onto the patch of grass.

Pippin stopped on the brick walkway, maintaining some distance. "Is everything okay?"

He turned and forced a little laugh. "Sure, sure. Everything's fine."

If she had to choose one word to describe him in this moment, it was shifty, and she did not believe him for a second. Just because he told her that he'd been friends with her father didn't actually make it true. She had learned to take things with a grain of salt.

He waited, as if she might hop over the flower bed and follow him, but she stayed put, hands on her hips.

Finally, he sighed and walked back to her, keeping to the grassy side of the flowers. "It's a rather sensitive topic," he said. "Prying eyes and all that."

"There's no one here to pry," she said, even though she didn't really believe that. It seemed there was always someone nosing into her business—Salty Gallagher, Jimmy, Monique Baxter, and Zoe Ibis to name just a few. The walls had ears.

He took her comment at face value. "I think you're wrong there. You have to be careful who you trust on this island."

She dipped her chin and crossed her arms over her chest. "And am I supposed to trust you?"

"Yes," he said without hesitation. "I was a good friend of your father's. He didn't trust many people, so he relied on those he did. I was one of those people, Pippin. You need to believe that."

She gave a derisive little laugh. "Unfortunately, he's not around to corroborate that. And to be honest, *Jed*, your word isn't enough to make me trust you."

He cupped his hand behind his beefy neck and looked upward, as if the sky had all the answers. "Point taken," he said, looking back at her. "What can I do to prove it to you? Your dad was a great guy. Devoted to your mother. Devoted to you and Grey. I had a hard time believing he just walked away from you both." He looked across the yard at the space on the driveway where Leo's fishing boat had been dry-docked for twenty years. "I'm glad he didn't—I mean him dying isn't a better scenario— Christ, this is not coming out right."

She cut him a little slack. "I know what you mean."

"Let me just cut to the chase. You and your brother, you have to be careful. Max Lawrence dying. Then that Baxter woman, and now..." He paused. Regrouped. "Listen, it's not over."

"What does that mean, it's not over?"

"Your dad was onto something when he died," Jed said. His low voice echoed what Hugh had told her. Even at a low level, his voice boomed. "These people, whoever they are, have proven they're willing to kill for whatever it was your dad knew or had."

Pippin raked her hand through her hair, dislodging the clip that held it up in the back. She yanked it free of the tangles, wound up her hair again, and snapped the clip back into place. "I don't know what you're talking about," she said, her voice more brusque than she had intended. The idea that people were coming out of the woodwork to find the treasure they were sure existed seemed surreal. She felt as if she was living in a Nicholas Cage movie.

Jed moved toward her a step. The toes of his shoes stopped at the edge of the grass. "The moment you and Grey reappeared, the curse was awakened."

A chill danced over skin. Those were almost the exact words Aunt Rose had used in her letter. "What curse?" she demanded, feigning ignorance. This was not going to be one of those: '*You know about the curse?' Answered with a cavalier, 'I didn't until you just confirmed it*' moments. No, Jed Riordin needed to explain himself.

He pulled a face, his mouth going askew. "Come on, Pippin. The curse on your family. The men drown, the women die giving birth. I know about it all. Your dad tried everything to save your mom, and you and Grey are being threatened now."

"Well, I'm not pregnant, so—"

"That's good, but surely you know that's not the most imminent danger. He entrusted a small group of people to help him," he said.

She stared. "He...what?"

"He couldn't do it alone—"

She pressed her hand against the base of her throat. There was no evidence that Leo had worked with anyone, but of course that didn't mean it wasn't true. She looked at him, trying to catch any glimpse of dishonesty. His face was a mask. "And you were one of those people?"

"Yes. I was, yes. Pippin, your father, he discovered something."

Her first meeting with Jed Riordin came back to her.

He'd asked about her father's things, but he hadn't said a thing about being in some trusted inner circle. Her skepticism flared. "Let me guess," she said. "You don't know what he discovered."

He heaved a sigh. "No, I don't—"

She scoffed. "So much for the inner circle."

He ignored her and kept on. "Whatever he discovered, it doesn't matter. I don't want to know. That's not why I'm here."

"Then why are you here?" she demanded. She wanted this conversation over and done with.

"Like I said. You're in imminent danger."

"From whom? You?"

It sounded so dramatic. Okay, so she wasn't only in a Nicholas Cage movie. Will Smith was in there, too, upping the stakes. Jed locked his eyes to hers, holding her gaze with the force of a magnet. He folded his arms like an armor that could deflect her skepticism. "I wasn't the only one your father trusted," he said like a teaser at the end of a movie.

She waited, then rolled her hand in the air to prod him. "Okay. So, who else?"

He paused. His Adam's apple moved in his throat as he swallowed. Finally, he spoke. "Connell Foley."

CHAPTER 16

"K*eep your friends close, keep your enemies closer."*

~Niccolò Machiavelli

PIPPIN WALKED TOWARD THE STREET, away from the house. Jed Riordin was on her heels. "Connell Foley was murdered," he said ominously.

She spun around to face him. "No. No he wasn't."

Jed's expression was tight and unwavering. "He was."

She let every last bit of air leave her lungs with her exhalation. That couldn't be true. "The sheriff thinks he probably had a heart attack, or maybe a stroke. He says he hit his head on the corner of the table as he fell."

Jed ignored her denial. "Pippin, listen to me. Someone killed him so he couldn't talk to you."

Pippin felt her skin turn clammy. "But how? How would that even be possible? Erin didn't see anyone going into the book room—"

"Did she see Foley go in?"

She hadn't, because she had been dealing with spilled milk and crying children. Her face revealed her answer, and Jed's mouth drew into a tight line. "Your witness is unreliable. Obviously, he did go into the book room. Unseen. Someone else went with him. Twenty years ago, Foley and your dad were looking for something. I don't know what, exactly, but I think Connell may have finally found it. I think he was murdered because of it."

Murdered. The idea choked Pippin's insides. "How did my father know him?" she asked.

"He said it was serendipity. They met at an estate sale they both attended. Connell was something of an expert on the Irish and late middle ages—thirteenth, fourteenth, fifteenth centuries. He collected books from that era. The Irish thing lassoed them together. Your dad trusted him, and Connell pretty much gave up everything else to help Leo."

The air slowly left Pippin's lungs. A connection to her father explained why Connell had the compendium of Tuatha dé Danann. A distant caw came from a solitary crow gliding through the air far overhead. She lowered her voice and hissed. "Are you saying someone *killed* him because of what he knew? Because of my family?"

"That's *exactly* what I'm saying."

Pippin felt like throwing her hands in the air and giving up. None of this made any sense. Her father had discovered something. Something *else* other than the necklace.

And now, according to Jed, yet another person had lost their life because of it.

"What am I supposed to do with that?" she said, her frustration mounting. "I don't know what to do with that. I don't know how to figure out what my dad knew."

Jed rooted himself to the ground with his heels. "I've been thinking about something Leo said. It's bothered me all these years, and, well, maybe you can make sense of it."

Pippin felt a flare of anticipation mixed with suspicion. "Okay."

"He told me early on about the curse. I mean, not when we first met, but once he felt he could...you know...trust me."

"Right. I got it."

Jed's nostrils flared with his heavy breaths. "He said there was a betrayal and a pact with an Irish god. That that is where the curse came from, and that he had to go back there—to the origin—to stop it."

"Right," she said again. It's exactly what she thought, and what she'd tried to do by offering Lir Titus's sword hilt.

"But shortly before he died, he said something else. At the time, I didn't think anything of it, but now...I'm not sure."

"What did he say?" she prodded.

Jed exhaled another heavy breath. "He said he couldn't break the pact with Lir. He said it had to do with a man."

Pippin's brows pinched together. "With what man?"

Jed shrugged. "He was in his own world, researching. It seemed like he'd made a discovery, but he didn't explain it and I didn't ask. But maybe you can make sense of it."

Pippin turned this over in her head. Leo couldn't break the curse with the god himself. What did that mean?

The hope that she might have a new clue to work with dissolved because a curse made by a god couldn't be broken by a man.

CHAPTER 17

"I think talking about one's love life is always... It's a Pandora's box, best kept in journals."
~Emma Caulfield

PIPPIN MET Jamie at the front door, letting him in and holding a finger to her lips. The house was quiet, all the guests had gone to bed. Her need to debrief everything that had happened was eating away at her. At long last, they had time to process. "Straight to The Burrow," she said, her voice low. *Prying eyes,* Jed had said. *The walls have ears.*

The unexpected sound of someone stirring came from the couch, stopping Pippin and Jamie in their tracks. Sailor kept going, heading for the kitchen and her water bowl, as usual, her nails clicking against the hardwood floor.

Pippin tiptoed up to the couch and peered over. Lil was stretched out on it, sighing lightly in her sleep. A paperback copy of a book on tarot fell to the floor. Quietly stepping back to Jamie, Pippin put a finger to her lips then pointed to the kitchen.

They left Lil sleeping, waited for Sailor to finish lapping up some water, then passed through Pippin's bedroom to the hidden access in the built-in shelves. Jamie and Sailor headed straight up the narrow staircase. Pippin closed the secret door behind her and followed.

"My father knew Connell Foley," she said in a rush once they were safely tucked away in The Burrow. She recounted her conversation with Jed Riordin.

"Do you believe him?" Jamie asked.

She had been at war with that question all evening. "Honestly, I don't know. He seemed sincere, but I don't think I'm the best judge of character."

"Don't sell yourself short, Pip. You have to learn to trust your gut and your instincts." He scanned the room, his gaze landing on the short stack of books that had surrounded Connell Foley. "Try one of his books."

She had begun to realize that everything happening in her life was tainted by the curse and completely intertwined with it. If Connell Foley had known her father, then, logically, his death was related to the curse. Jed Riordin certainly thought so. If it was, then starting with one of the books he'd been found with seemed like a good place to start.

She looked at the stack. None of them called out to her. She flipped through the thin paperback about Tuatha dé Danann, then went through both the index and the glossary. She hadn't expected to find Seamus O'Dulany's name there among the list of ancient Irish gods, but now it was firmly eliminated. She set the book aside. She held up the three fiction novels. "One of these, I think," she said.

One was as good as the next, so she started with *Captain Blood*. She sat on the rug in the middle of the small room. Before she could go through her ritual, the book slipped from her hands, as if pushed by some unseen force, and fell open. On the page full of letters and words and sentences, only one stood out to her.

> *"Peter Blood judged her- as we are all prone to do- upon insufficient knowledge."*

"So, someone you know was—or is—wrongly judged." Jamie said.

Her mind whirled as she mulled over the line. She had been trying to judge if Hugh and Jed were trustworthy. She didn't have a final verdict yet, though she was leaning toward untrustworthy. Was she wrong?

"Try another one."

Pippin set aside *Captain Blood* and picked up *Treasure Island* instead, the word 'treasure' drawing her to it. She directed all of her focus only on the Robert Louis Stevenson novel in her hands. Jamie sat down opposite her, watching her, expectant, his amber eyes bright behind his glasses and beneath the playful sweep of his hair. All of a sudden, a sliver of nervousness spread tiny tendrils inside her under his watchful gaze. What if it didn't work? What if her bibliomancy failed her?

"You can do it," he reassured her, as if he sensed her doubt. His voice was soft. Encouraging.

She blew out the breath she had been holding, a deep release that expelled her insecurity. The cover of the book was worn, but was basically in good shape. Still, she handled it with care, placing the spine on the floor in front of her. *"Ask me anything,"* Hugh had said. *"I'm an open book."*

Possible questions flapped around in her mind like the wings of a hummingbird, too fast to catch and hold onto one. Finally, the most obvious one surfaced.

"Who is Seam—" she started then stopped. Of course, the book couldn't give her an answer to such a specific question. She rephrased. "What do I need to know about Seamus O'Dulany?"

Then she dropped the sides of the book, letting them fall to either side. The pages settled and a single sentence darkened and undulated.

His stories were what frightened people worst of all.

SHE STARED AT THE WORDS, trying to make sense of them.

"Do you see something?" Jamie asked.

She read the line aloud to him. "I have no idea what that means. Seamus's stories? About what?"

She tried again, closing the book, posing the question, and letting the pages fall open. The same quote was revealed.

"Try a different question," Jamie suggested.

She went through the process again, pondering what to ask. It came to her like a bullet. "Can I trust Hugh?"

The book fell open to a different page. The words peeled off of the page.

I could not doubt that he hoped to seize upon the treasure, find and board the Hispaniola under cover of night, cut every honest throat about that island, and sail away as he had at first intended, laden with crimes and riches.

SHE READ IT ALOUD, then spun the book around for Jamie to see. "Seems like there's only one way to interpret that," he said. "He's a foe."

Her hand went to her naked neck, then her gaze settled on her father's safe where Cassie's necklace was safely hidden. She took the book back from Jamie as another question begged to be asked. She balanced the book on its spine. "I don't know what to do next," she said, then asked, "What do I do?"

We must go on, because we can't turn back.

HER SKIN EXPLODED WITH GOOSEBUMPS. There was no ambiguity in that message. She got up from the floor and sat in the chair, her heart pounding in her temples. She might not know what to do, but she couldn't stop. She couldn't turn back.

Jamie looked at her. "Are you okay?"

"I can't turn back," she said, pointing to the book. "It says I can't turn back."

"You weren't going to anyway," he said. "I've seen your determination. You're going to finish what your dad started, Pip. And I'm here with you. I'll help however I can."

She looked at him, more uncertainty filling her. Jamie the historian. Jamie the bookseller. Jamie the academic. Was he here for the treasure, too? Or for the anecdotes to history, courtesy of Pippin's ancestors? "Why?" she asked, her voice low. "Why are you here? Why do you want to help?"

He looked at her, puzzled. "What do you mean?"

Her years of trusting only Grey had kept other people at arm's length. She had begun to trust Jamie, but now doubt had wormed its way in. What did she have to offer him? What could he possibly see in her? "I mean, what's in it for you? Why do you want to help me? You're..." She fluttered one hand in the air, as if it could magically summon up the words she was trying to say, but Jamie had stood and come closer to her.

"I'm what?" he asked.

"Smart," she blurted. "You're so smart. And you light up when there's history, and this—" She waved her hand around again— "This is living, breathing history." She felt herself deflate as she spoke, because she didn't want to find out he was only here because of the history. Mathilda's observation about Jamie's and Pippin's feelings for one another—and Jamie telling Pippin that his daughter was right—drifted past. She tried to cling to it even as her voice cracked and she asked, "Is that what it's about?"

"Because I want to know about the history?" he asked, pushing his glasses up. "I mean, of course the history is fascinating. Your family is fascinating. But that's not why I want to help you. That's not why I'm here." He moved closer and put his hands on the arms of her chair, hinging at the waist until his face was inches from her. "I'm here because I'm crazy about you, Pip. You're on my mind all the time. All. The. Time."

An electric charge crackled inside of her. "But you're so educated, and I'm —"

And then his lips brushed hers, stopping her from finishing the statement.

She tried again. "And you've got the girls and your mom—"

And again, his lips stopped her from finishing.

"And I'm cursed," she weakly managed to say, because, after all, *this* was the biggie. *The* reason she couldn't give in to her feelings for Jamie. Except she *was* giving in, wasn't she?

He moved his head until his mouth was next to her ear. "And I'll be by your side until it's broken."

"You shouldn't—"

"But I am—"

"Jamie," she murmured.

"I'm not going anywhere, Pip," he said, his breath warm against her skin.

"You can't risk it—" she started to say, but his lips had found hers again, and the words dissolved into nothing.

And that was that. She gave into the kiss. She gave into her feelings for Jamie McAdams. And Pandora's Box opened.

CHAPTER 18

The Tuatha dé Danann came "without ships or barks, in clouds of fog [over the air, by their might of druidry]".

~Lebor Gabála Érenn, *The Book of the Taking of Ireland*

WHEN PIPPIN CRAWLED INTO BED, long after Jamie had gone home, all the anxiety she had managed to shove aside for the past two hours came flying back with the force of a bullet. She felt like she'd fallen in over her head, but she couldn't stop. That quote from Treasure Island repeated in her head:

We must go on because we can't turn back.

The curse had taken Leo. It had taken her grandmother, Annabel. Neither death was a direct result of the curse, unlike her grandfather, Edgar's, or Cassie's, but they died nonetheless.

She couldn't let that happen to Jamie. She couldn't let Heidi and Mathilda become orphans. She wouldn't let anything bad happen to them. She drifted off to sleep with her determined thoughts in her head.

She awoke, hours later, to the sharp sound of glass breaking. She was up and out of her room in seconds. Where had it come from? The house was still dark. The kitchen was silent. The door to the mudroom and to Hazel's small room beyond was closed. No light shone from beneath it.

She crept through the great room, starting on the left and following the perimeter of the room. The sun was just beginning to rise, soft rays of sunlight dappling the walls and the wood floor. Instead of easing her mind, the uneven patterns of light filled her gut with anxiety.

Trust your gut, Jamie had said.

Right now, it was telling her that something wasn't right.

She walked slowly past the fireplace. Past the staircase. Past the archway leading to the reading nook at the far end of the kitchen. Nothing was out of place. No knickknacks had fallen and broken.

She walked along the wall on the east end of the room. Past the door leading to the downstairs powder room. Past the little alcove where she stored snacks and water bottles for the guests. She cut across the corner and headed toward the foyer and the front door. That's when she saw it. Her breath caught. The front door was open a mere crack. A sliver of morning sun marked a vertical line between the door and the molding.

Had one of the guests gotten up early? Gone for a walk and accidentally left it open? She reacted without thinking, grabbing the handle, wrenching the door open, jumping back.

Nothing happened. No boogeyman leapt in front of her.

She blew out her breath as she inched forward, then poked her head out to look up and down the street. All was quiet.

She stepped back in, shut the door, and turned—and came face to face with Hazel. She bit back a scream. "Oh my God!" she said with a hiss, then slapped her hand over her mouth. "You scared me!" she said, her words muffled.

Hazel looked just as spooked. She wore a white, long sleeve nightgown that stopped mid-calf. She clutched a handful of the cotton fabric in one hand, the other arm stretched out, fingers pressing against one of the foyer pillars to steady herself. "You scared me!" she whispered. "What broke?"

Pippin let out another sharp exhalation. "I don't know. But the door was open."

The color drained from Hazel's face. "Open, open?"

Pippin didn't know what the alternative to open, open was, but she didn't ask. "Yesss—" She trailed off when she noticed her office door slightly ajar. It was impossible. She had a keyless entry handle installed with a code only she knew.

She grabbed Hazel's arm and pointed, but her thoughts suddenly stuttered. How had she not heard or seen Hazel walking across the great room? Could Hazel have come from her office?

She dismissed the idea just as quickly as it had surfaced. She knew she had locked the door, and Hazel didn't have the code.

No one could have been in her office. It was impossible unless...

...unless it had been opened from the inside.

She crept forward again, toward her office, Hazel right behind her. The floor was cold against her bare feet. At the door, she hesitated. She didn't have a weapon or any way to defend herself or Hazel. If someone was still in there...

It would be smarter to call the sheriff. Report a possible break-in. She started to back away, but in a flurry of movement, Hazel rushed past her and careened against the door with a grunt. The door flung wide, and Hazel tumbled into the room and onto the floor. Pippin froze. No one appeared. No one jumped on Hazel or barreled past them.

Her breath left her lungs in a rush. She hurried into her office and helped Hazel up. She immediately spotted the shards of glass on the floor, and once again, her heart was in her throat. Someone had broken into the inn. The question was, why?

PIPPIN CALLED the sheriff's department to report the break-in. In forty minutes, a deputy had arrived and taken all the information, told her he'd be back in touch, and left. "That's it?" Hazel asked when Pippin came into the kitchen.

"That's it."

They worked side by side, each lost in their own thoughts as they served breakfast to the guests. Pippin delivered plates to June and Heather. "Are you okay, honey?" Heather asked.

Pippin's shoulders dropped. She thought she had covered the dark circles under her eyes enough to mask her sleepiness and had stifled the adrenaline that still pulsed through her.

Apparently not. She forced a smile. "Just tired."

She spent the rest of the breakfast service keeping that smile pasted on her face. The minutes crept by, but finally it was over, and the kitchen was clean. She needed to get out.

To get some fresh air. "I'm going to go—" she started to say to Hazel, but the ringing of her phone cut her off. She pulled the device from her back pocket. Jamie's name practically shouted at her from the screen. Instead of going into her room, she went to the reading nook on the opposite end of the kitchen, sinking into one of the armchairs.

"Hey," Jamie said after she answered. "Good morning."

She pushed the break-in to the back of her mind for a moment. "Good morning to you," she said.

He paused for a long second before saying, "Listen, Pip. About last night—"

Her mind stuttered. About last night. Nothing good ever came from a sentence beginning with those three words. He was beating her to the punch. "Mmm hmm," she managed.

"It got me thinking about Connell Foley. What if he went to other rare book dealers before showing up at The Open Door?"

What if... The vice around Pippin's heart loosened. She knew she had to set boundaries with Jamie, but he hadn't called to say it had all been a big mistake. She breathed easier—at least for the time being. That conversation could wait. "That's an interesting idea," she said.

"I woke up thinking it was possible. So, I made a few phone calls this morning to a couple dealers I know. Two in New York have gone out of business, but three answered and are still in business."

Pippin sat up. "What'd you find out?"

He chuckled. "I thought this might interest you."

"It does. It definitely does."

"Well, I didn't find out much...yet. One of them had never heard of Connell Foley—"

"But the other one did?"

"Oh yeah. He has." Pippin could hear the smile in his

voice. "He got a phone call from Foley about ten days ago, and a week ago, Foley came to his store."

"Was he looking for the same books? *Treasure Island* and *Kidnapped* and *Captain Blood*?"

"That's the thing, Pip. He wasn't interested in the classics. He was looking for books on Irish lore and history. That validates what Riordin said about his expertise."

She felt her brow furrow. "I don't understand. Are there rare books on Irish lore?"

"Sure. Name a subject and there's probably a rare book on it somewhere. But he wanted something specific. A history of Irish curses."

She let those words sink in, then said, "From Tuatha dé Danann?"

"Yup. Specifically, about Manannán."

She repeated the word. "Manannán. What's that?"

"Not what. Who. Manannán mac Lir."

"Lir, as in...Lir? Our Lir?"

"As in 'son of...'" he said. "Manannán mac Lir is the Son of the Sea. He's a warrior and is king of the Otherwold. Here's the thing, though. He's the over-king of the surviving Tuatha dé Danann after humans and Christianity came along."

"So he's still around, this Manannán mac Lir?"

"Depends who you talk to. The general belief is that most of Tuatha dé Danann are gone, but Manannán rules over those who are left. He's said to use féth fíada—the mist of invisibility—to hide from humans."

"Féth fíada." Pippin let the sounds roll off her tongue, doing her best to capture the Irish sounds the way Jamie had. "Invisibility. Like the Invisibility Cloak in Harry Potter? Is that where it comes from?"

"You mean did JK Rowling borrow the idea of the Invisibility Cloak from Irish mythology? Maybe. It's pretty similar. The difference is that féth fíada is a magical mist, or a veil, not an actual cloak. When the members of Tuatha dé Danann enshrouded themselves with it, they became invisible to mortals. Manannán mac Lir is said to have given a fairy mound, to dwell in, to each member of Tuatha dé Danann, raising the mist of invisibility to keep themselves hidden."

These new pieces of information bumped around in Pippin's mind. Morgan Dubhshláine's pact had been with Lir. But...

Jed had said Leo "couldn't break the pact with Lir. He said it had to do with a man." Her heart expanded to bursting. Not man...but...Man. As in Manannán. "He couldn't break the pact with Lir," she murmured. "He had to go a man."

"Pip? You okay?"

She heard Jamie's voice, but it sounded far away, her thoughts in front of it, louder. Clearer. If Manannán mac Lir was now the god who ruled over the sea, that meant the pact might now be with him. That's what Leo had discovered.

"Pippin?"

This time, Jamie's voice in her ear brought her back. "He couldn't break the pact with Lir," she said. "He had to go to man. With Man. With Manannán mac Lir."

"Oh, shit."

Exactly.

The very idea brought up a slew of new questions. Could Manannán mac Lir, ruler of the sea, break the pact? Would he? And even if he could and would, how was she supposed to find an Irish god who concealed himself from the human eye?

She didn't have any way to answer the questions, so she

went back to what she could process. "If Connell Foley was looking for Irish curses related to Manannán mac Lir, Jed Riordin must be telling the truth. He knew about us. About the Lanes."

"Your gut told you Foley was connected to you and your family," Jamie said. "You were right."

She switched her phone to her other hand. "He had to have known my father is dead. So why was he here in Devil's Cove? And why was he at your shop?"

Of course, Jamie didn't have answers to those questions.

Bernadette! Connell's wife of nearly thirty-six years might know what her husband had been up to.

"What if Foley was murdered?" Pippin blurted, starting to believe what Jed Riordin had told her. The break-in was front and center again. "Hugh. Some other member of the treasure hunting club Salty Gallagher and Monique Baxter were part of. Someone else lurking around, hiding in plain sight." Her mind strayed to Hazel Hood. The woman had appeared out of nowhere, showing up just when Pippin needed her the most. How? Why?

She shook the suspicion away. Surely history wouldn't repeat itself.

"That presupposes that he knew something," Jamie said, sounding like he'd already processed through various scenarios.

"Jed thinks he did, though." She went on to the other question circling around. What did the two Robert Louis Stevenson books or *Captain Blood* have to do with anything? Aunt Rose and Jed Riordin both said that the curse had awakened. What if Connell Foley knew that? "

What if what Jed said is true? If my father told him that it wasn't Lir, but Manannán mac Lir, and Connell Foley really was a friend, then Leo probably told him, too, right? If he figured out the curse was active again—because it did try to take Grey, right?—then maybe he was looking for some old book about Irish curses to figure out how to break it."

Her eyes widened with realization as the answer came to her. "He was still trying to help Leo...help Grey and me," she said. "Jamie, he wasn't stealing from you. He was trying to help."

"You think he knew you're a bibliomancer?" Jamie asked, his skepticism traveling the airwaves from The Open Door to her.

"Maybe. I mean, probably. Wouldn't Leo have told him that? The women are all bibliomancers. And they're cursed to die," she intoned like a fortune teller might. "I mean Jed knows. Hugh knows. Maybe the entire treasure hunting secret society knows. Why not someone who was actually on Leo's side?"

"But why the other books? The Stevenson and Sabatini books?" Jamie asked.

She didn't have an answer to that, but the messages the books had communicated to her came to mind. The first, about someone seizing the treasure, still seemed to be about Hugh. He was after it himself. The one about judgement puzzled her completely.

But it was the other one that sent a chill up her spine. *We must go on, because we can't turn back.*

Connell Foley gave his life up for the past.

"What's going on?" Jamie asked.

"Hang on." She raced past Hazel and to her room. She closed the door behind her before hustling up to The Burrow. She dropped her phone on the desk and grabbed *Treasure Island*, the book that had given her the other messages, but no, that wasn't right. She had used it already. She exchanged it for *Captain Blood*, feeling the weight of it in her hand. Once again, she replaced it, though, choosing *Kidnapped* instead. She set it on its spine and asked the question at the forefront of her mind. "What do I need to know about Connell Foley?"

She dropped the sides and let the pages flutter. A line immediately appeared to her.

THERE ARE two things that men should never weary of, goodness and humility; we get none too much of them in this rough world among cold, proud people.

SHE PICKED up her cellphone again, breathless. "Jed was telling the truth. He was trying to help, Jamie. Connell—he really was trying to help."

CHAPTER 19

"Never a good sign, he thought, when the crows showed up."

~Justin Cronin

THIRTY MINUTES after Pippin called Grey to tell him about the break-in and her theory about Connell Foley, he was at the inn; wood, hammer, and nails in hand. His arms were flecked with dried wood stain and a thin layer of wood dust covered his work clothes, remnants of whatever project he'd been working on. She leaned against the wall in her office watching him while he boarded up the window from the outside until the wood blocked him from view. In so many ways, he was Pippin's other half. As kids, they'd created a special language that only they understood. Even though they did not use their secret language anymore, they still used their childhood nicknames for each other. Whenever she and Grey were in the same room together, a sense of calm settled over Pippin. Grey's presence had that effect, even now when he was tense and worried because danger was, once again, darkening their doorway.

He came inside to secure it from that direction. "Peevie, you gotta be careful. If that coin is worth what we think it is, whoever wants it isn't going to stop till they find it."

"I'm going to open a safe deposit box at the bank," she said. "It's the only way to keep it from getting into the wrong hands." The Burrow was the safest place in the house, but people knew about it. Some of the treasure hunters knew about it. It wouldn't stay secret for long. She was surprised no one had broken into it yet given that Salty and Jimmy Gallagher both knew about it.

The thought that Camille might also know about it, courtesy of her incarcerated husband, crossed her mind. Could Camille have broken the office window in hopes of getting into The Burrow?

"I'll go with you," Grey said.

Pippin scurried back to her room. Up to The Burrow. She caught a glimpse of the crow on the windowsill outside. Hattie thought the black bird was a sign of good luck, but Pippin wasn't so sure. It felt ominous the way it hung around, always turning up and stirring the anxiety living inside her. "Shoo!" She waved her hand at it, but it didn't budge. It angled its head and looked directly at Pippin. For the first time, she noticed the blue tint to its eyes. She inched closer to get a better look, but the movement spooked the bird. As it opened its wings, Pippin thought she caught a glimpse of a single white feather. No. Impossible. She clamped her eyes shut for a second, then opened them again. The crow was gone.

Good. She didn't need a harbinger of doom hanging around. She unlocked the safe. Before storing the necklace there, she had wrapped it up and tucked it away in an empty jewelry box, trading places with the silver necklace her grandmother had given her on her twenty-fifth birthday. Her hand went to her neck. She wore that now, instead of her mother's necklace. It didn't offer the same comfort or connection to Cassie, but it was from someone who had loved her, and that was enough.

She pocketed the little velvet box and hurried back to Grey. He drove them in his truck, and twenty minutes later he sat next to her while she filled out the form to rent a safe deposit box. Ten minutes after that, she and Grey took one last look at the necklace before locking it up.

As they left the bank, she felt as if the weight of the world slipped right off her shoulders. "I didn't know I'd feel so relieved. We should have done that sooner."

"Hindsight. It's done now," Grey said.

Pippin's cell phone rang when they were halfway back to the inn. It was Jamie requesting that she and Grey come talk to Cyrus about Connell Foley. Cyrus was part of the small circle of people Pippin trusted. He'd known her parents. He'd been helping her parents. And he was helping her. "We'll be there in a few minutes," she said. Grey changed routes and headed to Main Street.

CYRUS'S LIVING room was as familiar to Pippin as Sea Captain's Inn. She had been here many times as a child, the first time on the day an old woman had dropped a copy of *The Odyssey,* the book which foretold Leo's death. Since then, Cyrus McAdams had tried to help Pippin's parents unravel the curse that plagued their family.

His flat smelled like a spring day on the coast after a

sudden rainstorm. The simple style of his living room fit him perfectly. The living room opened to the bedroom, a framed archway separating the two spaces. Black and white photographs hung on the walls. Black open-backed bookshelves took up one entire wall. Cyrus had a collection of nonfiction books—history, archeology, biography, plus entire shelves filled with old books whose histories were both written on the pages and woven into the fabric of the binding, telling the story of those who had held the book before.

The color scheme throughout was black and white and gray. Once inside, Grey stood with his back to the bookshelves, a little away from the group, hands in his pockets. "Don't want to get your furniture dirty," he said.

Cyrus nodded. "Good man."

Pippin sat on the modern gray couch across from Erin, who'd already arrived. She was pale and subdued, compared to her usual bubbly self. Still shaken over discovering a dead body, Pippin thought.

Cyrus took one of the low-profile white chairs. He was ageless. Snowy white hair and a receding hairline; bright blue eyes that formed slits and angled down on the outsides. On someone else, those eyes might have looked menacing or eerie. On Cyrus McAdams, with the puffy half-moons underneath them, they made him look mysteriously ruminative. With his signature three-quarter zip black sweater and neatly trimmed salt and pepper goatee, the man was dashing personified.

Jamie stood next to Grey. He wore a plain white t-shirt under an open chambray button down and jeans. He suddenly moved, walking to the east-facing window, which overlooked the sound, then back. His wire-framed glasses slipped as he paced. Suddenly, he spun to face Cyrus as he shoved them back into place. "Something's been bugging me, Grandad."

As Cyrus's lips curled into a smile, more crow's feet mushroomed from the corners of his eyes. "I know it has."

If Jamie was surprised by his grandfather's observation, he didn't show it. He launched into his question. "When Lieutenant Jacobs asked if you knew that dead man—Connell Foley—you said you didn't know him. Was that the truth?"

Cyrus sat back, his smile turning wry. "Jamie, my boy, of course it was the truth. No, I did not know the man. But I did find something interesting."

Pippin leaned forward. If Cyrus McAdams founds something curious, she wanted to know more. "What is it?"

"It is just...his name. It is Irish, which, in and of itself, is curious. A coincidence since we are in the thick of an Irish mystery, are we not? But Foley..."

"What about it?" Grey asked.

Instead of answering the question, Cyrus waggled a finger in Jamie's direction. "Put that cellphone of yours to good work. Look it up, would you?"

Jamie obliged, slipping his phone from the front pocket of his jeans. He navigated to a browser app and typed with his thumbs. He read, then summarized. "It comes from the Irish 'Ó Foghladha'," he said, pronouncing the Irish name as 'Oh-Fu-la-ha', "which is derived from 'Foghlaide'. 'Foghlaide' is a plunderer or a pirate."

Cyrus leaned his head back, but in the low-profile chairs, he had nothing to rest it against. He brought it upright again. His eyes narrowed. "Just as I said, curious."

Jamie shoved his phone back into his pocket. "Curious how? The guy didn't choose his last name."

"Assuming it is his real name, which I believe it probably

is, then you are right. He didn't choose his last name. But it does reflect his ancestry. You said he was working with Leo. The question is '*Why*?'"

Jamie thought for a moment. He took his glasses off and rubbed his eyes. When he put them back on, his face had cleared. He looked at Pippin for a beat before turning back to his grandfather. "It could be."

"What could be?" Pippin asked. She had the same lost feeling she'd had through school when all the other kids read circles around her while she struggled to sort out the letter sounds. She wanted to understand, but it wasn't coming together for her as quickly as for Cyrus and Jamie.

Jamie had a masters from the National University of Ireland in Galway, and a doctorate in Medieval Irish Literature from Maynooth. Plus, he had a second doctorate in anthropology. Something about the conquering of the Irish. He'd had to explain to Pippin that Galway is in the west of Ireland and Maynooth is in County Kildare. Not that that helped much, in and of itself. She'd had to look it all up on a map to get her bearings.

The fact was the man was highly educated. He sold books for a living by choice, but his brain was always working, and it seemed as if he had retained everything he'd ever learned. Pippin listened intently as he launched into a history lesson. "The Irish were among the first of the European countries which adopted fixed hereditary surnames. The first fixed surname recorded in Europe is from the year 916. O'Clery, which is derived from Ó Cléirigh."

He spun around and started pacing again, past Grey, around his mother, circling the couch where Pippin sat, then looping back to where he'd started. "Incorporating Ó, with an accent, means 'grandson'. So O'Clery now could be traced back to Ó Cléirigh, which means the grandson of the clerk. More specifically, it was the death of Tigherneach Ua Cléirigh. He was a lord of Aidhne in County Galway. Ó Cléirigh is an occupational name. In America it would be like Baker or Smith. By the eleventh century, surnames had two common elements. They all began with O, which had previously been Ua, or Mac. The second part was the personal name, usually for the ancestor being honored. It's the equivalent of Johnson—son of John, or Robertson, son of Robert. Back to the eleventh century. Brian Boru was simply known as Brian, High King of the Irish. We can thank his grandson, Teigue, who adopted the surname Ua Brian. Literally grandson of Brian, to honor his lionized grandfather."

Pippin raised her hand to interrupt. "Um, who is Brian Boru?"

"He was the Irish king who is credited with ending the Viking's domination in Ireland," Jamie said, making another loop.

Erin had been sitting quietly. Bit by bit, the color had returned to her face. "Jamie, my love, you're going to wear a track in the floor." Jamie frowned but stopped pacing. He folded his arms over his chest but tapped his fingers against his forearms. Pent up energy.

Erin cleared her throat. "For the fourth-year students in the back, what does this history lesson have to do with the dead man, Connell Foley?"

Jamie shot her a glance that silently chastised her for the self-deprecation, but he adjusted his glasses and continued. "Irish surnames generally fit into two categories—descriptive or occupational. If we trace the surname Tracey back to Ó Treasaigh, we can assume the original honored someone who was formidable. Possibly dangerous or feared."

"A tough bastard," Cyrus interjected.

"Precisely. Descriptive. Treasaigh stems from treasach, which means 'warlike'. Now take Duff. The original person in a family with that surname would likely have had dark features. The root of Duff is 'duhh', which is black or dark. Also descriptive. So, what makes Connell Foley interesting is that it stems from Ó Foghladha', who was a plunderer or a pirate."

Cyrus looked at Pippin. "You were looking at the books surrounding the man," he said.

"Yes."

"Was there something about them?" he prodded.

Honestly, she couldn't say for certain. Part of it was intuition. Her gut reacting. She said this, then added, "I feel like they have something more to tell me."

Grey had his eyes firmly on her. "You need to listen to your gut," Grey said.

Cyrus cupped his hand beneath his chin as he nodded his agreement. "I agree. Intuition is powerful. Of course, we make connections based on the lens we see things through. Your ability to glean deeper meaning from the pages of a book influences how you see books. It is in a very different way than, for example, I see them."

Pippin circled back around to Cyrus's original curiosity. "But we think Foley was helping Leo, so even if his name means thief or plunderer, that wasn't what he was doing. So, isn't it just a coincidence that his name is Foley? I mean, there's a big Irish influence on the East Coast, so..."

"That is true, my dear," Cyrus said. "The original plunderer, Ó Foghladha, may have absolutely nothing to do with anything specific..."

"But..." she pressed, because it was clear Cyrus wasn't so willing to just write it off as coincidence.

"But it is worth considering. Perhaps his history is connected to the Dubhshláine's. It's neither here nor there, but it is interesting to think that perhaps that is why he was helping Leo."

Jamie had stopped pacing. He stood next to Grey. "Pip," he said, using the nickname again. "Your family's history dates back to the first century. We *know* that to be true. You said Jed Riordin told you Connell Foley was especially interested in some medieval centuries. Which ones?"

"The thirteenth, fourteenth, and fifteenth," she answered.

Cyrus snapped his fingers, as if he realized where Jamie was headed with his thinking. "And, according to Jed Riordin, Leo and Connell Foley meeting was pure coincidence? At an estate sale."

Pippin nodded slowly, the pieces of the puzzle rearranging themselves in her mind, and a chill running up her back. Grey voiced the same question she'd formulated. "You don't think it was a coincidence, do you?"

"I don't put much stock in coincidences," Cyrus said, his voice thoughtful. "If there is a logical reason to be found, I'll go with that every time."

"So, you think that Foley figured out a way to put himself in our dad's path?" Grey asked.

"I do," Cyrus said, "which, once again, begs the question why?"

CHAPTER 20

"In every conceivable manner, the family is a link to our past, bridge to our future."
~Alex Haley

THEY LEFT CYRUS, retreating to The Burrow. A short time later, Pippin was back to not trusting Jed. She had believed Foley had been helping Leo because Jed had led her there. For all she knew, Foley had checked into the inn to gain access to The Burrow. Like his name implied, maybe his sole purpose had been to steal the coin. Something about the idea didn't sit well. "He could have been making amends," she suggested.

Grey nodded. "I agree. Just because his ancestors may have been thieves doesn't mean he was."

Pippin processed through what Jamie had said about the evolution of Irish surnames. If he was right, then the oldest known Irish surname was Ó Cléirigh. She zeroed in on the 'Ó', then on her family name, Dubhshláine. Pippin didn't know what year, precisely, her ancestor Morgan had lived, but based on her father's research, it was in the first century, give or take. "Part of the name must be wrong," she said.

"What name?" Grey asked.

"Dubhshláine. Morgan Dubhshláine. Shouldn't it be Ó Dubhshláine?"

"Logically, yes. But part of the scroll is missing," Jamie said, referring to the fragment her father had hidden away —an old letter written from Morgan to Titus. Aunt Rose had said there was another part that had been tucked away in *The Secret Garden*, but it hadn't been with the book she had mailed.

"You think the Ó's torn away?" Grey asked, voicing her very thought.

"It's possible," Jamie said. "If Ó Cléirigh is the oldest recorded Irish surname, then we know Morgan and Titus lived after 916 AD. Knowing the timeline helps trace the history of your family. What is interesting," Jamie said, "is that the most common evolution of Dubhshláine is Delaney."

Grey's eyes narrowed and he tilted his head. "Not Lane?"

Jamie shook his head. "Not Lane. At least not usually."

They were silent for a beat, then Grey said, "We know our great-great-grandfather entered America as Artemis Lane."

"What if he was Delaney before that?" Pippin leaned against her father's bookshelf, thinking aloud. "Morgan is the first Ó Dubhshláine we know of. At some point over the centuries, someone in the family probably dropped the Ó, then later, the name itself was changed to the more common Delaney. Why would Artemis have changed it again?"

"We know there were errors, mostly unintentional, as people were processed through Ellis Island. They processed millions of immigrants—four or five hundred a day—so it's possible it could have happened there," Jamie said.

"So maybe not Artemis's decision at all?" she said.

Grey put his hands in his pockets. "Unless he changed it to hide from—"

"—from the treasure hunters," Pippin finished.

Pippin and Grey looked at each other. She could see the question rise in him at the same time it did in her. "So, Artemis must have known how valuable the coin was," Grey said.

"And here's something else to think about," Jamie said. "Was he running from Ireland for a better life, or to hide from the treasure hunters?" Jamie asked.

Pippin only knew one person who might be able to answer that question. "We need to talk to Aunt Rose."

As Pippin searched for the phone number for Books by Bequest, the lighthouse bookstore run by the West Coast Lanes, a flurry of memories darted in and out of her mind.

Cassie had told Pippin and Grey the story about her childhood on the Oregon coast in a small house connected to an old lighthouse. Their great-great-great grandfather, Artemis Lane, had built the lighthouse, which he called Cape Misery, as a memorial to his son, Trevor, whose boat was lost at sea—a victim of the curse.

Aunt Rose and Pippin's grandfather, Edgar, were Trevor's children. Pippin hadn't even known about Edgar until after Leo and Cassie were both gone. At Cape Misery, Pippin and Grey's cousins, Lily and Cora, had shared some parts of the Lane family history the twins had never heard about. Edgar married Annabel, and when he took over the lighthouse in the mid-1960s, he and Annabel converted it into a bookstore.

Like his father before him, Edgar was taken by the sea, dying in a boating accident. And even though she wasn't Lane by blood, Annabel had died giving birth to the twins. She had delivered Cassandra and died after Lacy slipped out. Aunt Rose gave the girls the names their parents had chosen for them, and she had raised them as her own.

Finally, clearing her head of the ghosts of memories, Pippin found the number. Jamie and Grey watched her with their undivided attention. She turned her back to them. Held her breath as the line rang once. Twice. Three times. Finally, on the fifth ring, a harried voice said, "Books by Bequest."

Pippin hesitated for a moment. She didn't recognize the voice. Then again, why would she? It had been twenty years.

"Is this...Rose Lane?"

"This is *Cora* Lane," the voice said warily. "Who's this?"

Cora. Pippin's cousin. Another collection of memories tumbled over one another. The four cousins. Two sets of twins. Cora and Lily, with their blond ringlets and knowing gray-green eyes, sitting next to their younger cousins on the rocky beach at Cape Misery. Pippin and Grey had been just nine when Grandmother Faye sent them away so she could deal with her son's death. Cora and Lily, at twelve, were so much more worldly. That evening, they had shared some of the secrets of the Lane family. The secrets they knew, at least. That was the moment Pippin realized that every family had a story. That every *person* had a story. The natural extension of that, which she had recently started to realize, was that every *book* had a story, but how its characters and setting and plot were understood depended upon the lens through which it was being read.

She heard Cora's voice from so long ago like a distant echo in her head. Names of family members she hadn't thought of again, not until she had seen their names in Leo's study. Siobhan, their great-great-great grandmother, had died in the crossing from Ireland with Artemis by her side. Artemis had made his way west and raised their children, Trevor and Ruth. "Artemis went mad after Trevor died," Lily had whispered. "He built the lighthouse and kept the light lit, hoping his son would find his way home."

Remembering the story now, a shiver crept up Pippin's spine at the thought of Artemis standing on the catwalk at the top of the lighthouse, leaning over the railing, calling out for his son and his wife, both lost to the sea.

The rest of the story went from random pixelated thoughts to concrete images. Ruth discovering her bibliomancy. The curse taking Lacy. Taking Cassie. It took everyone.

"Cora," Pippin said, overwhelmed by the memories and connections, her voice scarcely more than a breath.

Grey was by her side in a flash. Pippin put the call on speaker. "Grey's here. And—" She wasn't sure how to introduce Jamie. "And a friend who's helping us. I put you on Speaker," she said as Grey crouched down to listen.

"That's fine. I *knew* it was you when the phone rang," her cautious tone blown away in the wind. "I *knew* it!"

"How?"

"Pft. How do you think?"

Ah. Of course. "So, you practice?" Pippin asked, then added, "Bibliomancy, I mean. Do you practice bibliomancy?"

"Every day."

"You were lucky to be raised with it," she said, tamping down the speck of jealousy that flared. Cassie had run away from Cape Misery. She had turned her back on her gift, and that meant Pippin had spent her entire life, until just a short time ago, knowing nothing about the divination and the power that coursed through her.

"Aunt Rose is the expert but...but she's..."

Something in Cora's voice raised an alarm. "What?" Pippin prodded, a feeling of dread spreading through her. "Is she okay?"

Cora's voice broke. "No. She...uh...she died, actually."

"Aunt Rose is dead?" Crouched next to her, Grey sucked in a sharp breath.

"Yeah. It's been two weeks now. I...I came to see her and I...I found her."

Pippin's whole body turned to rubber. If she hadn't been sitting, she would have sunk to the floor. She didn't remember much about her great aunt, but their brief correspondence had brought her back into her orbit. And now she was gone again. For her cousins, the loss was so much greater. "I'm so sorry, Cora."

They fell silent—a moment for Aunt Rose.

"Are you staying at Cape Misery?" Pippin asked, breaking the silence.

"For now. I guess. I mean, I don't really know what to do."

"About the bookstore?"

"The bookstore. The lighthouse. The property. The cemetery. All our family is buried here. My mother. Emily. Annabel. And then there's Lily. I need to be here if she ever comes back."

Pippin's memories of Cora and Lily were as thin as the ones of Aunt Rose. Images of them played like a slideshow in her mind, but she couldn't conjure up a full image of any of them or what they might look like now. "What do you mean, if she ever comes back?"

"My sister left. Disappeared years ago. Aunt Rose thinks —thought—she died. Maybe of the curse. I keep hoping she was wrong."

Grey looked at the phone as if he could see Cora through it. "Hey Cora, this is Grey. I'm really sorry about Aunt Rose."

A few seconds passed before Cora replied with a soft, "Thanks."

"Why did Aunt Rose think the curse got Lily? Was she... pregnant?" he asked, his tone conveying the delicacy of the question.

"I have no idea," Cora said. Pippin thought she detected the faintest trace of bitterness in her cousin's voice. "She left so long ago. I waited and waited for her to come back. I always hated it here. Never wanted to do any bibliomancy, but Aunt Rose made us, of course. Lily was always pissed off. She wanted a mother and father, and we had neither. Aunt Rose used to say, 'Lilith is just like your mother. She wanted to run away from her troubles, but it won't do any good.'" Cora's voice cracked; lost in the memories of the only parent she knew. "'*You play the hand you're dealt*,' she used to say, '*not the one you wish you had*'."

"Was she trying to escape the curse?" Pippin asked. That's why Cassie had left Laurel Point. It seemed reasonable to think Lily might have left home for the same reason.

Cora dismissed the idea. "She knew we couldn't escape it. Our mom couldn't. Your mom couldn't. Edgar and Annabel couldn't." She let out a shaky breath. "*We* can't."

"We *can*," Pippin countered with more conviction than she felt.

Cora ignored that proclamation. She said, "I read your

letter, probably a hundred times, you know. I was going to call you. You beat me to it. You're teaching yourself bibliomancy, huh? Your mom didn't teach you before she... before she died?"

Pippin shook her head to herself before answering. "My mom didn't want to have anything to do with it."

"Yeah, that's what Aunt Rose said. Is it working for you, though? Because it can be really amazing. To be able to tell something about the past or the future? It's like we're witches, only instead of spells with frog's legs and eye of newt, books are our cauldrons."

That was one way to look at it, Pippin thought. "It's starting to work. At least I think it is. Sometimes it's hard to know."

"Yeah. The more you do it, the better you get at understanding the messages."

"Makes sense."

"I'm sorry about your dad," Cora said. "Your letter said he was trying to break the curse."

"He left a lot of clues," Pippin said, "and we're trying to piece it all together and decide where to go from here."

"Grey and you?"

"Yes, and a few...friends."

There was a beat of silence before Cora responded. "Friends who...know about the curse?"

"My mother and father came to trust a few people over here. People who helped them—"

"And now they're helping you," Cora finished.

The list of people who were invested in helping Pippin and Grey flashed through her mind. Cyrus McAdams. Jamie McAdams. Max Lawrence, who'd died for his efforts. Hattie Juniper Pickle. Daisy Santiago. Ruby Monroe. Even Collette de Maurin from Charcuterie had been influential.

Combined, they created a network of people around Pippin and Grey. A net underneath the tight wire they were on, there to catch them if they fell. The unknowns were Jed Riordin, Hugh, and Connell Foley. "They are," she said.

Sound reverberated in Pippin's ear. It sounded as if Cora was walking through a field of noisy aluminum sheets. "And?" Cora said.

"And...what?"

Through the phone, a door slammed closed and the cacophony stopped. The wind, Pippin realized. Cora had been outside, but now she was inside. "Have you figured anything out? About the curse?"

"I know that it's true," Pippin said.

Cora gave a forced laugh. "I could have told you that. I just have to look at the cemetery filled with mostly Lane women and the headstones marking empty graves where the men should be lain to rest...instead of where they are at the bottom of the ocean."

That was a good enough segue into the main reason for the call. "Cora, my mother had a necklace. She always wore it. All these years, I thought it was buried with her, but—"

"I know. It's in your letter. You found it. But then you said someone tried to steal it from you?"

Her father's killer, yes. "Right. Do you know anything about it?" she asked.

"About the necklace? Sure. I know that my mother had one, too. Aunt Rose said they were just the same. But it's long gone. We could never find it."

Pippin let this sink in. There were two necklaces. Two Roman coins, each worth a fortune. "What do you think happened to it?"

"God, I have no idea. Aunt Rose was frantic looking for it. I remember her tearing the place apart, saying, *It has to be here. It has to be here.* Finally, she gave up and just said it was lost."

A wave of nausea passed through Pippin. What if they needed *both* necklaces to break the curse with Manannán mac Lir —both of the Roman coins—they were screwed.

"Of course, Aunt Rose was a little flighty. When she couldn't find it, she said maybe it was buried with our grandmother."

"With Annabel? Would Artemis have given it to his daughter-in-law?"

Pippin could almost sense Cora's shrug. "Hell if I know. Seems to me that anything is possible. For all we know, Edgar took the thing out with him on his last fishing trip to, I don't know, offer it back to the sea. Maybe it's lost out there."

"I don't think so," Pippin said. Cyrus's comment about logical answers had taken root in her. "If there are two necklaces out there, the offering would need to be with both. Edgar knew there were two."

Cora was quiet for a beat then said, "Oh, shit. You're serious? Like they need to be given back to the sea and we'll be freed?"

"It's possible."

"Okay, but why?" Cora said after a long second. She sounded skeptical, and Pippin couldn't blame her. "Why would some Irish sea god want some stupid necklaces?"

"Because they're more than just necklaces," Pippin said slowly, emphasizing each word. "They're Roman coins.

Cora sputtered. "Holy fu—Then we are *totally* screwed."

"You said maybe the necklace was buried with Annabel?" Pippin said, thinking aloud. "Is there any way you can find out?"

Cora snorted. "What, like exhume the body? Yeah, I don't think that's gonna happen."

She'd meant with research, but really other than looking in the coffin, what *were* the other options? "Did Aunt Rose leave any journals? Letters?"

That snort again. "Pippin, if you could see this place... there's a lifetime of letters and journals here, and God knows what else. Aunt Rose never got rid of anything."

"Cora, the scroll—"

"Riiight. The scroll."

"Aunt Rose mentioned it in the letter she wrote me, but she didn't send it with the books. With my mother's books."

"*I* sent the books," Cora said.

"You?"

"She had the books in an envelope, addressed and ready to go. I found them and mailed them."

"The scroll wasn't with them," Pippin said.

"Oh. Hmm. I can look for it, I guess..."

There was something in her voice. Hesitancy. "Is there something else? Are you okay?"

Silence for a beat, followed by a shaky sigh. "Yeah, Pippin, there is. My mother's gone. I have no idea who my father is. My sister's been gone for...ever. I don't know if she's dead or alive. Aunt Rose is gone. And she's...I'm..."

"What is it, Cora?" Pippin prodded. She felt the weight of Grey's and Jamie's attention. They were fully focused on her side of the conversation.

The weighty silence stretched endlessly before Cora finally gathered her reserve and spoke again. "She's dead, and I'm here alone."

Pippin's hand found Sailor's head. She wove her fingers through her dog fur, just leaving them there. "Can you call someone?" Pippin asked. "Someone to stay with you?"

Cora gave a heavy sigh. “My friend is here. I’m sorry, Pippin. I didn’t mean—"

“It’s fine. I’m sorry for calling and bringing this all up for you. Reopening a wound that wasn’t anywhere near healing.”

“I just…I don’t understand how it happened.”

“What do you mean?” Pippin asked.

“It doesn’t really make sense,” she said. “Aunt Rose grew up here. She knew this place better than anyone. She wouldn’t have gone out to those rocks alone. She drilled that into our heads, Lily and me. She certainly wouldn’t have gone—not with the high tide coming.”

Pippin’s first thought was wondering if Aunt Rose had drowned like the Lane men. “She died in the water?”

“A head wound, technically. They think she slipped and fell.”

“Maybe she went out there earlier, well before high tide.” It could explain why her great aunt would have done the very thing she warned her nieces not to do. “Accidents happen. She might have slipped…”

“Maybe,” Cora said, but Pippin heard the doubt in her voice. “She called me, you know. She said she had a secret she needed to tell me. I hadn’t gone back to see her in a while. I put it off, but finally I went. I went, only, by the time I got there, it was too late. I couldn’t find her. I searched and eventually I saw her—" She broke off. Gulped in a stabilizing breath of air. “I saw her body. A yellow bundle draped over a rock at a tidal pool. I…I can’t shake the image of her hair. It sort of swirled in the water. Like sea foam.”

The image seared itself into Pippin’s mind. They fell into a respectful silence. A quiet sob escaped from Cora, and Pippin could feel her cousin’s pain from across the country. Aunt Rose had raised her. She was as close to a mother as

Cora had. "I'm so sorry," Pippin said. She hesitated before asking, "Do you think...could it be about the curse? Aunt Rose's death, I mean?"

"The curse didn't take her," Cora said. "She didn't have kids. She didn't die in childbirth. And the sea doesn't take the women. Only the men."

"Except it took Annabel, and she wasn't Lane by blood," Pippin said slowly.

Cora's breath grew heavy, but she didn't say anything, so Pippin dropped it. "You said she had a secret to tell you. Do you have any idea what it was?"

"None," Cora said. "Whatever she wanted to tell me, she took it to her grave."

Pippin took the next few minutes to tell her cousin about the treasure hunters. About Salty Gallagher and Monique Baxter. About how they discovered the Roman coin. "And it's happened again," she said. "Another man is dead."

"Holy fu—" She stopped and took a breath. "How many people know about all this?"

"We don't know."

"Who died?" she asked.

"A man who might have known my father. A rare book dealer named Connell Foley. He—"

Pippin sensed Cora freeze from across the country. "What the—what's his name?" she asked, her voice sharp.

"Connell Foley. "Why—?"

Cora cut her off. "I'll be right back." She dropped the phone with a clatter and was back in mere seconds. Cora's voice shot into Pippin's ear. "Found it. I *knew* I'd seen the name. It's on a business card on Aunt Rose's desk. Connell Foley. Heritage Rare Book Dealers."

"Connell Foley was there? At your bookstore?"

"Looks like it."

Grey let out a low whistle. Jamie cupped his hand at his jaw.

And Pippin sat there, stunned. Because why would a man found dead at Jamie's bookshop have visited Aunt Rose clear across the country?

CHAPTER 21

"Somewhere in her brain a wall formed, a wall that kept out further consideration about what was happening here."

~Ann Brashares, *Sisterhood of the Traveling Pants*

AFTER THE REVELATION FROM CORA, nervous energy surged through Pippin. She debated with herself. Should she march up to Bernadette Foley's room and demand answers? Or should she wait. Calm down. Think logically.

For the time being, while Bernadette chose to stay put in her husband's reserved room, Pippin stood sentry at the registration desk. She was lying in wait and ready to pounce the second Bernadette Foley appeared at the top of the stairs. The woman hadn't been out of the room since Pippin had taken her up there days ago. She hadn't even come down for breakfast. They left trays for her outside her door. When they came back to collect them, the food was picked at, but only sparingly.

Thirty minutes passed as she waited with one eye out for

Bernadette. June and Heather had headed out straight after they'd finished breakfast. Heather held up one sandaled foot and wiggled her toes. "Manis and pedis," she announced, "then crab cakes...*somewhere*."

June gave the tiniest roll of her eyes and chuckled. "Guess she wants crab cakes."

Heather gave her mother's arm a light backhand. "You know I do. You cannot come to the North Carolina coast and not have crab cakes."

"I agree. You should try—" Pippin broke off when she caught movement from upstairs.

Heather and June followed the direction of her gaze. Pippin hid her disappointment that instead of Bernadette slowly making her way downstairs, it was the Jeffersons, each of them gripping the handrail. "Ahoy there!" Jefferson called, one frail arm in the air.

"Ahoy to you, too," Heather boomed.

Pippin turned back to June, who tucked a wayward strand of her wiry hair behind her ear. June was at the tail end of her seventies, but she looked decades younger. "Sorry about that," she said about being sidetracked.

Heather flapped one hand in the air. "Oh jeez, no worries. I flop around from one thing to the next, and before long I've forgotten what I set out to do in the first place."

"It's true," June said. "She's been like that since she was a little girl."

"Crab cakes!" Heather exclaimed. "You were saying we should try..."

Pippin snapped her fingers. "Right. Amberjack Grill. It's a little hole in the wall place off of Main Street. If you go south, toward the pier about a mile or so, you'll see it. It doesn't look like much on the outside, but it has the best seafood around."

"Isn't that always the case?" June said. "Best kept secrets. There's that TV guy—"

"Literally *guy*," Heather said with a laugh. "Guy Fieri. He made a whole show out of the concept—"

"Right! Diners, Drive-ins and Dives!"

Pippin loved the way they finished each other's sentences—the same way she and Grey did.

"We've been there," Sue said as she and Jefferson finally approached the registration desk. "It is outstanding. Their fish tacos...I had them three times last time we visited Devil's Cove."

Heather and June made eye contact with each other, each giving one succinct nod. They were in agreement. "Then Amberjack Grill, here we come!" Heather proclaimed. She turned on her sandaled heel, slid her arm through her mother's, and a second later, they blew through the door, leaving a trail of energy in their wake.

"We're off for the day, too," Sue said.

"Where to?" Pippin asked conversationally.

"We're driving down to Cape Hatteras and then to the shipwreck museum," she said. "Have you been?"

"I haven't," Pippin said. Given the curse on her family and how many of her male ancestors had given their lives up to the seas and oceans, reveling in the history of shipwrecks along the North Carolina coast was the last thing she wanted to do. To get there, the Macons would have to cross the old swing bridge connecting Devil's Cove to the mainland at Sand Point, drive north until they crossed back the other way, drive through Roanoke, hit Nags Head, and turn south to drive down the narrow strip of barrier island. The sixty-mile trip would take close to an hour and a half if they didn't stop. "It's a bit of a drive."

Sue held up an unlit cigarette. "Which is why I need to

light this up before we go. Filthy habit, I know, but after sixty-five years, there's no point in stopping."

"I guess not," Pippin said with a smile. Old habits and addictions were hard to break.

Another thirty minutes passed before Nancy and Peter Kernoodle came down, both of them wearing the same dour expressions they had at breakfast. Nancy had complained about running out of creamer. Peter had griped about the fact that the Devil's Cove Gazette was filled with too many ads. Nancy had grumbled that the toast was too toasted, then, when Hazel remade it, she'd sent it back for not being toasted enough. They seemed to suck all the positiveness from a room. No matter what, Pippin had decided, there was no pleasing these two.

Unlike the other guests, Nancy and Peter Kernoodle headed straight for the front door with nary a glance in her direction. Pippin pasted a smile on her face and repeated her service mantra to herself. *The customer is always right. The customer is always right. The customer is always right.* To them, she said, "Have a good day," keeping her voice bright and cheery.

Nancy stopped and turned. "You cannot order someone to have a good day, you know. Either we will or we won't, but it has nothing to do with whatever you *tell* us to have."

Pippin kept her smile in place. *The customer is always right. The customer is always right. The customer is always right.* "I suppose that's true. I *hope* you have a good day," she amended, although inside she couldn't really care less how good their day was. They were ill-mannered and abrasive people.

"If we do, it's no thanks to that woman's prattling," Peter Kernoodle muttered.

Pippin tilted her head and drew her brows together. "What?"

"Corner room," Peter said irritably. "Talking and crying all. Damn. Night."

"That poor woman," Hazel said after the Kernoodles left. "Maybe we should call Dr. Wilkenson again."

Pippin suspected that while Hazel wanted to make sure Bernadette Foley was okay, she also wouldn't mind seeing the good doctor again. "Let me see if I can talk to her first," Pippin said.

She left Hazel to answer the ringing phone. "Sea Captain's Inn. How can I help you today?"

Hazel's voice faded away when Pippin got to the top of the stairs. She strode to the guest room rented by Connell Foley and occupied by his wife. She stopped and pressed her ear to the door. Whatever prattling Peter Kernoodle had overheard had stopped. She was met with silence.

She rapped her knuckles on the door. "Mrs. Foley?" she called. "Are you in there? Are you okay?"

Nothing.

She tried again, knocking louder this time. "Mrs. Foley? Bernadette. It's Pippin. The innkeeper? Can I get you something to eat?"

Still silence.

She stood back, torn on what to do. On the one hand, she had a master key so she could open the door to check on her. The woman was clearly distressed, and Peter Kernoodle reporting her crying all night felt like good cause. On the other hand, Bernadette had hung up the Do Not Disturb sign. The woman was grieving. Maybe she had cried herself to sleep. If that was the case, Pippin didn't want to disturb her. She retreated back downstairs. She would try again in a few hours, and if she got no answer, she'd call the doctor.

Those hours passed by at a glacial pace. Finally, come late afternoon, Pippin made her way upstairs once again, knocking on Bernadette's door. This time, after the second knock, the door opened, and Bernadette stood there looking forlorn and ragged. "Oh, Mrs. Foley," Pippin said, rushing toward her. "Can I...you look...Mrs. Foley, what can I do for you?"

Bernadette stepped back into the dark room, leaving the door open for Pippin to follow. The bedding was in disarray. Bernadette probably *had* been asleep, but she didn't look like she had slept at all. She sank onto the desk chair and stared off at nothing, her eyes just as vacant as they'd been last time Pippin had seen them.

"Are you hungry?" Pippin asked, wondering if Bernadette even registered her presence.

Bernadette blinked and awareness came back to her. "I can't eat anything. My stomach is in knots," she said. A puzzled expression slipped onto her face. "Why is it in knots?"

Pippin stared. Faltered. So, nothing had changed. The woman's hold on reality was tenuous, at best. "Mrs. Foley, what can I do for you?"

Bernadette wrung her hands. "Connell's out just now. He's off to see about a book. He's always seeing about a book. Our entire house is filled with his books, did you know that? This book is invaluable. That book will change history. Another one will sell for thousands. What is he looking for? I can't remember." She looked at Pippin, her mouth pulled down in consternation. "Do you know? I hope he finds it. He's been on the hunt for so long. I hope he finds it."

"It's something about Irish curses, I think," Pippin said, answering the only question she could because the more she spoke with Bernadette, the more she realized that dementia drove her thoughts in every which direction.

Bernadette cocked her head to one side and looked at Pippin curiously. "You know it? The book he wants? He'll be so happy!" She flung her head this way and that. "Is it here? You must get it so he can see it when he comes back." The next second, her face fell. "Do you know when he'll be back?"

Pippin drew in a bolstering breath. She had no idea what to do. What to say. "I don't," she said. "Bernadette, you said someone is coming to help you?"

"He gets lost in his books," Bernadette said, ignoring Pippin's question. "Needles in haystacks. I've told him I don't know how he expects to find five-hundred-year-old books, but he insists he will." Her expression took on a childlike quality. "Do you think he will?"

"I don't know—"

"Oh! But you said you found it!"

"Mrs. Foley," Pippin said, trying again. "Is there someone I can call for you?"

Her face lit up suddenly, like a bulb had been turned on from inside. "Yes. Call Ruthie. She'll know what to do. She'll know where Connell is."

"Ruthie?" Pippin asked, hoping Bernadette would give more information this time.

"Our daughter. Our lovely daughter." Her chin quivered and for a second, Pippin thought maybe Mrs. Foley was remembering, but then it stopped. "Call Ruthie," she said again. "Her number is in the diary."

Ruthie—their daughter! Relief flowed through her. She needed to call Ruthie. "Where's the diary?" Pippin asked.

"Connell's diary," she said, a trace of impatience in her tone. "He left it here for me, but I can't see where he is."

Bernadette walked to the desk and laid her palm on a small navy hardcover book. “He was at the bookshop, then was to meet someone. I suppose *that’s* where he is.”

Pippin’s heart stuttered. She was torn between calling Ruthie immediately and learning more about Connell’s diary. “Mrs. Foley, who was he going to meet?” she asked, because whoever it was could have something to do with his death.

Bernadette picked up the book, holding it with both hands. She flipped it open to a random page, the hours of the day running down the side, lines filled in with neatly printed notes. Pippin watched her, realizing that it wasn’t a diary like a *journal.* It was a diary like a *calendar.*

“He’s fastidious, my Connell,” Bernadette said, quietly, as if she were reminding herself about her husband’s qualities. She flipped through the pages until she landed on the entry she’d been looking for. She turned the book around so Pippin could see, pointing to the three o’clock space.

Eight words. That’s all it took to knock the wind from Pippin’s lungs.

The Open Door—Seamus O’Dulany has the answers.

SHE STARED at the name from the slip of paper Hugh had handed her. Her heart stuttered. Who in the hell was Seamus O’Dulany?

CHAPTER 22

" 'S*on,' his father said, leaning forward. 'Stories don't always have happy endings.' "*

~Patrick Ness, from A Monster Calls

THE NAME SEAMUS O'DULANY was going to start haunting her unless she could figure out who he was.

Why did Hugh give her a slip of paper with the name written there?

Why did Connell Foley have the name written in his diary?

And what did this Seamus O'Dulany have to do with her?

Jed Riordin had insisted they leave the house before they talked. "*The walls have ears,*" he'd said. Everyone, with the exception of Hazel Hood and Lil Hart, was out for the day. She looked around the bedroom, a thought suddenly occurring to her. Could the inn be bugged? Could Jed have been referring to that?

Other than tearing every room apart from top to bottom,

Pippin didn't have the faintest idea about how to figure out if listening devices had been hidden here. That was something to think about later.

"Mrs. Foley, please come with me," Pippin begged. The only thing that mattered at this very moment was Bernadette. If whoever killed Connell realized that the dead man's diary might hold incriminating evidence—and God, she hoped it did—then she had to get Bernadette someplace safe. Only then would she stop to call Ruthie.

The problem was, Bernadette hadn't budged. She looked rooted to her chair, heavy and motionless. She held the diary open and looked at Pippin with wide eyes. If Pippin snapped her fingers right in front of the woman, she wasn't sure she would even blink. She wasn't all there.

"Will you come with me?" Pippin asked again.

Bernadette's smile grew even wider, if that was possible. "To see Connell?"

The question left Pippin tongue-tied for a few seconds. Bernadette looked hopeful. Innocent and suddenly buoyant. How could she shatter the woman's world? "I—I have a friend I'd like you to meet," she said.

It was enough to get Bernadette to stand. "I need lipstick," she said. "Connell—he's always loved it when I wear lipstick."

Bernadette took a few minutes to spruce up. She finished by applying a heavy layer of coral lipstick, then she followed Pippin with the diary still clutched in her hands. Down the stairs. Out the front door. Into Pippin's ancient gas-guzzling Land Rover after making a quick detour to her office to grab her purse and cell phone. Now her thumbs flew over the screen as she texted Jamie that she was heading to the bookshop to see his grandfather. Cyrus didn't live his life with a cell phone in hand. If he had one of his own, she had never seen it.

She shoved her phone into her purse before seeing if Jamie replied. She didn't want to give Bernadette a chance to change her mind. She threw the car into reverse, backing out of the driveway, then directed it towards town. Behind her, a car appeared out of nowhere. She glanced in the rearview mirror. In the waning afternoon light, the car's high beams glared like menacing eyes. She quickly adjusted the mirror to redirect the light as she turned onto Main Street. The car followed. As she pulled into the closest parking lot to The Open Door, it passed by, slow and ominous.

Get a grip. She shook her head, chasing away her agitation. It was all in her imagination. No one was following her. She threw the car into park and was out and around the car, yanking open the passenger door before Bernadette seemed to register that they'd stopped. "Is this where Connell is?" she asked.

Pippin couldn't answer the question. She offered her hand. "Let me help you out."

A few minutes later, Jamie opened the bookshop door to them, locked it again, and led them up a flight of stairs which led to a short hallway. Just as they reached the top, the door to Cyrus's flat opened. The man himself startled when he saw the three of them standing there, but only for a quick second before his eyes widened and his forehead crinkled. "My, my. What do we have here?"

"This is Bernadette Foley," Pippin said.

"Mrs. Foley," he repeated. The surprise at seeing them disappeared as he smiled politely at the newcomer. He dipped his head slightly. "Delighted to make your acquaintance. Please. Come in."

He stood back while the three of them entered. Cyrus sat with Bernadette on the low-profile sofa. As he spoke to her in low, soothing tones, Jamie pulled Pippin as far away from them as he could, leading her to the large east-facing window in Cyrus's bedroom, Roanoke Sound silently flowing by below. Jamie and Grey had only left Sea Captain's Inn a few short hours ago. Now here she was again. "What's going on?" he whispered.

"I think she's in shock."

"Okay," he said, "but we knew that. So, what else happened?"

Pippin had a fleeting thought about how well Jamie seemed to know her already. He knew she wouldn't have brought Bernadette Foley to Cyrus without a specific reason. "I went to talk to her. She has her husband's diary—his *calendar*. Jamie—" No one else was here, but she lowered her voice to a whisper. "He came to the bookshop to meet with —get answers from—*Seamus O'Dulany.*"

The name of the elusive Seamus O'Dulany shocked Jamie into silence for a moment. "If Jed is right, and Connell was murdered, then maybe *he* did it," Pippin said. "And if Connell put information about him in his diary, then Bernadette could be in danger. I can't have another person dying because of me and this curse."

"We need to find Seamus O'Dulany," Jamie said.

"I've Googled him," she said. "Nothing. There's a Seamus O'Duan. Seamus O'Dolan. Seamus O'Neil. Seamus O'Reilly. Seamus Hanlon. But no Seamus O'Dulany."

From the other room, Bernadette let out a low cry, like a wounded animal. They both swiveled their heads. "Maybe Cyrus got through to her," she said, her gut wrenching at Bernadette's pain.

Pippin and Jamie moved at the same time. The black,

gray, and white color scheme was the complete opposite of Sea Captain's Inn. Despite that, it normally filled Pippin with ease and comfort. It was a safe space.

Not right now, though, with the sounds of grief pouring from the couch. Bernadette was doubled over, her head between her knees, her back heaving. The low animalistic cry had grown to something even more primal. Even more brutally devastating. Pippin rushed to her. She crouched and put her hand on her back, rubbing gently and making low, soft, soothing sounds. Nothing she said would lessen the woman's grief, so she just let Bernadette cry.

Jamie spoke in low tones to his grandfather. Pippin craned to hear. "She knows what happened now?"

Cyrus gave a taciturn nod. "She does."

"Call Ruthie." Bernadette's low, broken voice brought Pippin's attention back to her. She had forgotten about her daughter. Bernadette managed to sit up. Her face was pure anguish. Drawn and pale and suddenly ten years older. She pushed her husband's diary into Pippin's hand. "Call Ruthie," she said again.

"I will. I'll call right now," Pippin said. She took the small hardcover book and stood. She left Bernadette with Jamie and Cyrus, retreating to the outside hallway to make the call. She walked to the end of the hall and out the backdoor. A small landing overlooked a dumpster and asphalt alley shared by The Open Book and Devil's Brew. Beyond that were the waters of the sound.

She flipped through Connell Foley's diary, looking for the section where he'd written phone numbers. She found them in a note section at the end. For a younger man, it would have struck her as unusual to find a handwritten list of phone numbers, including one for his own daughter, but for someone in the profession of studying old things, it didn't surprise her that Connell Foley hadn't relied on a cell phone's contact list.

Connell's writing was small and neat. It angled slightly left, and he wrote in all caps. Pippin often thought that how a person organized their cellphone apps, or their calendar, was a reflection of how their mind worked. Apps put into folders equaled an organized mind. Apps with no particular order skewed more to the chaotic or creative.

She was looking at Connell's diary, not his phone, but the take-away was the same. His calendar and notes were ordered. So, she thought, was his mind. She ran her finger down the list of names, stopping when she came to Ruthie Barringer. She quickly searched the 412 area code. Pittsburgh, Pennsylvania. She punched the number into her phone and pressed the call button. It had barely finished one ring when it clicked and a distressed voice said, "Hello?"

"Is this Ruthie Barringer?" Pippin asked. "Connell and Bernadette's daughter?"

"Yes. Yes. Who's this?"

"My name is Pippin. I'm calling about your mother—"

"Oh my God. Oh, thank God. Is she...is she okay?"

"She is! She's okay," Pippin said quickly. "She's had a shock—"

The woman on the other end of the line heaved. Her voice sounded tinny, like she had her phone set to Speaker. "Someone from the police called and told me. My dad—"

So, she knew about Connell's death. "Yes. I'm so sorry. Your mom asked me to call you—"

"Oh my God, I'm so glad you did," Ruthie said, relief flooding her voice. "She called to tell me about my dad. Where is she now?"

"She's in Devil's Cove, at the bookshop. Well, above it, in an apartment—"

"Oh thank God," she said again. "She's been so paranoid. She shouldn't be alone. Is she..."

"She was in denial at first," Pippin said when Ruthie trailed off. "She was in shock, I think, but she seems to understand now...about your father."

Pippin heard her draw in a few strangled breaths. "She knows, at least on some level. She told me. But it comes and goes—" She broke off. Inhaled. Exhaled. "Her mind is getting worse, so she goes—" Another stabilizing breath,"—in and out of knowing what happened. This might push her completely over the edge."

Dementia, just as Pippin thought. It explained the severity of Bernadette's reaction, and the ebb and flow of her awareness. "She must have forgotten she called you, because she asked me to," Pippin said. "You're right, I don't think we can leave her on her own. Can you come?"

"I'm already on my way," Ruthie said. "I just passed through Virginia Beach. My GPS says I'm about two hours away. Can you stay with her until I get there?"

"Of course." Bernadette needed support from people who knew her. People who loved her. Pippin could keep her safe for the time-being, but they both needed Ruthie here sooner rather than later. She gave Ruthie the bookshop's address. "Call me when you're here so I can let you in."

"You said your name is Pippin, right?"

"Right."

"Listen. I just want to say...I mean, I don't even know who you are, but I can't thank you enough for watching out for my mother."

"I'm glad I was there."

"Where did you find her?" Ruthie asked.

"I run an inn on the island," Pippin said. "Your dad, he reserved a room, and your mom came to stay—"

Here demeanor changed, her voice suddenly sharp. “Wait. What?”

Pippin went on instant alert. “Your dad reserved a room at my inn. Your mom showed up—"

“At Sea Captain’s Inn?”

Interesting that Ruthie knew the name of the inn. It showed her father had been keeping tabs on Leo’s old house, or on her and Grey, and had shared at least that much information with his family. “No, she showed up at the bookshop where your dad...where he died. I happened to be there. I didn’t want to leave her alone, so I took her back to the inn with me.”

She murmured something under her breath, then more loudly, “It’s about the book. That’s why he was there.”

“What book?” Pippin asked, wondering for a split second if she’d been wrong and Connell had been after some old book all along—something that had nothing to do with the Lanes. But no, it was too coincidental that he’s been to Books by Bequest at Cape Misery, too. The thought was gone as quickly as it has appeared.

“I don’t even know. It’s like, five hundred years old, or something. He’s been looking for it for years. Years,” she repeated.

A five-hundred-year-old book. “Why did he want it so badly?”

“I don’t know. He was always so secretive about it. My mom said he gave up the search years ago. I mean, seriously, it nearly destroyed them. He was over it—or at least we thought he was—but then he brought it up again a few months ago. Said he had a new lead on it. I tried to get him to just drop it. It was around the same time my mom’s health started to...” She left the rest unsaid, finishing with, “But nothing was going to stop him. He was obsessed again.”

Three questions surfaced for Pippin. First, *had Connell Foley found the book he'd been searching for?* Second, *had he been killed because of it?* And third, *what, if anything, did the book have to do with the curse?*

"Ruthie, did your father know Leo Hawthorne?" Pippin asked, seeking confirmation.

"Of course he did. That's why my dad rented the room at that inn. Everything for the last twenty-five years has been about Leo Hawthorne and that stupid curse."

CHAPTER 23

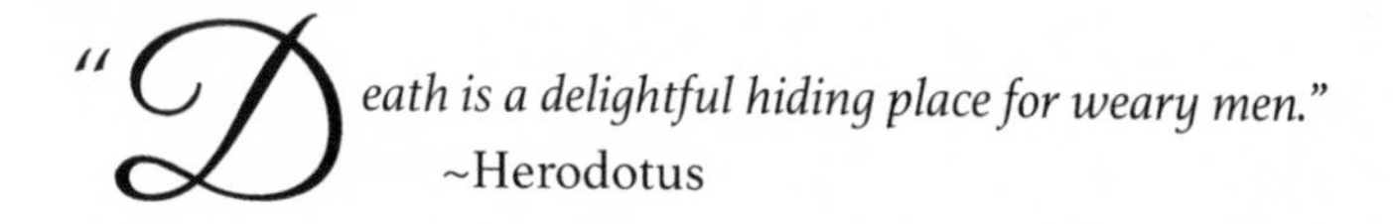

"Death is a delightful hiding place for weary men."
~Herodotus

AFTER HANGING UP WITH RUTHIE, Pippin stared at her phone. Stared at the pavement below. Stared at the sound.

Ruthie had confirmed what Jed Riordin had said. Connell Foley had known her father. Had known about the curse.

Which meant Jed's belief that Connell Foley had been murdered was all the more plausible. All the more likely that someone had been in the rare book room with him. The possible scenario she'd thought of, of Connell falling because someone had pushed him—suddenly became more believable. Connell had specifically told Hazel that he wanted to speak with Pippin. Jed believed someone wanted to stop that conversation from happening.

She pressed the heels of her hands against her temples, stifling the frustrated scream inching up her throat. Oh, how she wished her father had left explicit information about the curse that she and Grey could follow. She tried to let the thought pass right through and not let bitterness take root. She couldn't blame Leo for not leaving clearer evidence of what he'd learned, who he trusted, or what his next steps were going to be. He hadn't known he needed to.

A part of her did blame him, though. She tried to bury it. To knock it away. It was irrational and unfair, but it resurfaced, over and over. Leo had left her and Grey to fend for themselves. It may have been inadvertent, but he'd exposed himself to the wrong people, and it had cost him his life. It had orphaned his young children. And it had left a curse circling around them like a cyclone, ready to rip them to shreds.

A garbage truck rumbled loudly into view. Pippin let the reverberating sound of its diesel engine crowd into her consciousness. The *beep, beep, beep* it emitted as it backed up and repositioned itself to lift the dumpster brought her back to the moment. It shook reason back into her mind. Leo had done his best. He'd loved her and Grey, and he'd loved Cassie. She repeated this to herself, pushing the other wayward thoughts out. She turned to go back inside, grabbing the handle of the door and yanking. It didn't budge.

"Of course," she grumbled under her breath. *Of course* it would be self-locking. She should have checked before closing it. She should have assumed, because Cyrus and Jamie wouldn't leave a door with access to the bookshop unsecured.

She walked down the steps, the breeze whipping her skirt around her legs. She started to circle around the building but stopped when she saw another door. It had to lead to the downstairs hallway near the bathroom and

Jamie's office, she thought. She knew it would be locked, too, but she tried the handle anyway. It turned. It wasn't locked, and she stumbled backward when it flung open.

She stared down the dark hallway in surprise. She stepped in and closed it, examining the locks. The handle itself had a turn lock, and there was a deadbolt and a surface bolt that should have been extra security against the locks being picked. None of it worked if it wasn't locked, though.

She threw the deadbolt and pushed the surface bolt into place before racing upstairs and bursting back into Cyrus's flat. She didn't know what to address first—the book Connell had been searching for all these years, or the unlocked door downstairs.

The question was answered when Jamie looked at her face and strode to her, pulling her back into Cyrus's bedroom. "Are you okay? What happened?"

She told him about the door downstairs first, posing a possible scenario. "Lieutenant Jacobs said Connell had a probably had a heart attack and fell. But I'm beginning to believe what Jed said...that someone killed him. It would explain how the keys got back onto the counter. And if someone pushed Connell, then maybe they ran out the side door. That's why it was unlocked."

"The door's been unlocked since that man died?" Jamie closed his eyes and shook his head as if he couldn't believe it. Pippin could read his thoughts through the change in his expressions. He'd taken a few days off, leaving Erin and Noah in charge of things. And they hadn't checked to be sure the back door was locked when they'd closed up for the night. He shook his head, as if he could shake away his frustration. He could review closing procedures with his mother and Noah later. "It makes sense," he said, "although, who knows? If the outside door was unlocked, maybe the book room *was* unlocked. Now I can't swear it wasn't."

"Let's assume it *was* though. And that someone followed Connell. Whoever it was took the keys and unlocked the book room door."

"If it was just Connell, he'd have to put them back before slipping inside," Jamie said.

"If it was someone else, they could have put them back as they left."

"If it was Connell," Jamie continued, "he could have locked the door from the inside just in case someone decided to try the handle or unlock the door."

"If that's what happened, then his death would be an accident. A heart attack, and a fall that caused the head injury," Pippin said.

Jamie adjusted his glasses and cupped his chin. "If someone else was there, then that person followed Connell into the room and confronted him—presumably about the book he was searching for—"

"Or maybe found," Pippin interjected.

"Right. So, Connell tried to fight, but was pushed."

Maybe the intent hadn't been to kill him, Pippin thought. Jed thought it was murder, though. Of course, accidental murder is still murder, right?

Either way, Connell was dead. The main question Pippin was left with was, *Where is the book now?* Because, if it was an accident and Connell had been alone, then he'd put the book somewhere else.

And if it was murder—either by intent or accident—and Connell did have the book with him, did the killer now have it?

Pippin's feeling that Bernadette was in danger multiplied, because of the third scenario. If Connell hadn't had the book with him, then the killer was out there, still looking for it, and there was a good chance Bernadette could know where her husband might have stashed something so vitally important. Something that resulted in his death.

CHAPTER 24

"*Persons living with dementia are usually capable of more than we can imagine.*"

~Bob DeMarco

WHATEVER PROGRESS CYRUS had made with Bernadette had slipped away again. Reality was elusive. It seemed wrong to pry into Bernadette's failing mind, yet Pippin had no choice. Ruthie had arrived, but whatever animosity she had toward Leo and the curse had dissipated during the rest of the drive, replaced by concern for her mother. Her height fell somewhere between her mother's five-foot-three-inches and her father's taller, lankier frame. She looked weary after her long drive, but immediately rushed to her mother, comforting her as if she were consoling a child. Bernadette brought up stories about Connell's trips abroad to international book festivals, his passion for exploring every bookstore he ever came across, and his own store, and Ruthie went along on the trip down memory lane. They both referred to him with present tense verbs, the idea that he was gone completely vanished from their minds, the way a sandcastle is washed away by the rising tide, any evidence of its existence demolished.

Finally, during a lull, Pippin asked, "Can I talk with her?"

Ruthie answered by standing and giving Pippin her spot on the couch. Pippin sat next to Bernadette, Connell's diary in her lap. She flipped through the pages, looking for any other clue Connell might have left about the mysterious book he'd found, where he might have hidden it, or who Seamus O'Dulany was. "Did your husband—" Bernadette convulsed, and Pippin quickly rephrased. "Do you and Connell have a safe deposit box?" she asked, thinking that maybe he'd done the same thing she and Grey had done in order to keep their respective treasures safe.

Bernadette answered right away. "Oh, no. Never, Connell is old-fashioned. He trusts strangers as much as he trusts his family and friends."

"Bernadette," Pippin asked slowly, "where would Connell hide something important to him? Something he didn't want to fall into the wrong hands?"

Bernadette's chin pressed against her chest, her eyes cast downward. "The only valuables he has are his books."

Pippin pressed. "Where are his most valuable ones?"

"At his store, of course. They're on the shelves like every other book."

So. No safe deposit box, and no special location for the ultra-valuable books in Connell Foley's collection. She looked to Ruthie in case she had different answers to the same questions, but she just shrugged. "She's right. He did —" Bernadette made a choking sound and Ruthie quickly broke off then started again. "There are no secret hiding places."

Pippin moved on, mentioning the books Connell had pulled from the shelves, and which had been found next to his body. "Robert Louis Stevenson and Rafael Sabatini," she said.

Bernadette's head jerked up, as if a puppet master had yanked on an invisible string attached to the crown. She spoke, but to no one in particular. "My Connell, he loves Robert Louis Stevenson. He has first editions. I found a copy of *Treasure Island* while we were on our honeymoon." She beamed at the memory, but the light faded a minute later. "I held it hostage once." Her voice had turned quiet and soft, like it was far away. "Do you remember that, Ruthie? I was ready to tear out the pages, one by one. Oh, but he was furious."

Ruthie's voice matched her mother's. Sadness permeated the air. "I do remember it, Mom. It happened more than once."

Bernadette's face crumpled into puzzlement. "Why did I do that? I can't remember." She knocked her knuckles against her skull. "Why can't I remember?"

Once again, Pippin looked to Ruthie, this time with compassion for both the women. Ruthie sighed. She spoke softly so her mother couldn't hear. "This is sometimes how it goes with dementia. She can remember things that happened fifty years ago, but she might not be able to remember what happened yesterday, or what she had for breakfast today."

Pippin turned to Jamie and posed a rhetorical question "If he already had a first edition, why would he have been looking at one of your copies?"

Of course, none of them—including Jamie—had an answer to that until Bernadette spoke up again. "Connell has a philosophy that you can never have too many books.

Tell them, Ruthie. Isn't the house stacked to the ceiling with books?"

Ruthie got onto her knees in front of her mother with a gentle smile. "You're right. It is, Mom."

"Your dad's a good man, isn't he Ruthie? He'll give the shirt off his back, won't he?"

"He is, Mom," Ruthie said, but her face clouded. She turned to Pippin. "I'd started to become worried about him, too, though. For the last few months, he wasn't quite himself. Something was on his mind. It had him agitated."

"My assistant at the inn said he was kind of on edge when she checked him in," Pippin said.

"He's been acting that way more and more." She remembered to refer to him in the present tense, just like Bernadette was doing to support her mother's addled mind. She thought it was also a way to keep herself under control in her mother's presence. "Almost paranoid," Ruthie said. "He'd come home sure that someone had followed him or convinced that someone had broken into the store and had moved some books around. I thought he was imagining things, but—"

"But that did happen," Bernadette interrupted. "Someone broke into the shop and made a mess. The police, they thought it was kids running around vandalizing."

"That was so long ago," Ruthie whispered to Pippin. "Twenty years ago." Louder, so her mother could hear, she said, "I remember that. He never believed it was kids that broke in."

Bernadette tilted her head to one side and looked at Ruthie with wide eyes. "Did the kids break in again? Your dad's going to be furious."

Ruthie patted her mom's hand. "No, Mom. Nobody broke in. The store is fine."

Bernadette's lips curved into a vacant smile. "That's good," she said, then she stared off to the distance. "She's coming, you know. She'll come for me."

Pippin met Ruthie's eyes. Bernadette's random moments of clarity were jarring. She seemed so lucid. So aware. Yet the next moment she became childlike again and seemed lost inside her own mind. "I'm here, Mom," Ruthie said.

Bernadette blinked and for a split second, clarity showed on her face. "Here you are! Ruthie." The curtain fell again, though, and the light went out. "She's coming, you know. She'll help Connell. She'll take me into the light."

Pippin caught Ruthie's concerned eye and tilted her head, silently asking Ruthie to come with her for a minute. Ruthie followed her into the hallway. "It's late. You can stay at the inn with her," Pippin said. "I just didn't want to leave her there alone."

"I don't know how long we'll need to stay. I need to make arrangements to bring dad back home."

That hadn't even crossed Pippin's mind. Of course, they'd want to take Connell back to Pittsburgh to be buried near family and friends. "Your dad booked the room for a week, but you can stay as long as you need to," she said.

"A week?"

A week," Pippin said. Now that she knew Connell Foley was connected to her father, she wondered what he'd planned to do during those seven days. He'd taken that information to the grave.

CHAPTER 25

"Actually, I believe in everything, including astrology and tarot cards. All of it is just another way for people to try and tighten the link to the spirits in our universe. I believe it exists for all people."

~Billy Dee Williams

Lil sat on the couch, a pillow on her lap, a mini hardcover journal propped open on it, a stack of colorful cards in her hand. She bobbed her head along with whatever played on her earbuds. Pippin worked around her, fluffing the cushions, dusting the shelves, thinking about what to do next—not about the inn, but about her life and the curse.

Lil set the pillow aside as Pippin started dusting the shelves. She murmured something to herself then laid three cards on the table in front of her.

Lil murmured some more, then suddenly let out a screech. "It's time!" She flung herself back against the couch cushions, her arms outstretched. "At long last."

Pippin jumped and rushed over to her. "Lil, are you okay?"

Lil waved one of her arms around. "I'm fine. Fine! This is brilliant. Just brilliant!"

Pippin glanced over Lil's shoulder at the cards. "What, the cards? Is it tarot?"

"Exactly. I've been waiting for this day for so long. Years. I left everything behind to find the answers to the questions I had, and now, finally..."

"What does it mean?" Pippin asked when Lil trailed off.

Lil pointed to the three cards in turn, her silver rings catching the light, her bangle bracelets jingling on her wrist. "This card represents the past, the present, or the future, this one is about the situation. Or it could be about the action to take, or the outcome I'm seeking. And that last one is choosing the path to take." She turned to look at Pippin. "It's confirming that I'm doing the right thing. And that the time is right. The time is *now*."

The candle on the coffee table flickered as Pippin looked down at the cards. "How does it work?" she asked.

Lil looked up at her, her eyes bright. "Are you interested in tarot?"

Pippin didn't know if she was or wasn't. "I don't really know anything about how it works."

"Ahh, well, you've come to the right place. I'll do a reading for you!" Lil patted the sofa next to her.

Pippin hesitated for a second. The idea of tarot felt as mystical to her as bibliomancy. She imagined the person doing the reading saw everything through the lens of their own experiences in the same way she did when she tried to interpret passages from books. How valuable could that be? But if she thought in those terms, then how valuable was her own divination?

Why not? she thought. She had nothing to lose, so she sat.

Lil drew the cards together into a stack. "The cards draw energy. I don't usually let anyone touch my cards. Not casually, anyway. But I sense something in you. You have a strong energy."

Once again, her bibliomancy came to mind. Was that the energy Lil sensed? Was she that perceptive?

"When I got this deck, I slept with it under my pillow for seven days. It's called attuning. It helped me connect to my cards, and the more connected I am, the more accurate my readings are. The more insightful." She held the cards in one hand and fanned them out, then she gently blew on the edges. Next, she put them back into a neat stack, holding them with the same hand, and with the fingertips of her other hand, she knocked once on the top of the deck. "Now the deck is cleansed of any old energy," she proclaimed. "Now, close your eyes and take a few breaths. This will calm you and attune you to the moment." She heard Lil's calming breaths and followed her lead. "Now," Lil said quietly, "visualize white light. Picture it flowing from the crown of your head straight into the cards."

Pippin did as Lil said. Her mind wandered, and she thought maybe she should create a ritual like this before she practiced her bibliomancy. It could help ground her.

Lil handed her the deck. "You shuffle it."

Pippin held the heavy cards in her left hand, lifted sections up and out, then put them back to mix them all up. Lil took the deck back and fanned them out. "Using your left hand, choose one, then pass it to me. Do this three times."

Each card Pippin drew and handed to Lil, she placed face down on the table. "The past, the present, and the future," Lil said.

She turned the first one over, starting on the left top. The image was of a man hanging upside down, suspended by a tree. The Hanged Man, it read. That did not seem like a good omen. It felt ominous and deadly. Pippin swallowed, stifling her unease at the image.

"Interesting," Lil said. "Don't worry. It's not a bad card. On the contrary, it represents that the universe has had its own plan in the past, and that you've had to be patient. Your timetable didn't coincide with the universe's. You can't control that of which you have no knowledge."

This felt accurate to Pippin. For twenty years, she had wondered what had happened to her father. As a child there had been no way for her to find out. Grandmother Faye had kept every bit of information hidden away, including the house's existence, but they'd inherited it, returning them back to Devil's Cove. In the end, the universe had contrived to bring them here.

"The Hangman can also be telling you to be patient, and to try to see things from a different perspective. Look at it from a new angle."

Pippin nodded, letting Lil's message sink in. "So that's the past?"

"Yes. I'm doing a different type of reading than the one I did for myself. The middle card for you is the present." She turned it over, flipping it sideways, left to right. The image was of an angel with pink wings and a trumpet, a group of people, arms outstretched, gazing up at him. "The Judgement card," Lil said. "In terms of your present, it means it's time to come to some decision about the past. The implication is that change is on the horizon. Opportunities. Keep in mind, the idea of judgement isn't about other people judging you, but about how you judge yourself on your past, whether that means past actions, past believes, or past attitudes. The card is face up, which means you should, ideally, see your past in a positive light. You should recognize that you've acted with integrity. That you've always done the best you could." She looked around the great room, as if she was taking in all the details of the house at once. "I mean you just inherited this place, and now you have an inn."

A dark cloud slid over Pippin. "How did you know that? That we inherited the house?"

Lil raised her brows innocently. She shrugged. "I guess I overheard it somewhere," she said, then carried on. "The implication of the judgement card, when you look at it in terms of Home, is that you may be drawn to an old home or an old property you had a connection with. A place with happy memories."

Pippin's skin flared with goosebumps. She was wary of this woman, but so far, everything Lil had said was spot on. Eerily so. She pushed her concern aside for the moment and pointed to the last card. "And that's the future?"

Like the others, Lil flipped the card from left to right, revealing a young man sitting under a tree. Three cups sat in front to him. A cloud held the fourth cup, an arm extending it out to him.

"What does it mean?" Pippin asked.

Before she answered, Lil said, "You have a lot going on in your life right now."

That felt like a massive understatement. "I definitely do."

"Are you in a relationship?"

Jamie flashed in her mind, but she shook her head. "No."

"Okay. Well, given that, this card is telling you to open yourself up to your emotions. You may feel ready for love, or maybe you don't. Regardless, there is some past emotion that needs healing, but you *can* risk opening yourself up." She paused and closed her eyes for a beat. "There's something about the number four," she said after she opened them again. "Four friends? Four obstacles—"

"Four enemies?" Pippin said.

Lil shot her a look. "You have enemies."

A statement, not a question. "That's probably not the right word. People who think I'm in the way of something they want. Only they don't even know what that thing is."

"Interesting," Lil said, her voice quiet. Reflective. "But you know what they are after, don't you?"

A chill swept over Pippin's skin. This woman was too perceptive. "You said your cards were telling you that you're on the right path. That you're doing the right thing. Do you know what that means—?" Pippin started to ask in an attempt to redirect the conversation, but she broke off when a page in Lil's journal caught her eye. Half the page was covered with doodles, but one in particular caught her eye. It was familiar. It was a circle. Inside, with each end touching the circle's lines, was the letter V. And another image was cradled inside the V. A face, only it wasn't a face. It was a skull.

She'd seen it before—as a faded tattoo positioned between a woman in a bikini top and grass skirt, a rope and anchor, and a ship, sails billowing in the wind. It had been inked on the arm of her father's murderer. Her temples suddenly pulsed, adrenaline pumping through her body. She turned cold, as if a skeleton's hand walked up her spine. "What is that?" she asked, pointing to it. Her voice turned hoarse. "What *is* that?"

All Lil's exuberant animation settled into something more somber. "Have you heard of Venatores?" she asked.

Pippin shook her head. She slowly angled her body to look straight at Lil, moving slightly away from her at the same time. "That's what the V is for?"

"That's right."

"What does it *mean*?"

"The symbol? It traces back to the 1500s. And the word —Venatores? It's Latin. It means hunters."

The chill coursing through her turned icy. "As in treasure hunters?" she asked, her voice scarcely more than a whisper.

Lil's gaze bored into her. "You could call them that. They formed about five hundred years ago." She held out her hands and wiggled her fingers as if she were casting a spell. "Very woo woo. Hush hush. A secret organization with very few members who are after something very specific."

Pippin's head clouded. This woman, she knew about the treasure hunters. She had a name for them. Which meant she could be one of them. She probably *was* one of them. Pippin felt as if she was trudging through muck to pull Lil's words into the light. A five-hundred-year-old organization called Venatores. "Do you know what they're after?" she asked.

Lil leaned forward and dropped her voice to match Pippin's. "I know *one* of the things they're after." She looped a finger under the leather cording around her neck, pulling it out from its hiding place behind her white t-shirt.

Pippin stared at it. Sucked in a startled breath. Her heartbeat pulsed in her ears. What the—? How—? It was the coin. Her hand pressed against her neck, though she wasn't wearing her mother's necklace anymore. *Her* coin, but that was impossible. She and Grey had put it in a safe deposit box. "Where did you get that?" she snapped, suspicion and anger making her voice sharp.

Lil glanced around, as if looking for prying eyes. *The walls have ears.* She patted the air with one hand. "Calm down, Pippin. This isn't your necklace."

Pippin sputtered. "It's not...then whose?" The space behind her eyes ached. She wanted to run—to run from the house, straight to the bank, to check that Cassie's necklace was still there. Instead, she stayed rooted to the sofa, staring at this stranger who seemed connected to her in some way. "How do you *know* about my necklace?"

"I've always known." She fluttered her hand, the buoyancy of her personality resurfacing. "Well, since I was little, anyway."

She'd always known? Pippin scooted back, putting distance between them. "Who *are* you? Are you part of... that...group? The...the...Venatores?"

Lil glanced at the tarot cards on the table then got up and moved to perch on the coffee table across from Pippin. "I thought you might recognize me," she said.

Pippin's mind stuttered. What did she mean? They knew each other? "Recognize you?"

Lil nodded emphatically. "Pippin. I'm Lily."

Pippin stared.

And stared.

And then, in a flash, it came to her. Hart. As in Annabel Hart, her grandmother. Lil, as in Lilith Lane.

The woman sitting across from her...the woman with the necklace just like hers...this woman who read tarot cards in the same way Pippin's bibliomancy worked...this woman was her missing cousin, Lily.

CHAPTER 26

"*The voyage of discovery is not in seeking new landscapes but in having new eyes.*"

~Marcel Proust

THIRTY MINUTES LATER, Grey, Lily, and Pippin stood together in a triangle out on the beach behind Sea Captain's Inn. Sailor walked in a circle around them like a sentry. The twins considered the mysterious woman who claimed to be their cousin with trepidation and caution. The peaceful lapping of water on the shoreline belied the roiling hurricane in Pippin's gut.

Grey cupped his hand over his forehead, rubbing his temples. "Let me get this straight. This man was in Oregon and had an affair with your mother. Then he just happens to wind up here on Devil's Cove and *coincidently* befriends our father. In a movie, people would say that's too unbelievable to be true."

Lil wasn't deterred. She gave an annoyed shrug. "Whatever. Believe it or not, but it's true."

Grey glared at her. "You waltz in here and we're just supposed to believe everything you say?"

Lily folded her arms over her chest like a barrier, as if any of their skepticism would bounce right off of her. "You think I'm lying? That I'm making this shit up?"

Grey threw up one hand. "Why the hell not? How do we know you're not just another treasure hunter?"

Pippin started. That thought had crossed her mind, too. Lily...or Lil...had shown real sorrow when Pippin had told her about Aunt Rose. But, as she had learned, people showed you what they wanted you to see, and plenty of people were good actors. Pippin narrowed her eyes and stared at Lil. Did the woman standing in front of her resemble the kid she'd met twenty years ago? She sighed, letting go of the idea that she would be able to pull any recognition from her brain. It had been two decades since they'd last seen each other. She and Grey didn't know anything about their cousins. It was easy enough to fake curly blond hair. For all they knew, this woman who claimed to be Lilith Lane was another person out to take what wasn't hers.

"I'm not a treasure hunter," she snapped, answering Grey's question.

Pippin stared. Lil was saying that her biological father—a man she had never known as a child—was a bad guy in their family drama. "How did you find him?"

"I did one of those DNA tests—"

"And he showed up in the results?" Grey asked with another disbelieving laugh.

"No. God, no! Grey, would you just listen to me?"

Grey threw up both hands in mock surrender. "Go ahead."

"He did *not* show up in the results, but other relations

did. I tracked them down, one by one. It was like putting a puzzle together and my father was the missing piece. Eventually I figured it out though. Jed Riordin was the common link between those distant relatives and Cora and me. He *is* our biological father."

Lily's ingenuity was impressive. "That was pretty clever," Pippin managed to say through her shock.

"Yeah, well, there's more. The man is *not* our friend."

Those six words hovered like a dark cloud overhead. "What do you mean?" she asked slowly.

"My guess is, he never really cared for my mother. I think he was after something, used her, and when he didn't get whatever it was he wanted, he bolted."

"Are you saying Jed is a treasure hunter? Part of that group? The Venatores?" Pippin asked.

"The Latin word for hunters," Grey repeated after Lil explained the origin of the symbol and the meaning of Venatores.

Lil lifted the length of leather cord over her head and handed it to Grey. "Pippin said you have your mother's necklace. This was my mother's. This is at least one of the things the Venatores are after."

"And you know this how?" Grey asked, but the skepticism that had been coloring his words had faded. He turned the coin over in his hand, examining it.

"My mother kept a journal. For a few months leading up to the time she got pregnant with me and Cora, she wrote about the man she had been seeing. She was crazy about him. She referred to him by his initials—JR. So, when I did the DNA test and started talking to people and Jed Riordin's name came up a few times, I put it together.

"My mom wrote in her journal about how willing this JR was to help Aunt Rose clean the bookstore and organize all her old things. *He's such a curious person*, she wrote. *So interested in everything Aunt Rose has to say. She doesn't like him much, though, and I can't figure out why. When I asked her, she just shrugged. 'Just a feeling', she said.*" Lil's voice had changed as she imitated her mother's words, but now it was back to normal. "She described his tattoo. The circle with the V and the skull. She said it gave her the creeps, and when she ran her fingers on it and asked him about it, he didn't want to talk about it. He described it as the symbol for some fraternal organization he belonged to. I've been searching for anything and everything about it. All I know is what I've already told you. The V stands for Venatores. It's Latin for hunters—"

"What about the skull?" Grey asked, the Roman coin clutched tightly in his hand.

"That I don't know. A Roman god, maybe?"

A murder of crows glided by overhead, circling, and coming back before disappearing over the roofline of the house. Their caws hung in the air long after they were no longer in sight. "I still don't understand how you know Jed was after the necklace more than thirty years ago, and that he's after it now," Pippin said, feeling like she was playing devil's advocate. She hadn't believed in Jed...until she had, and now she was reluctant to let that trust completely evaporate.

"My mother's journal is equal parts writing and sketching. She would sketch the flowers in the cemetery at Cape Misery, and the flora around the house. She wrote poetry. She died young, but she filled so many journals with her writing and her art."

"The necklace..." Grey prompted, hurrying Lil past the memories she had fallen into from her mother's journals.

Lil reached into the folds of her maxi skirt, pulling out

her cellphone. A second later, she held it out for Pippin and Grey to see. "I took a picture of this page—of a bunch of pages, actually, but this one is a rubbing of the necklace at the top, and below that, she sketched the front and back of it." Lil scrolled through the photos and found another one to show them, only it wasn't another drawing, Pippin saw. It was the torn remnant of a drawing. "In the next entry, she was really upset. She said JR was gone. He'd ransacked the bookstore and then disappeared. And it was only that night that she realized he'd ripped the drawing from her journal. She said, and these are *her* words, *'He used me. All this time, I trusted him and loved him, and he only wanted the necklace. I only hope Aunt Rose remembers where she hid it.'*"

Pippin's nostrils flared and her heart seemed to swell inside her. What she would have given to have her mother's thoughts and feelings and recordings of her daily life. She pushed down the intense desire, though, focusing on her mother's sister, Lacy, and what Lil was recounting. "After I read all of it, I knew other people were going to come looking. Aunt Rose didn't remember where she put it. She had left herself obscure little clues. It took forever, but I finally pieced them together and found it in a jar of elderberry jam in the back of a cupboard. I took it with me. Leaving it would have put Aunt Rose and Cora in danger, and I couldn't take that chance. I had to find our father, and the necklace is my bait."

"Have you made contact?" Pippin asked, sounding like she was asking if Lil had been in communication with an alien spaceship rather than with her biological father.

"Not yet. You know how it goes when the thing you want is suddenly in front of you. Everything in my life for almost the past ten years has been about finding him. Now that I have, I'm not sure what to do next."

Neither Pippin nor Grey could help their cousin with that emotional burden, so Grey's response surprised her. "One step at a time," he said. "First, we need to make a plan. If your father...this Jed Riordin...was working against our father, does that mean he knew about the Lane curse way back before we were all even born? He knew about it when he was with your mom," he said, this time not as a question but as a quiet musing.

All the implications felt like fiery icepicks piercing Pippin's brain. She spun. Paced in a circle. She had let Jed Riordin into the inn. Had listened to him when he'd pulled her outside and told her that he and Connell Foley had both worked with her father, and that she and Grey weren't safe. He'd seemed so sincere. Scared, even. "He could have killed Connell Foley," she said. "If he really had figured something out about the curse or the necklaces or..." She trailed off. She knew there was more, she just didn't know what it was. "He may have killed Connell so he could keep whatever he found to himself."

CHAPTER 27

"*S**he is the only person left in the world who shares my memories.*"

~Lisa See

BEFORE THE THREE of them could decide what to do next, Pippin asked Lil one of the questions in the forefront of her mind. "Why haven't you called your sister all these years?"

Lil squeezed her eyes shut for a second, battling down the unexpected emotion the question brought up. "She wouldn't want to talk to me."

Pippin shook her head. "That's not true. I talked to her. She's there at Cape Misery, waiting, in case you come home."

Now it was Lil's turn to pace, her feet kicking up the sand. "I've thought about going back, but we...we weren't on good terms when I left, and I couldn't go back empty-handed."

Grey's eyes darkened as he studied her, as if he was

looking for some crack in her persona. "You mean proving that Jed Riordin is your father?"

"That, and our bibliomancy. Cora always wanted to pretend the curse wasn't real. She practiced bibliomancy when we were growing up." She gave a sharp laugh. "We didn't have a choice. It was a non-negotiable for Aunt Rose. But Cora never took it very seriously. She didn't really *believe* it. Not like I did, anyway."

Much like Grey, Pippin thought. But he'd come around, and from talking to Cora, she thought her cousin had, too.

"She didn't know I was going to try to find our father," Lil said. "I told her I was going to prove it was real, and I wasn't coming back until I did."

"When was that?" Pippin asked.

Lil gave a heavy sigh. "It's been more than ten years."

Grey lightly scoffed. "You were practically still a kid—"

Lil rounded on him. The pain flowing through her pores was clear, but she steeled herself. "Haven't you ever done anything you regret, but once it's done, there's no way to take it back?"

In fact, Grey had done that pretty recently with the purchase of the boat he was refurbishing, and his ventures into the sound, as a result of his total disbelief of the curse and his fate if he discounted it. Pippin avoided making eye contact with him. She'd gotten him to face the existence of the curse and they'd forged a shaky truce. After he'd nearly drowned in the Atlantic off of Nags Head during Pippin's attempt to break the curse with an offering to Lir, he had finally come around. But he still had the boat—was still working on the boat—, and Pippin wasn't entirely sure he wasn't still tempting fate with his kayak and fishing pole.

Grey did meet Pippin's eyes and he gave a heavy exhalation. Their connection was as strong as it had ever been, and she knew he was thinking the same thing she was. They'd been so connected from the moment they'd been born—and before, even—that the mere idea of being apart made anxiety pool in her gut. Cora and Lily were twins, too. Their separation from one another had to be tearing them apart at their very core.

The moment between Pippin and Grey passed and they both turned back to Lil. "You need to call her," Pippin said quietly, because she could feel the heartache emanating from her. She pulled out her cell phone and called up the number Cora had given her. She held her phone out to Lil. "Call her."

THE CONVERSATION between Lily and Cora quickly turned emotional. As much as Pippin wanted to hear every word, she dragged Grey up the beach, up the deck stairs, and to one of the bistro tables in order to give Lil privacy. They watched her kick the sand with one foot, then the other. Finally, she sank down on the sand, her arms wrapped around her knees. Her voice floated through the air, her words unintelligible, but laden with ten years of loss and sorrow and love.

"What do you think about Jed Riordin being their father?" Pippin asked Grey. "Do you think it's possible?"

"Sounds like she's done her homework," Grey said with a frown. "The DNA thing...that was damn clever. He's been hiding in plain sight and Dad never knew."

That's right. Leo had trusted Jed. He was part of his inner circle. And all along he'd been hiding in plain sight. *Hiding in plain sight*. Something about that phrase struck Pippin, but she couldn't put her finger on why. She stared at

Lil, who still sat on the sand facing the sound and the barrier islands beyond. Above her, the crows had returned, cawing and cawing and cawing. Jed had been right there, hiding in plain sight, and Leo hadn't known. Or had he? The question circled in her mind. Had Leo known Jed was a traitor?

Pippin had a sudden recollection of something Salty Gallagher had said to her when he'd had her trapped in The Burrow, he and his son, Jimmy, trying to get ahold of the necklace. A conversation with Salty came back to her in a burst. *"I looked everywhere for that. All these years I thought it was buried with your mother, then you came back to town, and I figured out Leo gave Max somethin'."*

Max Lawrence had been killed because of the necklace, but before that, he'd told Jed Riordiin about it. Jed had known about it. He'd known *all along*.

Her thoughts went back to her father. Leo had been on a mission to stop the Lane curse and save his wife and children from it. As a young child, Pippin had believed him to be invincible. That belief had waned when he vanished, but since learning the truth about what happened to him, his persona had ebbed and flowed in her mind, growing larger than life, then shifting to failure with the anger that sometimes materialized. She heard Grey's voice echoing in the back of her mind, but she frowned, her thoughts slamming against one another. Could Leo have known Jed Riordin was a Venatore, or had Jed duped him?

She blinked at a sound, then at Grey's fingers snapping in front of her. "Hello. Earth to Peevie."

She blinked again. "Sorry."

He watched her, familiar with the way she processed thoughts. "What is it? What's wrong?"

Pippin looked at him. "We're missing something. About Jed, maybe, or about the books Connell had? I don't know."

Pippin and Grey had left Lil alone, not wanting to rush her after the first talk she had had with her sister in a decade, but now Pippin tapped her foot anxiously. Her gut told her there were answers at The Open Door. Finally, Lil ended the call. She stared out into the distance for a solid five minutes before climbing the stairs to the inn's back deck. She handed Pippin her phone and gave a watery smile. "Cora's...doing okay. I'm going to go home," she said, then she rolled her hand in the air. "After we talk to Jed, of course, and, you know, stop the curse."

Pippin gave her a bolstering smile. Her cell phone pinged with an incoming text from Jamie. "I heard from my numismatist friend," it said.

"Maybe that'll fill in another piece of the puzzle," Grey said after she showed him the text.

"Okay. Glad we're on the same page there. She put her hands on the arms of her chair and stood. "Now. Let's go."

"Where to?" Lil asked.

"Back to the scene of the crime," she said, "because I think we'll find the answer to whatever Connell was trying to communicate in his last minutes there."

CHAPTER 28

"T*here'll always be serendipity involved in discovery.*"
~Jeff Bezos

The Open Door Bookshop was buzzing with activity. The fact that a murder had taken place there had been downplayed by The Devil's Cove Gazette, and if it had been picked up in the other Outer Banks news publications or the bigger news areas in the state, it certainly hadn't affected business. Pippin hadn't seen any of her current guests around town, but when she stepped inside the shop, the first people she spotted were Nancy and Peter Kernoodle. They'd seen her first. Pippin had made eye contact with Mrs. Kernoodle, but the woman broke it by turning her back to face the opposite way.

Pippin could see her mouth moving as she murmured something to her husband, but Mr. Kernoodle stood with his hand shoved in the pockets of his Dickies, wearing the same stern expression he always wore, not shining his gaze to Pippin at all. He kept his focus on his wife as she scanned the shelves.

If Mrs. Kernoodle sensed her husband's dourness, she didn't let on...or she didn't care. She was in the mystery section, perusing each and every title by pulling each one out, running her eyes over the cover, flipping it over to the back, then sliding it back into its position.

If either of them had looked her way, Pippin would have waved and smiled. But they didn't, so she didn't.

Grey led Lil to the register where Jamie waited on a customer. Pippin set down the books they'd found around Connell Foley on the counter. She took a second to walk to the archway connecting The Open Book and Devil's Brew. Ruby was busy behind the counter, the line six or seven people deep. At a table toward the back were Mathilda and Sasha. They sat across from each other, knees bent under them, each leaning forward on the table, their attention on the coloring books they had in front of them. A box of crayons had been emptied, and the crayons spread haphazardly across the middle of the table. Mathilda popped up on her knees and said something to Sasha, who broke into a fit of giggling. Pippin smiled to herself. Those two were good for each other.

She went back to the bookstore counter, leaving Ruby to her customers. Jamie had finished up with the person he'd been helping. He clapped Noah's shoulder. "I'll be back in ten," he said.

Noah flicked his head back to peer out from under the hair that swept across his forehead, offering some sort of silent communique that Jamie took as an "Okay, boss,"

Jamie wore his usual button-down shirt over a plain t-shirt, the sleeves rolled up. He wore a black watch, jeans, and with his wire-rimmed glasses, he looked the part of a bookseller to a T. "Mam," he called toward one of the stacks. Erin poked her head out, brows raised. "Keep an eye on the girls, would you? I'll be in the office for a few minutes."

"Sure thing, love," she said.

Heidi's precocious voice wafted from nearby. "Gram doesn't need to keep an eye on me. I'm eleven, remember? I am perfectly capable of taking care of myself."

Pippin raised her hand like she was in the witness box and had her other hand on the Bible. "I can attest to that," she said.

Heidi appeared at the end of an aisle, a stack of books in her arms. "Thank you, Miss Pippin."

"You're very welcome, Heidi."

Jamie's shoulders shook with his silent laughter. "There's another stack to re-shelve on the counter," he said

Heidi gave a mock salute. "Ay ay, cap'n," she said before disappearing into the stacks again.

Jamie started for his office down the back hallway. He had recently built bookshelves in his office and given everything a fresh coat of paint. Boxes of books sat against one wall, but other than that, he kept his space orderly. A set of stacked trays organized printed invoices and order forms. Another held printed catalogs some publishers still sent out. The computer cut down on a lot of the physical paperwork, but there was still plenty to keep sorted, and Jamie had a system for it all.

When they were all inside, he closed the door and turned, nodding at both Grey and Lil. He looked at Pippin, one corner of his mouth lifting in the sort of smile that made it clear he was glad to see her. She felt the same, but she tucked those emotions away to think about later. Right now, they had a curse to break. "Jamie, this is my cousin, Lily."

His chin dipped in surprise. "Your cousin from Oregon?"

What he'd left unspoken was: *The cousin you haven't seen since you were nine years old?* And, *the cousin who vanished?*

Lily answered the question he'd asked. "Right. My sister's still there. Cora."

"Nice to meet you," he said, managing to school his face and questions he had at being face to face with Pippin's long-lost cousin.

An awkward silence descended for a few seconds until Pippin broke it. "You know Jed Riordin?"

"Yeah, of course." He looked from Pippin to Grey to Lil, waiting for whatever was coming next.

"He's my father," Lil blurted.

He took a step back, shock on his face. "Whoa, what?"

Lil gave a mirthless smile. "He's my biological father."

"That is an unexpected twist," Jamie said.

"Another one," Pippin said.

"Why are we back here?" Lil asked, cutting to the chase.

"So. My numismatist friend," Jamie said.

Lil gawped. "Your numis-whatis?"

"He has a friend who's a money expert," Pippin said, summarizing, probably badly, what a numismatist was and did.

"Old coins and currency," Grey said with a bit more accuracy.

Lil flashed him a leery look. "You have a friend who *happens* to study old coins?"

"I do," Jamie said, ignoring the suspicion underlying her question. "She works with the Smithsonian's National Numismatic Collection in DC. Now, she prefaced her thoughts on this by saying she can't be sure of anything without seeing it in person, and that it's highly unusual for something gold to be covered in silver. The opposite is seen more often, with something silver covered in gold to make it seem more valuable than it is."

"Okay," Pippin and at the same time Grey said, "Noted."

Jamie went to his desk and grabbed a small sheet of paper torn from a notepad. "Okay then. She said that, without seeing it, it reminds her of a coin known as the *Aureo medallion of Massenzio.* She said there are only two that have ever been found." He paused and looked at them with an expression that conveyed they were about to hear something remarkable. "They're each worth about a million and a half."

Pippin and Lil both gasped. Grey muttered a quiet, "Damn," followed by, "Glad we locked that thing away."

Once the words were uttered, they all seemed to realize that only Pippin's necklace was locked away. Lil still wore hers on the leather strap around her neck, and right now, her hand was fisted around the coin.

"Lily, you need to get that thing into the safe deposit box," Grey said.

And pronto, Pippin thought. She circled back to what Grey had said about Jed Riordin. He'd been hiding in plain sight. So had the Roman coins. Even if they were worth just a fraction of these *Aureo medallion of Massenzio* coins, they still had to be unbelievably valuable. At least two people—Max Lawrence and Monique Baxter—had died in connection with it, not to mention Leo. And possibly Connell Foley. Jed Riordin knew about at least one of the coins. If he'd been at Cape Misery like Lil theorized, then he probably knew about both of them. There was no telling who else might know, but if Lily's true identity was revealed, she would be in danger. Getting her coin to safety was a priority. It was the only way to protect it, and her.

All the color had drained from Lil's face when Jamie had

told them how much the coins might be worth. Her whole body seemed to tremble. She understood the danger she was in, and also the risk she had been living with all these years, a million-plus dollars strung around her neck on a strap of leather. Grey lightly touched her elbow. "Come on, I'll take you to the bank. We can lock it up with the other one."

She nodded, eyes wide and spooked. "Okay. Yeah. Good. Thanks."

Like a little caravan, they left the room following Jamie back through the shop, where Jamie was immediately sucked into helping a customer. As Grey and Lil headed off, Pippin took a moment to stand back and take in the store. So many people came and went through the rows and rows of books. She'd seen June Rycliff and Heather Beadly here —was that yesterday? Or the day before? Her days were muddled together. She'd seen Nancy Kernoodle looking at books while her husband stood back and watched, first on the classic side, then at the mysteries. This led her to wonder about Jed Riordin. What if he'd followed Connell Foley in from Devil's Brew the day Connell died? A chill swept through her. Could Connell have known Jed was following him?

A yelp rose from one of the rows of books. Heidi. Pippin reacted, immediately calling out, "Heidi," then louder, "Heidi?"

"Over here." The girl's voice came from deep in the stacks.

Pippin tracked Heidi to the row that held classics from N through Z on one side and mysteries from A through M on the other. Heidi had dragged one of the stools in front of the C section of mystery novels. Standing on it gave her just enough height to slip the book that needed re-shelving into its spot.

Seeing her on the stool caused a memory to spark. A step stool in the aisle, knocked over—as if whoever had been using it knocked it over as they quickly stepped down. A scenario started to form in her head, playing in bits and pieces like an old movie being spliced together. She pictured Connell running into someone—Jed?—in the coffee shop, then trying to shake him in the rows of books.

Heidi gave a frustrated growl. She stood on her tiptoes on the stool and grabbed ahold of a book, yanking it out. "People are so dumb," she grumbled. She looked up as Pippin came up beside her. She held up the book she had removed from the shelf. "I mean, it's not, like, *hard* to put a book back where it belongs, right? So, you know, anyone who wants to find it can?"

"Right," Pippin said slowly, something about Heidi's words grabbing her. She thought again about Connell Foley and...

Pippin's gaze traveled to the empty space on the check-out counter where the stack of books for Heidi to re-shelve had been. She had set the books Connell Foley had had with him there when she'd come in. The space was empty now.

Those books. They were trying to tell her something, but what?

She scanned what she knew. Connell was an expert on medieval history. He'd been looking for—and had possibly found—a book that revealed something about Morgan Dubhshláine and the pact she had made with Lir. If he knew he was being followed and possibly in danger, he would have hidden it. The question was, where?

Something Lil said sent her thoughts in a new direction.

Lil had said Aunt Rose had hidden Lacy's necklace but couldn't remember where. She had started leaving herself little clues to remember. Clues that had led Lil to a forgotten jar of jam.

An image of Uncle Billy from *It's a Wonderful Life* flashed in her mind. He'd tied strings around his fingers as reminders.

These thoughts led her back to the books Connell had with him when he died. He had chosen them for a reason. She had used her divination to try to figure out why. Why *Treasure Island*? Why *Kidnapped*? Why *Captain Blood*?

From the corner of her eye, she saw Heidi drag the step stool to the other side of the row. She had her diminishing stack of books cradled in one arm. Robert Louis Stevenson's *Treasure Island* was clutched in her hand. As Heidi stepped on the stool, the answer hit her like a blow to the gut. Hiding in plain sight.

Pippin thought the books had to do with her bibliomancy, but she was wrong. Connell was being literal. They were meant to help him remember. That phrase came back to her again—hiding in plain sight.

"Wait!" she yelled, the word shooting out of her mouth with the force of a rocket hurtling toward the atmosphere.

Heidi jumped. The books fumbled in her arms.

Pippin hurried forward, arms outstretched to help catch any falling books, but Heidi caught them. "Miss Pippin, you *cannot* go around scaring people like that," Heidi scolded. "I almost dropped all these books."

"Heidi." Jamie's voice came first, followed by his footsteps, and then his appearance at the end of the row. He leveled a chastising gaze at his daughter.

Heidi's shoulders sagged. "Sorry, Miss Pippin," she grumbled.

"You're right, though, Heidi. I didn't mean to startle you." Pippin turned to Jamie. "It was my fault."

He must have caught something in her posture or the urgency in her eyes. "What's going on?" he asked.

She tried to still her thrashing heart. "I think I know where Connell hid the book he found."

Heidi moved to the side so Pippin could step onto the stool. She scanned the author's names. *Wide Sargasso Sea*, by Jean Rhys was followed by JD Salinger's *Franny and Zoe*, then Muriel Spark's *The Prime of Miss Jean Brodie*. Next was Robert Louis Stevenson's *Dr. Jekyll and Mr. Hyde*, then *Valley of the Dolls* by Jacqueline Susann.

She ran her fingers across the spines of the books. *Dr. Jekyll and Mr. Hyde* leaned at an angle against *The Prime of Miss Jean Brodie*, revealing the spot where *Kidnapped* and *Treasure Island* belonged. Pippin pushed the two books apart, widening the space. She reached her hand in. Her fingers grazed the hard cover of a thin book at the very back of the shelf. She held her breath as she pulled it out and her heart stopped.

It was bound in worn, mottled leather with faint gold embellishment and sprinkled edges. She carefully opened it and read the title page. Dagda and the Curse of Morrighan.

The author's name was Seamus O'Dulany.

CHAPTER 29

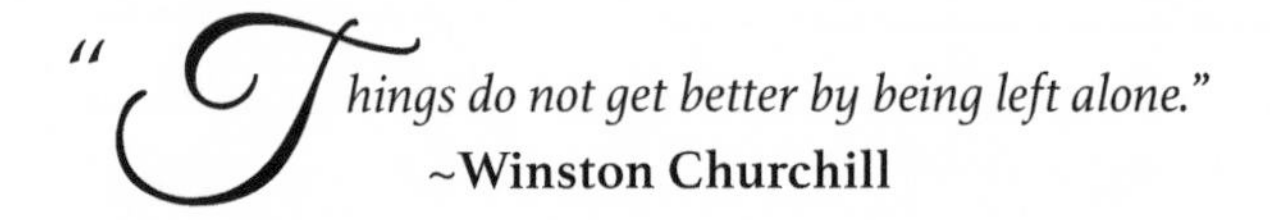
"Things do not get better by being left alone."
~Winston Churchill

"WHOA," Jamie muttered. He took a step back, then forward, then back again. "Whoa," he said again. They stood there in the middle of the row of books staring at the volume Pippin held. Her mind spun like a top out of control, wobbling on its tip and starting to topple, first this way, then that. Her thoughts smashed against each other. So, *this* was the Seamus O'Dulany Connell Foley had been referring to in his diary.

Connell had found the book and had come to Sea Captain's Inn. Holding it in her hand, Pippin knew with certainty that he'd been planning to give it to her, but when he knew someone was after him, he'd done the only thing he could. He'd hidden the book and left a clue so it could be found again.

Seamus O'Dulany. She repeated the name, letting it come faster and faster. "Jamie," she said suddenly, her voice low and urgent. "Remember the other day you said the most common evolution of the name Dubhshláine is Delaney?"

Jamie pushed his glasses up, then cupped his chin. "Yes, I do remember that," he said slowly, and Pippin knew he was making the same connection she had.

"So, the O was dropped. Dubhshláine became Delaney, which my great-great-grandfather eventually became Lane. But what if there was an in-between?"

"O'Dulany," Jamie said.

"O'Dulany," she repeated, then held up the thin book. "Which could make Seamus O'Dulany one of my ancestors."

"Can I finish reshelving these now?" Heidi asked, holding up the stack of books still in her arms.

"Yeah, Bean," he said, calling her the nickname he sometimes used.

Heidi set to work, climbing up onto the stool and sliding *Treasure Island* into the vacant spot. Jamie pulled Pippin aside. Seamus Dulany's name repeated in her mind. Her pulse thundered and her nerves made her feel as if her heart might burst right out of her body. Jamie took both of her hands in his, looking at her with so much concern in his eyes that she thought she might give into the tears that pricked at her. But no. She couldn't. She *wouldn't. She would not cry*.

He wrapped his arms around her and pulled her close. She could feel his heartbeat against hers. She breathed in, letting the coiled ball of tension inside her loosen and unwind. He held her steady until her pulse slowed. Finally, she pulled back, first resting her forehead against his, then lifting her eyes to his.

He tucked the book under his arm and put his hands on

her shoulders. “We’re going to get through this. Together. We’re going to figure it out.”

Oh God, her nose tingled. Her eyes welled. She screwed them shut to keep the tears at bay. It had always been her and Grey against the world. He’d been her only confidant. The only person she trusted implicitly. Slowly, Ruby and Daisy and Hattie had chipped away at some of the walls she had built long ago. And now Jamie had burrowed through completely. He squeezed her hand. “We’re going to figure it out,” he said again. “Let’s go upstairs.”

Yes, Pippin thought. Cyrus could be a sounding board to her new theory.

Jamie paused long enough catch Noah’s attention. “You good?”

“Yup,” Noah said, never missing a beat as he rang up a customer buying the first Harry Potter book.

Jamie grabbed a handful of cotton gloves from a drawer at the counter before taking Pippin’s hand and leading her to the stairs, but she dug in her heels, stopping suddenly. Icy fingertips crept up her spine carrying with them the eerie feeling that she was being watched. She peered at the customers milling around, looking for Jed Riordin. She didn’t see him, but that didn’t mean he wasn’t somewhere nearby. That he wasn’t following her. Her nerves knotted, pulled tighter at the idea that Jed might have killed for the book she now held in her hand.

As she turned back toward the stairs, she caught a glimpse of a woman’s head disappearing behind a free-standing shelf. Her gut constricted. Camille.

Pippin pulled her hand free, startling Jamie. She thrust Seamus O’Dulany’s book at him and took off. “Pippin, what the—"

“It’s Camille!” She raced back through the shop and

toward the place the woman had just been. "Camille!" she called. No answer. Pippin rounded the corner, pulling up short, stopping herself from plowing into Sue and Jefferson Macon. "Oh!" Sue blurted, hand to her heart. "Pippin! I... didn't expect to see you here. Are you quite alright? You seem rather...agitated."

"I...was there a woman here a second ago?" Pippin asked, peering around the couple.

"Someone just ran by—"

Pippin didn't hear what Jefferson Macon said next. His words faded to the back of her awareness as her attention zeroed in on the whoosh of the shop's door opening. She moved to the end of the aisle just in time to catch a glimpse of Camille Gallagher's figure hurrying down the sidewalk outside.

CHAPTER 30

"Parentage is a very important profession, but no test of fitness for it is ever imposed in the interest of the children."

~George Bernard Shaw

COULD Camille Gallagher be a treasure hunter? What if she was helping Jimmy and Salty from afar? What if they were all in cahoots with Jed, every one of them wanting to find some mysterious treasure?

Jamie stopped her at the top of the stairs leading to Cyrus's flat. "Do you think Camille Gallagher is involved in this," he asked, and from that statement, she knew that he'd surmised all the *What Ifs* circling in her mind.

"I just...I don't understand how these people know about any of this. It's *my* family and *I* didn't know about the coins or...or—" She gestured to the book in Jamie's hand. "—or that."

He didn't have any answers for her. They retreated into Cyrus's monochrome living room overlooking the sound.

She called Grey, telling him and Lily to come back when they were done at the bank. Before long, the five of them sat facing each other. The book, *Dagda and the Curse of Morrighan,* lay on the coffee table between them. "It has to be from the late 17th century," Jamie said.

"How do you know, my boy?" Cyrus asked. He'd welcomed them in without question, serving sparkling water and crackers while they waited for Grey and Lil. Jamie had made them all don the cotton gloves he'd brought up. He perched on the edge of his chair as each of them took a turn looking at the book. Jamie held onto it longer than the others, carefully examining the binding and the pages, barely containing his excitement at the five-hundred-year-old find.

He pointed to the gold tooling on the spine, and the golden edges of the pages. "This mottled treatment on the leather was pretty common for 17th century bindings. And the embellishment, and the green and white endbands," he said, pointing to the small cord attached near the spine. "It provides structural reinforcement. Also, look at the cover itself. Bookbinding became a lot easier in the 16th century. Wood was phased out. This one is definitely pasteboard. And it has endpapers."

"Kinda helpful to have a book nerd on the team," Lil said dryly.

Pippin gave her cousin wry grin. "You'd be surprised how often it comes in handy. He's also an expert in Medieval Irish literature. That's handy, too."

Lil cocked one brow. "I guess it is."

Pippin turned back to Jamie. "Why is everyone after it?"

"It's just like the coin," Jamie said. "Rare first edition books are..." He paused for a second. Shook his head. "Man, they're worth so much. The *Bay Psalm Book*, for example, was the first book printed in British North America. 1640, I think. There are only eleven first edition copies. That's all that are left—that are known to exist, anyway. One of them sold at auction, maybe nine or ten years ago? Fourteen-million dollars."

The two words stuttered in Pippin's mind. Fourteen million. Pippin imagined Lieutenant Jacobs clutching his palpating heart at the idea of a book being worth that kind of money. Shoot, *her* heartbeat hammered at that number. But she thought there was more to it...at least for her and Grey. For Lily and Cora. For their descendants. Connell finding this book for Leo was not about the money. It was about something else. "Who is Dagda?" she asked Jamie.

Jamie adjusted his glasses and went into full professor mode. "Dagda was the chief of the Tuatha dé Danann."

"Like Zeus?" Lil asked. "*The* God of the gods?"

"Exactly," Jamie said. "You name it, he probably had a hand it. Fertility. Agriculture. Magic. Wisdom. The druids. Time itself. And life and death."

"And Morrighan?" Lil asked him.

"Ah, Morrighan was the goddess of war. She was said to determine whether a soldier would walk off the battlefield. If you were a warrior, you did *not* want to see her, because that meant you were going to die."

"That's a pretty bad omen," Grey said.

"To some. People called her the Battle Raven. Some saw her as the mythic triple goddess, representing the maiden, mother, and crone cycle of life." He paused. "But that's pretty contested among scholars. Most see her as a deity who guides or protects a king. She was Dagda's wife, so in some ways his protector since he was, essentially, the king."

"Morrighan," Pippin murmured. Then she said it louder.

"Morrighan." She felt fire in her veins. She felt four sets of eyes on her. "Morrighan...*Morgan*," she said.

Lil fiddled with the bangles on her arm. "Okay, wait. What are you saying?"

"I'm wondering," Pippin said. "Could our Morgan Dubhshláine be connected to this goddess Morrighan? They sound the same, right?"

Lil stared. "As in maybe they're the same people?"

They sat in silence for a minute, considering the question. "Zeus and the Greek gods always disguised themselves as humans, right?" Grey said. "So, what if Morgan Dubhshláine was Morrighan the goddess's human 'disguise'?" He made air quotes around the word.

Jamie snapped his fingers and pointed at Grey. "Yes! That's exactly what she would have done if she was having a relationship with Titus."

Lil's eyes flashed. "Are you saying you think our ancestor is not Morgan Dubhshláine, but this Morrighan? That we're descended from mythological gods?"

Jamie sat back, one arm crossed over his chest and supporting the opposite elbow. He cupped one hand over his forehead. "If you would have asked me to believe that six months ago, I don't know what I would have said. Maybe *hell no*. But now? With your bibliomancy, Pippin, and with the curse in your family...now I say that, yeah, I think it's possible that Morgan is actually Morrighan."

Pippin shuffled this idea into the conglomeration of all the rest of the information she had surrounding the Lane family curse. "So, obviously, she bore a child by Titus."

"And what of the name Dubhshláine?" Cyrus asked, his voice circumspect.

"Titus died, so Morrighan gave the child a mortal name. The Dubhshláine name," Grey said.

"Why that name? Why Dubhshláine?"

Jamie considered the question, filing through his mental Rolodex of information. "It's an Old Irish name, derived from either 'dubh', meaning 'dark' or 'black', or from 'slán', meaning defiance. My guess is she had the affair and the child in defiance of Dagda."

Lil leaned forward. "If Dagda is the god of everything, wouldn't he be totally pissed that his wife had an affair, and with a mortal dude, no less?"

"She betrayed him," Pippin said, then added, more slowly, as if giving the idea time to percolate, "What if it was never a pact between Morgan and Lir?"

Grey sat up and finished Pippin's thought. "What if Dagda, in anger over his wife's betrayal, cursed Morrighan and Titus's descendants."

"Not Lir," Pippin said.

"Not Lir," Grey repeated.

If this version of their history was true, it changed everything. They didn't need to make an offering to the sea god Lir or his son Manannán Mac Lir. They needed to make an offering to *Dagda*. Only he'd be able to break the curse.

They all shifted their gazes to Seamus O'Dulany's *Dagda and the Curse of Morrighan* sitting in the center of the coffee table. Grey moved to the edge of his seat. "We need to read that book."

PIPPIN DIDN'T EVEN TRY. She had become a stronger reader since returning to Devil's Cove, but she still struggled. The thought of trying to read something written with a seventeenth century typeface, in addition to the odd phrasing and vocabulary of the time, was too daunting. With the added pressure of four people listening to her, she begged off. "I just want to listen and process," she said.

She sat back as the others took turns reading or summarizing the chapters of Seamus O'Dulany's book. It was just over a hundred pages and took the better part of two hours before they'd gone through the entire thing. Jamie read the last line of the last page:

"'Many will think this nothing but fanciful imaginings. Be assured, they are not. Dagda's curse of Morrighan is as real as Tuatha dé Danann. There is no falseness in the story. Bear it in mind. Both are true. I pray that the unpretended descendants of she who called herself Morgan Dubhshláine and Titus of Roma, within the dark side of Clann na Morrigna, return to Dagda what he so seeks and was taken from him. Only then will the curse that the truest god did place upon the children of the betrayers, and the unfortunate that came after, be broken.'"

"Read it again, please," Pippin said, the feeling that she was missing some nuance in the words. She closed her eyes as Jamie read the last lines again. When he finished, they sat in silence for a long minute. Finally, it hit her. She sat up suddenly. "Children. Seamus said children."

Grey spoke. "Children as in the descendants—"

Pippin cut him off. "But he mentioned the unpretended descendants. That means us. The real descendants, not the Ventatores or treasure hunters. That last line," she said, trying to articulate what she thought it meant. "Dagda put a curse on the children of the betrayers. The children of Morgan Dubhshláine and Titus. Not child," she said with emphasis. A chill swept through her. "Children."

"Twins," Grey said. "They must have been twins. If Morgan...or Morrighan...was pregnant by Titus before he left Ireland, then he died, she had to have had twins."

Lil drew in a sharp breath. "That's what this O'Dulany guy meant when he said that thing about strife from within and a resulting separation."

Earlier in the text, Seamus O'Dulany had used an old Celtic word when he'd written about discord that had been sown between two people named Aisling and Aoife. Pippin looked at Jamie. He seemed to read her mind. He carefully looked back through the pages until he found the passage in question. "Deirfiúr," he said. "He calls them sisters, and he says they're like Ceridwen's children."

"Who is that?" Lil asked.

"Ceridwen was a Welsh sorceress. She was a white witch in Celtic mythology. She used her power only to help others. She possessed poetic wisdom, inspiration, and the gift of prophecy. The source of her magic was her cauldron, which was a strong presence in Celtic mythology and with the Tuatha dé Danann."

"What's the point?" Grey asked when Jamie paused.

"The point is that there is a strong sense of good and bad in Celtic mythology. Kind of a yin/yang thing. Ceridwen had two children. Well, three, actually, but the third is a whole different story. The first two were Creirwy and Morfran."

He went back to the compendium Connell had had about the Tuatha dé Danann, finding another passage and reading it aloud before tapping his finger on the page. "It's right here. He's saying that Dagda cursed the offspring of Morrighan and Titus before birth, and that curse damaged —or maybe divided—the sisters. He likens Aisling to Ceridwen's daughter, Creirwy, beautiful and pure. But Aoife was like her son, Morfran, who was slow-witted and disfigured."

Pippin plugged all this new information into place. With a jolt, she remembered the passage her bibliomancy had revealed to her from *The Secret Garden.*

"It is the child no one ever saw!" Exclaimed the man, turning to his companions. "She has actually been forgotten!...Poor little kid!" he said. "There is nobody left to come."

SHE HADN'T UNDERSTOOD it then, but now it took on new meaning. No one had realized there were two ancestors at the beginning of the Lane family tree. Aoife was the forgotten child. Not anymore, she thought. Aloud, she said, "So Seamus O'Dulany is saying that Aisling and Aoife were opposites just like Creirwy and Morfran were."

She completely mangled the Irish names, but it didn't matter, and Jamie didn't correct her. He tapped his finger on the page again for emphasis as he read. "'They split apart, two parts of a whole, separated forever. Morrighan and Titus begat Aisling, and the purist line called—" He looked at Pippin and Grey— "Dubhshláine." He read the next line to himself, then looked at them again. "It's just like Ceridwen's third child, Taliesin. Aoife was wrapped in a leatherskin bag and pushed out to sea."

"By her mother?" Lil asked, horror etched on her face. "What a bitch," she muttered, but Jamie shook his head.

"Not by Morrighan," he said. "By Dagda."

"But Aoife didn't die," Pippin said. An eerie dread spread like ink through her insides. "She didn't die, and she had children, and those children are cursed, too."

Pippin remembered what Hugh had said...that he was a descendant of Titus. That Titus had left a woman in Rome pregnant, and Hugh was from that ancestral lineage. But his knowledge of the Pippin and Grey and the Lane curse didn't make sense if he didn't have a connection to Morrighan. "He lied," she said, more to herself than to the others, but they all waited for her to continue. "Hugh...or whatever his name is. He said we had a shared ancestor. Titus. But he knows too much. He's cursed, too. Which means—"

"Which means," Pippin said, "that we do share Titus as an ancestor, but we also share Morrighan. His line comes from Aoife."

CHAPTER 31

"I believe in mythology. I guess I share Joseph Campbell's notion that a culture or society without mythology would die, and we're close to that."

~Robert Redford

PIPPIN REVELED in the momentary glow of success. They'd discovered something their father hadn't. Thanks to Connell finding Seamus O'Dulany's book, they had a real chance at stopping the curse.

"But the book doesn't say how to break the curse with Dagda," Lil said, bringing Pippin right back down to reality.

"And we still don't know what happened to Connell. Was it Hugh, or are we still thinking it was Jed?" Jamie asked.

Or could it be Camille Gallagher? Pippin added silently. She felt the woman's eyes boring into her even when she wasn't present. She kept that thought to herself and turned to Jamie. "What about the letter?"

In the bit of ancient parchment they'd found hidden

away by Leo, Morgan had told Titus that she had waited for him. That their love transcended the obstacles they faced. "What if she really did love him. What if the biggest obstacle was that Morrighan was married to Dagda?" Pippin said, thinking aloud.

Jamie spun around and paced. "There has to be more," he said. "Dagda cursed the descendants of Morrighan and Titus. But Titus was lost at sea. Coincidence?"

Pippin inhaled sharply. "Aunt Rose said the other part of the scroll fragment said something about Lir, the pact, descendants, and an offering or sacrifice. We've been thinking it was Morrighan who made a pact with Lir, but what if it was Dagda? What if he wanted Titus dead?" Her mind spun. "What if Lir took down Titus's ship because Dagda wanted him to?"

"Dagda wasn't known as a vengeful god," Jamie said, then more slowly, "but it's possible."

Cyrus cleared his throat. "Go back to the last passage of the book," he said, his voice deep and resonant.

Jamie opened to the last page and read aloud:

"'I pray that the unpretended descendants of she who called herself Morgan Dubhshláine and Titus of Roma, within the dark side of Clann na Morrigna, return to Dagda what he so seeks and was taken from him. Only then will the curse that the truest god did place upon the children of the betrayers, and the unfortunate that came after, be broken.'"

Jamie gave a sudden and incredulous laugh. "Oh my God."

All eyes turned to him. Pippin was the one to ask, "What?"

"If Dagda made a pact with Lir to take down Titus's ship, then Titus must have stolen from him. To Morrighan, their love might have been real, but Titus betrayed her if he stole from her husband. I can imagine Dagda being in a fury about that."

The scenario reminded Pippin of Jed and Lacy. Lacy, like Morrighan, had been in love, but just as Titus used the goddess, Jed used Lacy. Everything came back to treasure. Jed's treasure was the necklace, while Titus had been after something powerful. The hair on the back of Pippin's neck raised. The books on Irish lore. Connell Foley had left a message about where he'd hidden Seamus O'Dulany's book, but the book he'd had on Irish history also told a tale. "Connell was trying to help us," she said. He left clues for us to find this book, and he left the book on the Irish gods so we could connect the dots."

Jamie exhaled. He looked like a man who'd just discovered the meaning of life—shaken and low-key thrilled at the same time. "It's all connected." He paced again, like he was trying to realign the pieces in his mind.

"Tell us, my boy," Cyrus said.

Jamie held his hand up. "Wait. I'll be right back." He set Seamus O'Dulany's book on the coffee table and left, returning not two minutes later with a different book in his hands. Pippin recognized it immediately. It was the book about the history of Tuatha dé Danann found near Connell Foley's body. He flipped through the pages until he found what he was looking for, his chest rising and falling heavily with his breaths. "Okay, listen. "Historically, there are four treasures of the Tuatha dé Danann. Magical treasures. At first it was thought that they were brought by Tuatha dé Danann either from the Celtic Underworld or out of heaven. Later, it was said they were brought from the greatest cities of Tuatha." He tapped his finger on the open page. "The Stone of Destiny; the Invincible Spear; the Shining Sword; and the Cauldron of the Dagda."

"What do they do?" Lil asked.

"*Lia Fail*—the Stone of Destiny—is said to cry out in a thunderous voice, or roar with the power of the ocean when the rightful monarch stands upon it. It was brought to England in the thirteenth century," he said. "It's said to be the Coronation Stone in Westminster Abbey. Then there's the *Sword of Lugh*. The Invincible Spear. It's the sword of Lugh of the Long Arm. Lugh was the first king of the Tuatha. He was called the Long Arm because of the spear. Think of it like Zeus's lightening rod. It would grow so hot that it had to be kept in a vat of water so it wouldn't burn the earth."

Jamie's eyes skimmed over the next two pages, then continued. "Next is the Sword of Nuada, or the Shining Sword. The light of the sword is said to represent sacred knowledge and wisdom. And lastly, there's the Cauldron of the Dagda, which is a bottomless vessel which never runs dry. It provides a never-ending supply of whatever is needed. It's thought to have the ability of rebirth and regeneration. It belonged to Dagda, who was considered by most to be the greatest among the Irish Gods."

"So the stone is in England. Supposedly. What about the rest—the spear, the sword, and the cauldron?" Pippin asked.

"Lost to history," Jamie said. He put down the book and picked up Dagda and the Curse of Morrighan. Once again, he turned to the last page and read: "'I pray that the unpretended descendants of she who called herself Morgan Dubhshláine and Titus of Roma, within the dark side of Clann na Morrigna, return to Dagda what he so seeks and was taken from him. Only then will the curse that the truest god did place upon the children of the betrayers, and the unfortunate that came after, be broken.'"

"Surely Dagda thought using and betraying Morrighan was a bigger betrayal than some object," Lil said. "So what, are we supposed to return his beloved wife to him?"

Pippin wasn't so sure Lil was right. "Morrighan's betrayal would have been huge," she said, "but would Dagda have considered a valuable object like the spear or the sword or the cauldron to be more important? So important that, in his anger, he cursed Morrighan's female descendants, so they'd all die in childbirth—"

Lil raised her brows and nodded. "That would certainly be a constant reminder to her of her betrayal," she said.

"—and then he made a pact with Lir to swallow Titus."

"Throwing in a curse on Morrighan's male descendants for good measure," Grey said dryly. "Lir gets to drown us all."

"Morrighan prophesied it, but couldn't stop it from happening," Jamie said.

Pippin felt the force of all the air leave her lungs, as if she had fallen flat on her back, the wind knocked clear out of her. The lore of Tuatha dé Danann was real, and they were a living breathing part of it. She pressed her hands to her temples, trying to wrap her mind around what they had to do. "So we have to figure out what Titus took, find it, and return it?"

Grey muttered under his breath, clearly as shaken as Pippin was. "And just how in the hell are we supposed to do that?"

CHAPTER 32

"Anyone can lie. One need only have the requisite intention - in other words, to say something with the intention to deceive. Faking, by contrast, is an achievement. To fake things you have to take people in, yourself included."

~ Roger Scruton

THE BANK WAS CLOSED by the time they'd worked through the meaning in Seamus O'Dulany's book. "The Burrow is the safest place for the book," Grey said. "Dad's safe is there."

Grey, Lil, and Pippin left together, the small ancient book deep in Pippin's purse. She walked between her brother and cousin, holding her bag tightly against her chest, her arms crossed over it as if she was Wonder Woman and could ward off any attack that came at her with her fisted hands.

They walked the few blocks in record time. Lil stayed in the great room, Grey stood sentry outside Pippin's door with Sailor, who had popped up the moment she'd seen Pippin enter the kitchen, and Pippin raced up to The Burrow and locked *Dagda and the Curse of Morrighan* safely away.

Hiding the book had alleviated some of her anxiety, but plenty remained to stir trouble in Pippin's mind. Grey left to make a delivery. "This table's been in the back of my truck all day. I'll drop it off, then come back," he said, making her promise to lock the doors and be vigilant. After all, Jed Riordin and Hugh, descendent of Aoife Dubhshláine, were still out there and willing to do who knew what in order to steal their treasures.

Downstairs in the great room, Pippin sat next to Lil and scratched Sailor's head. She had been thinking about Hugh again. "Why did he lie?"

The question was rhetorical, but Lil came up with an answer. "If he didn't have Seamus's book, then he doesn't know the whole story, right? So maybe he really thinks we're only related through Titus."

It was a good theory. She buried her face against the back of Sailor's head. "So, what now?" she whispered.

"Are you talking to me or the dog?" Lil asked.

"You," she said, but maybe also to Sailor. The dog *had* been instrumental in saving the day after Dr. Baxter's murder.

"Maybe Jed'll just show up again and try to kill us for the damn book," Lil said.

Pippin frowned at her. "Comforting thought."

They both froze at a knock on the inn's door. Sailor stayed by Pippin's side as she went to the foyer. Pippin shot a backwards glance at Lil and murmured a silent prayer that it wasn't Jed or Hugh standing on the other side. She peered through the peep hole to see Camille Gallagher. She flung the door open just as Camille raised her hand, knuckled poised to knock. There was just a split second between the moment the door opened and the moment Camille lurched backward, but it was enough time for Pippin to register the shock and determination etched on the woman's face. The events of the past few months had taken their toll on her. Her softness was gone, replaced by hard lines and hollows in her checks.

Pippin was just as shocked to see Camille as Camille seemed to be seeing Pippin—even though Camille was the one standing on the porch. This woman lurked around town constantly. Pippin felt the invisible strength of her stare everywhere she went. And now here she finally was. They locked eyes, neither one speaking.

Finally, Pippin broke the silence. "What do you want from me?" she demanded, and just like that, the hardness of Camille's stony face melted into something tragic and sorrowful. It collapsed and a painful mewl escaped her lips. She glanced around the porch, averting her eyes, letting her gaze settle on the rocking chairs, then on Pippin's boarded up office window. "A break-in?" she asked.

Pippin waved the question away. "Yeah. No. It's nothing. Just waiting for the window to be replaced."

Camille turned back, the window forgotten. "I...I guess I want to...to say *I'm sorry.* I am so, so sorry."

Pippin held tight onto the door, the statement nearly knocking her over. An apology was the last thing she had expected. "Sorry for what?" she asked.

The anguished twist of Camille's face gave her the answer even before the woman replied. "For Salty. For Jimmy." She flung her arms wide, as if they could encompass the entirety of everything that had happened twenty years ago all the way up to the present moment. "For all of it. I've been wanting...trying...to work up the nerve to say it to you. Every time I see you in town, *I think this is it. I'm going to do it.* But I just haven't been able to." Her face crumpled. She looked at Pippin through watery eyes. "I didn't know. You have to believe me."

Pippin felt a wave of guilt flow through her. That night, after the break in, she had briefly considered if it could have been Camille. And every time she saw Camille, anger and trepidation warred from within. But here she was, apologizing.

"I do believe you," Pippin said, surprising herself. She knew the kind of sorrow Camille was experiencing. The young mother had lost her husband—and her children's father—to prison. Pippin had lost both her parents. It wasn't the same kind of loss, but the source of grief didn't matter. Loss was loss was loss, and she could see the depth of it written on Camille's face.

"I made up my mind to talk to you weeks ago, but I haven't been able to," Camille said. Her gaze shifted to some distant spot over Pippin's shoulder. She spoke, her voice a little distant. "I kept trying to talk myself into it, and I was looking for a sign. Something to help me get there. And then a few days ago I was in Devil's Brew, then I went into the bookstore with my kids...and I heard two men talking about you. One of them was saying how you and your brother didn't deserve what was happening to you—"

Pippin froze. "What two men?"

Camille's wrung her trembling hands together. "Jed Riordin...and the one...that man who...who died."

A conversation between Jed and Connell, in the bookshop. "What day was this?"

Camille tried to still her hands, clasping them together until they turned blue. Her voice dropped to a hoarse whisper. "The day before the man was found...dead."

This was it. This was proof that Jed Riordin was present

when Connell Foley died. He'd been present at the scene of the crime, and Camille was a witness to that. Pippin was brought back to the current conversation.

"Hearing the one man say you didn't deserve what was happening, well, it made me think. We're the same, you and me. Neither of us deserve what's happened to us. I didn't want to be another problem in your life, and what Salty and Jimmy did...it was all about opportunity, you know? Jimmy watched you, and when you weren't home—Well, you know what happened. It didn't pan out for them."

It was sort of an apology, as much as Camille probably felt she could apologize for her husband and father-in-law. She was right. The opportunity *hadn't* panned out. It had ended up with both Salty and Jimmy awaiting trial for murder.

"That day at the bookshop, I didn't want Jed to see me, because he still talks to Salty, you know, and then my son spilled his milk, and a woman was trailing after her husband, crying and carrying on about her ruined vacation and it was grating on me, and then the woman who works at the bookshop came to help me. For a minute, I escaped to the bathroom and I thought I might actually lose my mind, but then, you know, sometimes when one door closes, another one opens. Jimmy and Salty, they're gone, but I'm still here." She paused, as if she was trying to figure out how to say what her thought process had been. "I thought Jed was one of the good ones, you know? He tried to help Jimmy. Or at least I thought he did. He told him that his dad was on the wrong side of things." Her lower lip quivered, and her voice cracked. "Things might have turned out different if Jimmy had listened."

"And if Connell hadn't trusted him."

"Right," Camille said. Her face clouded. "Trusting people is a mistake."

Absolving Camille of any responsibility for her husband and father-in-law's actions wasn't actually in Pippin's power to give, but Camille accepted it anyway. She exhaled, and while the color didn't return to her face and the dark rings under her eyes didn't dissipate, Camille was visibly lighter. "Thank you," she said, the two words more of a sigh than anything else. She turned to leave, one hand holding onto the stair railing as she walked down the first set of steps, but stopped and turned back to Pippin. "How's the man's wife doing? Is she still here?"

Pippin glanced over her shoulder toward Bernadette's room, as if she could see through the walls. "Mrs. Foley? Yes. Until her daughter makes arrangements for Mr. Foley. She goes in and out of understanding. She's having nightmares, but her daughter's here."

"Dementia?" she asked. Pippin answered yes, and Camille gave a sad nod. "I thought so."

Pippin watched Camille get into her car and drive off, her words echoing in her wake. Jed tried to help Jimmy. That single statement threw a wrench in the notion that Jed was the killer. Was he a good guy or a bad guy? Had he *really* tried to help Jimmy? Had he *really* tried to help Pippin, for that matter?

The fact was, people came in and out of the bookshop all day long, every day. She'd seen most of her inn guests there. Half the town shopped there. Jed's presence there before Connell's death didn't definitively prove anything. The fact that he was Lil's biological father certainly cast him in a bad light, but it wasn't proof of anything.

She wandered back inside, back to the sofa. Lil was gone, probably to her room. With Sailor curled up at her feet, Pippin thought about Connell hiding the book in the stacks. Was he hiding it from Jed?

She came back to the idea that Connell must have gone willingly into the rare book room. There would have been a scuffle, otherwise. Surely Connell would have put up a fight...unless he didn't suspect a problem. But then why would he have hidden the book?

It felt like an unsolvable paradox.

Camille said she had seen Jed leave, but what if he had come back while she'd been distracted with her son and his spilled milk, or while she'd been in the bathroom? Nobody had witnessed those crucial minutes when all hell had broken loose in the bookshop, which had given Connell Foley and someone else the opportunity to slip into the rare book room unnoticed. But if Jed wanted the book, and Connell had it, why would Jed kill Connell before getting what he wanted?

Plain and simple, he wouldn't.

So...Connell might have gone into the book room with Jed, but to what end? And Connell had no other connection to anyone in town.

One of the passages her bibliomancy had revealed from *Captain Blood* shot back into her mind. Unbidden, but with power as if it was the answer to the riddle.

> *Peter Blood judged her- as we are all prone to do- upon insufficient knowledge.*

She still didn't know what it meant, but her subconscious had brought it forward, so she started to work through it. First, she replaced her own name with Peter Blood.

Pippin judged her- as we are all prone to do- upon insufficient knowledge.

Who was the *her* that she had judged? The obvious answer was Camille, but that had resolved itself. Was there someone else? She ran through all the women in her world at the current moment. Hazel. Her inn guests; Nancy Kernoodle, Sue Jefferson, June Rycliff and Heather Beadly. Erin McAdams. Collette de Maurin from the Cheese Shop, but Pippin hadn't seen her lately. Daisy and Ruby. Hattie Juniper Pickle. She had formed some opinions about Nancy Kernoodle, but she thought they were pretty warranted. The other guests hadn't struck her one way or another. They were fun and pleasant. Hazel had shown up at the inn just when Pippin needed her—and she was a godsend. No judgement there.

Daisy, Ruby, and Hattie were her people. Of everyone in Devil's Cove, they were the ones she turned to.

Slowly, the low murmur of voices drifted into her consciousness. They came from the only other women in Pippin's immediate world—Bernadette and Ruthie.

Had Pippin passed judgement on them? It was true, they both seemed to have begrudged Connell his passion for books. Ruthie seemed to resent the time her father had spent away from her when Connell had been helping Leo. Bernadette's memories of the past, when her mind wasn't fully in the here and now, were more positive than her lucid moments, minus the times she had tried to hold his books hostage.

Pippin came back to Connell being either forced into the rare book room at The Open Door or going willingly. "He would have gone with his wife," she thought.

But no. Bernadette didn't arrive until later. She tried to dismiss the idea, but there was something making her cling to it. Whatever it was, it floated just out of reach.

Hazel ambled into the great room, light on her feet, humming a Michael Bublé song. She clutched her recipe binder against her chest. "Hey," Pippin said.

Hazel jumped, the song abruptly cut off. "Good golly gosh, you scared me!" she shrieked, adding the 'good' to her quirky exclamation. "I didn't know you were back."

"Yeah, for a little while now."

Hazel gathered her nerves and sat down. "Is everything okay?" she asked as she opened her binder, propping it on her lap. "You and Lil rushed out of here so fast, it made my head spin."

There wasn't a simple answer to Hazel's question. There were layers to it. On the one hand, the Roman coins that Artemis Lane had brought with him to America were safe. Seamus O'Dulany's book was hidden in The Burrow. So, sure, in that respect, everything was okay.

But she had no idea what to do about any of it, especially with the theories she and Grey and Lil and Jamie had floated. Things were very much *not* okay with all of that.

"Hmm," she answered noncommittally. It was the best she could do.

Hazel was blissfully unaware of the Lane family drama. She paged through the recipes she had collected over her years in the bed and breakfast business. "I wish it was still blueberry season," she said. "I have the best dang recipe for blueberry coffeecake. I mean, I could use frozen blueberries, but they're not the same as North Carolina homegrown, are they?"

"Hmm," Pippin said again, then asked the question that was burning her tongue. "Hazel, when Connell Foley checked in, he was alone, right?"

Hazel looked up. "That's right. Remember I told you he was on the phone with his wife. She wanted to stay for a vacation, but he wasn't having anything to do with that."

Pippin called up the exact words Hazel had used to describe the Connell Foley's check in. She had said Connell's wife was upset she couldn't stay because she liked the look of the inn. That implied she had seen the inn, didn't it? The day Hattie rode her trike, Rizzo, came back to her. It was Connell Foley she had seen leave the inn and drive away. Another car had pulled out right in front of Hattie, cutting her off. A car driven by a woman. A car that had made the same turn Connell had. "Did you get the feeling she was here, on island?" she asked, because she suddenly had a strong feeling that the woman in that car had been Bernadette Foley.

Hazel considered the question for a solid few seconds before answering. "Now that you say something, it *did* kind of sound that way. He told her to go on home, that he'd see her there. That sort of sounds like they might have been together, but he made it clear he was working. From his side of the conversation, it sounded like her vacation plans were ruined."

A ruined vacation. Camille had just said something about someone's ruined vacation. Pippin closed her eyes for a beat, trying to remember. Camille had been talking about the commotion in The Open Book the day Connell Foley died. Her son spilled his milk. Erin had left the front counter to go help her. "And a woman was arguing with her husband, crying and carrying on about her ruined vacation," she said aloud.

Hazel leaned forward, angling toward Pippin. "You sure you're okay?"

The new idea that Bernadette had been in Devil's Cove when her husband died was starting to take root. But could she be behind his death? *Would* she have killed him? And if she was involved somehow, it didn't explain why Connell had hidden Seamus O'Dulany's book.

"Pippin?"

She slid her fingers through Sailor's soft hair, absently scratching. With her other hand, she waved at Hazel and gave a quick nod of her head. "Sorry, yeah, I'm fine."

Hazel didn't look convinced, but she went back to her recipes. Pippin leaned back on the couch and let her mind sort through everything she knew about Bernadette, which, admittedly, wasn't much. But then something Bernadette had said when Ruthie showed up bubbled to the surface. Bernadette talked about how she had held Connell's books hostage when she was mad at him. How she had come close to ripping out the pages.

She closed her eyes and tried to imagine the scene. Bernadette, with her battered mind, showing up unexpectedly and calling her husband.

Connell telling her to go home, and that he'd see her there.

Connell going to the bookshop and hiding Seamus's book before meeting with Jed, a man he hadn't seen in years.

Connell taking *Captain Blood* and *Treasure Island* to

remind him. Ruthie had said he'd been forgetful lately, so it made sense.

The conversation with Jed at Devil's Brew, and then at the bookshop. Jed leaves, then Connell goes to retrieve Seamus's book.

Except, there's Bernadette. She's carrying on, according to Camille, about her ruined vacation, following him around. Connell wouldn't have taken the book out of hiding because Bernadette was mad and not in her right mind and she'd threatened to rip the pages from his old books before. This old book was a particularly sensitive subject for the entire family.

Erin was distracted with Camille and her son. Connell spots the door. Sees the keys on the desk. Goes into the rare book room with his wife so she'll calm down.

What happened inside the room was less clear. More arguing, perhaps. Maybe it really was a heart attack, or maybe Bernadette, in her anger, gathered up enough strength to shove Connell off his feet. The end result was the same. His head had caught the edge of a table on the way down.

Bernadette locked the door, wiped the keys, and ran. And then her already addled mind worked overtime to help her forget what had transpired between her and her husband.

Pippin sat up, spine straight. Shook off the sharp crackle of nerves alighting. The more she thought about it, the deeper the tendrils of the scenario grew. She let the idea settle until it slowly overtook the notion that Jed or Hugh were behind Connell's death.

She peered upstairs as if she could see through the walls and into the room where she could hear Bernadette and Ruthie speaking in low tones.

After another few seconds, she made up her mind. She felt Hazel's eyes on her as she stood, straightened her sweater, tucked her hair behind her ears, and headed upstairs.

She rapped lightly on the door. A moment later, Ruthie opened it. The second Pippin saw the dark rings under her bloodshot eyes, her sallow skin, and over Ruthie's shoulder, Bernadette in a heap on the bed, she knew she was right.

Ruthie could see it in Pippin's face, too. She closed her eyes for a long second before standing back and holding the door open wider so Pippin could enter.

The room was dark, and with the pall of death hanging on around it, the cozy charm of the inn was cloaked in shadows. "It was an accident," Ruthie said quietly. "She didn't mean to do it."

CHAPTER 33

"Pandora's Box could not be unopened, no one could return to Eden."
~Selena Kitt

LIEUTENANT JACOBS HAD SHOWN up to speak with Bernadette and Ruthie in mere minutes. It was as if he'd been circling the block—like Camille Gallagher seemed to do—waiting for just such a call. "She confessed?" Pippin asked him when he ambled back downstairs thirty minutes later.

"As much as a woman with only half her mind can," he said. "It's enough, at least for now. They got into an argument. She followed him into the room. His heart gave out. What happened next is still murky. She may have pushed him. He may have fallen. She can't remember. The ME report says Foley died of asphyxiation."

Asphyxiation. That made no sense to Pippin unless Bernadette had fallen on top of her husband in a fit of despair, not realizing he was still alive. She voiced the thought aloud, but Lieutenant Jacobs just shrugged. "Anything's possible. She said she went for help, then she started talking about her nightmares and being underwater and going into the light. Then—" he snapped his fingers— "she's back to saying he just fell and nobody could save him. She's all over the place. The bottom line, Ms. Hawthorne, is that all of it is unprovable, and she won't be of any help. Her confession isn't enough, and it isn't reliable. Testimony from those with dementia—" He shook his head. "What she thinks happened may be entirely different from what actually happened."

From all that, Pippin just kept coming back to the idea that Connell Foley might have lived if only Bernadette had gone for help, but what Lieutenant Jacobs said stuck with her. What Bernadette thought happened might be entirely different from the truth.

PIPPIN WAS familiar with the feeling of being watched. The treasure hunters had done their fair share of watching. Then there was Camille Gallagher, Jed Riordin, and Hugh—descendant of Morrighan and Titus through their daughter Aoife. She had been watched by friend and foe alike.

But this time, she was the one doing the watching. At her request, Jamie had planned a Synkéntrosi meeting at The Brewery.

"Do you announce a topic ahead of time?" she had asked.

"We plan the calendar every January with the six topics for the year. Sometimes we change, though, or hold special meetings."

"And does Jed Riordin usually attend?"

"He does," Jamie said.

At The Brewery, Gin White, a native islander who claimed to be a descendant of Eleanor Dare, drew pints of beer behind the bar. The owners, Chuck and January Wagner, played their own parts. Chuck sidled from table to table, greeting people with hearty slaps on the back or shoulder squeezes. No matter the temperature, he wore a Brewery t-shirt, cargo shorts, and flip-flops. Pippin often wondered if he owned a single pair of long pants. His blond hair, darker now since his sun highlights had faded with the fall weather, fell in loose waves.

While Chuck was the welcome wagon for the business; January was the brains. She handled all the behind-the-scenes stuff. Behind the softness of her North Carolina accent, she was hard as nails. Pippin waved to her from the back table she, Lil, and Grey had taken. It gave them a clear view of the Brewery's interior. January brought over a pitcher of a pale ale they had on draft and three frosty mugs. "Let me know if I can get you anything else," she said, and then she was off to pick up and deposit another order at the bar.

By seven o'clock, nine men had gathered, including Jamie and Cyrus. They sat at a group of tables Chuck had helped Jamie pull together. Jed wasn't among them.

"Maybe he's not coming," Lil said.

Pippin deflated at that. Jamie said Jed always came to the Synkéntrosi meetings, but that had been when several of the members were trying to find what Leo had hidden. But things had changed. The Venatore group wasn't quite out in the open, but it wasn't hidden, either. People were in prison for their part in Leo's death. And others were dead.

Jamie and the other men sat around their tables, sipping beer and talking. Quincy Ratherford, the lead reporter for the Devil's Cove Gazette, barreled through the door wearing a coral button-down shirt, his signature plaid pants, and a brown corduroy beret. "Ahoy there!" he called, standing with his back to the door, holding it open. "Sorry to be late, but the news waits for no one."

Pippin read between the lines, taking his words to mean that he'd written about Bernadette and Connell Foley. She wondered how he'd spun the story because whatever confession Bernadette had made, it had been only to Ruthie and Lieutenant Jacobs.

So that was that. Connell Foley was dead, Bernadette Foley had withdrawn into her mind, and Ruthie had lost two parents.

And Jed was a no-show. "Maybe he got wise and blew town," Grey said.

"Maybe not," Pippin said as Jed suddenly strode in.

Pippin and Grey watched as both Quincy and Jed headed toward the Synkéntrosi group. Jed scanned the room. He stopped the second he laid eyes on the three of them. He showed no particular reaction to Lil but gave a small nod of acknowledgement to Pippin. It felt like they were in a game of chicken. Who would move first? If Jed joined the Synkéntrosi group, then they'd wait until the meeting was over to confront him, keeping their eyes on him the entire time. If he fled, they'd go after him.

Lil grabbed Pippin's hand and squeezed. Lil wanted Jed to acknowledge her as he had Pippin, but he showed no recognition. He hesitated, as if deciding what to do. Quincy had already made his way to the Synkéntrosi group. He sat and jumped into the discussion as if he'd been there the entire time. Jamie was the only one who wasn't engaged. His attention was glued to Jed.

"Ten bucks says he bolts," Grey said under his breath.

"That would be too obvious," Pippin said. "It would make him look guilty."

"Guilty of what? He didn't do anything," Lil murmured, and she was right. Pippin was in conflict about Jed. On the one hand, her father seemed to have trusted him. But on the other, he'd shown up at Cape Misery more than thirty years ago, and according to Lacy, he'd been searching for something.

Whatever Pippin had expected Jed to do, it wasn't what he actually *did*. He didn't turn and retreat. He also didn't join his friends, though a few beckoned him.

No, he turned and strode toward the three of them, pulled out the fourth chair at the table, and sat. "Should I be worried?" he asked, directing the question to Pippin.

"I think we should be asking you that question. You met with Connell Foley just before he died."

"I told you, we both worked with your father—"

"You left out the part about you meeting him the day he died. Did he tell you what he discovered?"

Slowly, Jed shook his head. "He did not." He bristled under the weight of their collective stare. "We met and I left him at the bookshop. I didn't kill him if that's what you're thinking."

They knew that, of course, but they still didn't know if he was friend or foe. "Camille Gallagher told me you tried to help Jimmy," Pippin said.

Jed exhaled a shaky breath. "Of course I did. I tried to help them both. To talk sense into them. But Salty's crazy. He has a strong hold on them."

"How long have you known about the coins?" Lil blurted.

His eyes narrowed as he stared at her. "What?"

"The coins," Lil repeated. Her voice turned brittle.

Harsh. "You went to Cape Misery and seduced my mother. You *used* her so you could find them, and then you just vanished. She fell in love with you, and you just left her like she was nothing. She *died* because of you."

Jed jerked back as if she had dealt him a physical blow. He turned pallid. One second he'd been flesh-colored with pink in his cheeks. The next, as quickly as water being sucked down the drain of a sink, he was ashen. "You're...are you...Cora? Or Lily?" he managed.

Pippin's eyes pricked from hearing the anguish of her cousin's emotions. The whites of Lil's eyes turned red along with the tip of her nose. Her voice cracked. "You know about us?"

"Only after I met Leo," he admitted. "Once we became... friends...once he trusted me, he told me about Cassie and Lacy. Not everything, but enough."

The pricking behind Pippin's eyes spread to her head. She felt like a pressure cooker ready to explode. "You've lied to us from the beginning. To him—"

"No!" Jed said. "I did not lie to Leo. He knew who I was and what I'd done."

Pippin leaned forward. "What do you mean? What did you do?"

Jed sat back, as if the air shifting between them forced him backward. "There's a group of people...they're hunters. Treasure hunters—"

"Venatores," Lil said. "Yeah, we know."

Jed's brows shot up. "How...?"

"My mother kept a journal, *Dad*," Lil said, forcing invisible daggers into the word Dad. "She wrote all about you. She drew the Venatore symbol."

Jed's right hand went to his opposite forearm and Pippin knew he had the same tattoo she had seen on Salty and

Jimmy. He seemed to deflate, his voice and his body losing air and volume. "I was a different person back then. My father was obsessed with the Venatore group. I joined when I was sixteen, but..." He ran his hand down his face again before continuing

"But..." Lil prompted.

"But I thought it was like a Dungeons and Dragons kind of thing. Role playing. Pretend. I went to Laurel Point—to Cape Misery—and I...When I left there, I felt like shit. Lacy was a nice girl and I really liked her. And her aunt...they were both...good people. Genuinely good people. And I came and messed with their lives. When I found out Lacy died—"

Lil sat up straight, her spine practically cracking with tension. "But you *knew*. Leo told you. You *knew* she gave birth to me and Cora. You *knew* she died."

Pippin could hear all the unspoken words. He'd known about her and Cora, yet he'd never come for them. He'd never showed up to be their father.

"I know you might not believe this, Lily, but I started working with Leo *for* you and Cora. So you wouldn't suffer the fate your mother did. He knew about me. About you. About...us. I did everything I could to help him with his research. To help him figure out how to stop it. When he disappeared, I couldn't believe it. I thought, no way would he abandon his kids." Lil blew a raspberry at that. "I know," he said. "Ironic, because it's what I did. But he was different. He really loved Cassie. He had a relationship with his kids. I spent all those years trying to make up for what I'd done. How could I show up on your doorstep without a solution to the problem I'd created for you? Because of me, Lacy died. Yes, yes, it was the curse, but I got her pregnant, didn't I?"

Pippin didn't know if Lil would ever believe Jed...or

forgive him. He hadn't asked for her forgiveness, but from the slump of his shoulders and his glassy eyes, it was clear he'd unburdened himself of thirty-two years of guilt.

It might have been naive, but Pippin believed Jed Riordin's story. She wasn't about to bring him into *her* inner circle, but knowing he hadn't killed Connell Foley was enough to give him the benefit of the doubt. For now, anyway.

She had to think about next steps. Knowing she and Grey—and Lil and Cora—had to find something of Dagda's had given her new hope that they *would* be able to finish what Leo had started. That they *would* be able to break the curse. But knowing was only the beginning. The bigger question they now faced was how they were supposed to go about finding whatever lost treasure Titus might have stolen two thousand years ago. They had to go back to Leo's study. Back to the compendium Connell had when he died. Back to the story of Morrighan and Titus, and Aisling and Aoife. Back to Seamus O'Dulany and his book.

And they had to find Hugh, because whether he was friend or foe, he was part of the story.

But all that could wait until tomorrow. Today held different plans.

The doorbell rang and the promise of the future rose inside Pippin alongside a kaleidoscope of butterflies flapping in the pit of her stomach. The feeling of hope was welcome, and night and day from the fear that had resided inside her for so long. She took a quick moment to stop in front of the mirror that hung behind the door of her office. Her green eyes shown like emeralds, enhanced by the soft strawberry-hued curls framing her face. A few faint freckles danced across her nose and her cheeks wore smudges of pink.

Hazel poked her head into the office. "He's here!"

Pippin felt a new flurry of nerves alight inside her. Felt the heat spread from her neck to her cheeks. She gave Hazel a wobbly smile. "Why am I so nervous? It's just Jamie."

They both darted glances toward the front door when doorbell rang again. "It's your first official date, though, right?" Hazel smiled. "It's been a slow rollout."

"What if it's a mistake?" Pippin murmured, a single thread of trepidation materializing. When she pushed her emotions aside and stopped to think, she knew that nothing had changed. Not getting involved with anyone had been one of her diehard rules. She was still cursed, after all. So how was a date with Jamie McAdams a good idea?

"Love is never a mistake," Hazel said as if she'd read every one of Pippin's thoughts. "Look at me and Doc Wilkenson. The second I laid eyes on him, I knew."

That was a love connection Pippin still didn't quite understand. The doctor was as curmudgeonly as curmudgeonly could get, but when he was with Hazel, the brittle edges of his personality softened a little bit. And their budding romance meant Hazel was hanging up her traveling innkeeper boots and sticking with Sea Captain's Inn and Devil's Cove. Pippin couldn't deny how happy that made her.

"And look at your friends Daisy and Kyron," Hazel continued. "Love just happens, Pippin. You can't fight it."

That was true enough. She knew the story of Pandora, who was created by Zeus as a punishment for humans. From the gods, Pandora received the gifts of beauty and wisdom, peace and kindness, health and generosity. But Zeus tempted her with the gift of a jar and a warning to never open it. How could she resist the temptation? She opened it, and out flew life's miseries—greed and envy, hatred and pain, hunger, diseases, and poverty, as well as war and death. Only hope remained.

By steering clear of relationships, Pippin had viewed her heart as Pandora's Box...or jar, as the case may be. Closed and safe. Jamie had broken the seal and now her feelings for him were out in the world. They couldn't be hidden away again.

But hope...hope remained in Pandora's Box, just as it remained with Pippin. They would figure it all out. Jamie was instrumental to that. Without him, Pippin and Grey wouldn't know half of what they now knew about the Lane family, the curse of Morrighan, or Dagda and his lost treasure. He'd come into her life for a reason. But her feelings for him now went beyond how he'd been able to help them.

Outside her boarded-up window, the crow, Morgan, perched on the casing. She spread her wings, the single white feather catching Pippin's eye. She'd stopped trying to shoo the bird away. She didn't know if the crow was a harbinger of doom or a good omen, but she was here to stay. "Wish me luck," Pippin said.

The crow cawed in response.

The bell rang again. Pippin exhaled all of her anxiety and squeezed Hazel's hand. Hazel winked. "I won't wait up," she said, locking up after Pippin left. Minutes later, she and Jamie were in his silver Audi. She glanced in the passenger side mirror as he drove up Rum Runner's Lane, past Hattie's house and her old orange pickup truck parked along the edge of the street. Past the next two brightly painted beach houses.

Behind them, she saw Hattie appear. She threw her leg over Rizzo's center bar, positioning herself on her trike. She pedaled off, tossing her hand up as if she were waving at someone. Pippin traced an invisible line from Hattie to the inn's driveway but didn't see anything. Jamie flipped his turn signal on, ready to turn at the corner. The same corner Connell had turned on the day he'd died. The same day Bernadette had followed him in another car. Followed him to the bookshop.

Pippin's phone pinged. A text from Hattie flashed on the screen. Should I get my key and let Camille in?

Pippin's brows pulled together. What? she typed.

Camille's on the porch. Should I let her in for you?

If Camille was at the inn now, she had to have seen Pippin leave with Jamie not two minutes ago. So why was she—

Her thoughts flew around her head, careening into each other. Something Jed said resurfaced in her mind. She had commented about Camille saying Jed had tried to help Jimmy. When Jed replied, he'd said he tried to help them both. Pippin thought he'd meant Jimmy and Salty, but what if he'd meant Jimmy and Camille? Jed had said Salty had a stronghold on *them*. Not *him*. Not just Jimmy. But *them*.

"The angel of death," she muttered. NO! she typed, at the same type she grabbed Jamie's arm and said, "Stop!"

He glanced at her. "What?" he asked, but the expression on her face made him pull over. He turned in his seat now, watching her.

"Bernadette's having nightmares. She sees the angel of death taking her husband." A slew of thoughts marched through her mind. Connell had a heart attack but died of asphyxiation. Suffocation. The only reasonable scenario involving Bernadette was that she had fallen on him, trying to help, and smothered him. But she said she had gone for help.

All this time, Pippin had been thinking that Jed was present when Connell had died. *But so was Camille.* The spilled milk. Opportunities. Camille had stood on the porch of Sea Captain's Inn and told Pippin how Jimmy had watched her. Waited for opportunities. Those crucial few minutes… An image slammed into Pippin's mind. The angel of death. "Ohmygod ohmygod ohmygod."

Jamie grabbed her hand. "Pip, what's going on?"

"She went to the bathroom."

"Who went to the bathroom?" Jamie asked.

The pieces of the puzzle careened against each other in Pippin's mind, making it hard to get the words out. "Camille! Camille! Camille! She was in the bookshop. She was there. She told me she went to the bathroom."

Bernadette kept talking about her nightmare. After Ruthie had arrived, Bernadette had said, "She's coming, you know. She'll help Connell. She'll take me into the light." She'd said she had gone for help. Had she run into Camille? But instead of helping Connell, had Camille actually seized the opportunity, trying to finish what Salty and Jimmy had set out to do? Only, when Connell didn't have any treasure, she smothered him. The angel of death.

If Camille was working with Salty and Jimmy…if she was a hunter…then she was at the house to look for the treasure, or…

…Or she was there to tie up a loose end. Bernadette.

"Turn around," Pippin said, flapping her hands in the air, then said more emphatically, "Jamie, turn around!"

Jamie threw the car into gear, flipped a u-turn, and sped back to the inn. The fading sun made Hattie a blurry image ahead in the distance, already halfway to Main Street, but she was making a wide turn, directing her bike back toward home.

Jamie stopped abruptly in front of the inn. Camille was nowhere in sight. Pippin was out of the car before Jamie even cut the engine. She flew up the walkway. Up the steps. Her hand shook as she pressed the numbers on the keypad. It gave an obnoxious buzz and flashed a red X when she entered it incorrectly. She tried again, this time getting it right, nearly falling as she stumbled through the open door. Jamie was on her heels. "Bernadette!" Pippin hollered as she raced for the stairs.

Hazel appeared from the reading nook at the far side of the great room. "Pippin? What's going on?"

"Did you let Camille in? Is she here?"

Hazel's brows shot up. "No. Nobody's been here."

Pippin hardly broke stride, racing up the stairs, rounding the corner at the top and skidding to a stop at Bernadette's door. She pounded her fist on the door. "Mrs. Foley! Bernadette!"

She pounded and pounded and pounded. Jamie and Hazel stood back behind her. The Kernoodles appeared at their door. "What's going on?" Peter Kernoodle demanded.

Before Pippin could reply, Bernadette's door opened and the disheveled widow stood there looking groggy, but alive. Pippin heaved a relieved sigh. Maybe Hattie had been mistaken about seeing Camille. Maybe Pippin's thinking had gone off the rails, and Bernadette's confession was the only true explanation for Connell's death. Pippin nearly left it alone, but her stomach roiled and she suddenly couldn't. "Mrs. Foley, who is the angel of death? From your nightmare, who is she?"

Bernadette's lips pulled into a deep frown and her eyes glazed. "The angel of death. She...she took Connell."

"But who is she? Do you know her?" Pippin suddenly remembered Bernadette staring out the window at Devil's

Brew after Camille had left with her sons. "Have you seen her? In town…have you seen her?"

But Bernadette stood frozen. If she knew anything more, she wasn't saying.

She and Peter Kernoodle both retreated back into their respective rooms. Pippin, Jamie, and Hazel stared at each other before finally turning and going back downstairs. "You think it's Camille?" Hazel asked with a hiss, putting the pieces together.

"She was there when Connell died," Pippin said, "but I don't know. Maybe not."

They stood in silence for a moment before Hazel shooed them away. "Go on, you two. I'll keep an eye on her. Go have your da—"

She broke off at a sharp bark coming from the back of the house. Sailor. They shot each other a look and then the three of them took off at the same time. Sailor barked again, then appeared before them. Pippin fell to her knees, wrapping her arms around her neck and giving a squeeze. "It's alright, girl," she said with a shaky voice as she looked over Sailor and toward the door to her room. "Is someone in there?" she asked the dog, knowing, of course, that Sailor could only feel the vibration of her voice, but not hear the words.

"Sailor was in there?" Jamie asked quietly, notching his head toward the closed door.

Pippin nodded. Hazel backed away, one arm folded over her chest, the opposite hand pressed against her mouth. "Is someone here? In your room?"

Hazel didn't know about the secret access to The Burrow, but Camille would. Jimmy and Salty had been there. Icy fingers crept up Pippin's back. The break-in the other night. It very easily could have been Camille. Hadn't she given a pointed look at the boarded-up window and commented on it? There are lots of reasons for a broken window. How had she known it was from a break-in?

Pippin let Sailor go and walked with Jamie, side by side, to the door of her bedroom. She always locked it when she left, but the handle turned, and she slowly pushed the door open. Instantly, she saw the broken glass from one of the squares on the French doors, which had allowed it to be unlocked from the inside. The door stood wide open now.

Pippin's eyes shot to the bookshelf containing the secret entrance to The Burrow, and felt short-lived relief that it was still closed. So, either Camille hadn't managed to figure it out, she was up there now, or she had spooked when Pippin and Jamie had burst into the house, hollering, and left before they could catch her.

Pippin's bet was on the latter, but she strode to the bookshelf and pulled open the hidden door. Hazel gasped. She stood at the threshold, wide-eyed and spoke in a hushed voice. "I heard some rumors in town, but I didn't believe it. A secret room."

Jamie poked his head into the secret stairwell, cocking his ear upward to listen. "I don't think anyone's up there," he whispered, but he quietly mounted the steps to check. A second later, he jogged back down, shaking his head.

In unison, their heads all swiveled to the open French door. Pippin stepped onto the screened porch, instantly spotting the gaping hole in the screening. As she pointed at it, a harrowing screech came from the street followed by Hattie bellowing something unintelligible at the top of her lungs. Jamie backtracked into the room and barreled past Hazel, Pippin on his heels. In seconds, they flew through the great room, out the front door, and down the porch steps. They pulled up short at the scene before them. Camille was trapped against Hattie's old pickup, pinned by Rizzo. Hattie held onto the trike from the street side, her rainbow legs spread wide and pressing into the road, her upper body nearly vertical to the ground as she held Rizzo in place. The trike acted like a cage, the big tires like an open jaw threatening to chomp.

Camille jabbed her head forward and growled, feral and crazed. "Let me go, you crazy—"

Hattie bared her cigarette yellowed teeth. "You best watch what ya say, darlin'. I have me a very long memory. Now, if I'm not mistaken, you're responsible for that poor man's death." She swung her head to look at Pippin. "Did I get that right?"

Pippin looked in awe at Hattie Juniper Pickle. The woman was a force to be reckoned with. "I believe you're correct, Hattie." She turned to face Camille. "That was a very sweet act you put on the other day, with your apology and all. You missed your calling to the stage. Trying to point the finger at Jed? Good touch." Camille spat, but Pippin continued. The more she said aloud, the more sense it made. "He may not be a completely good guy, but he's not a murderer, is he? I think *you're* a treasure hunter right alongside Jimmy and Salty. Still watching me for them. Trying to seize your opportunity to search my house."

"Let me go," Camille growled.

"No can do, sweetheart," Hattie said, her mangled cigarette hanging loosely from her lipstick-stained mouth.

Camille glared at Pippin. "You don't even know what you're doing—"

"I know plenty, Camille. I know, for example, that you're part of the Venatores, just like Jimmy and Salty—

Camille blew a harsh raspberry. "Jimmy and Salty and me are the least of your worries."

Pippin ignored her. "I know that you broke into my house—twice."

Camille scowled.

"And Connell Foley," Pippin said. "He had a heart attack and Bernadette freaked out, didn't she?"

Camille shrugged. "Right place, right time. Salty drilled it into me and Jimmy. Look for opportunities."

"But why kill him?" Pippin asked, genuinely stumped by the question. "He didn't have to die."

Camille thrashed, trying to break free from her tricycle cage. Hattie held tight. "He wouldn't tell me where the book was—"

"He was having a heart attack!"

"If he would have just told me, then Jimmy could go free—"

Pippin stared. Sputtered. "Wait, what? How is that possible?"

Camille's face contorted. "Salty already warned you, Pippin. Be careful who you trust because we're everywhere."

Pippin's blood turned to ice. "Are you saying someone in the legal system could get the charges against Jimmy dropped if—"

"If that stupid man would have told me. I said I'd help him if he would just give me the book, but he wouldn't. He kept saying something about the treasure on the island, and I kept saying, 'I *know* it's here on Devil's Cove, but *where*?'" She was crying now, big ugly mascara-tinted tears staining her cheeks. "He wasn't making any sense and I just...I just... finally I just made him stop."

Pippin's heart ached for Connell Foley. He hadn't been saying there was treasure on the island. He'd been telling her where to look. Next to *Treasure Island* on the bookshelf.

"He did tell you, though. You just didn't know what he meant," she said sadly.

"How did you know he found a *book*?" Jamie asked.

But Camille didn't answer. Her attention had been pulled to something in the distance, as if the crown of her head had been caught by a fishing line and whoever held it was trying to reel her in. Pippin followed the line of her gaze and drew in a sharp breath. A hundred yards down Rum Runner's Lane stood Hugh. His figure was blurred and dark in the waning light, but there was no mistaking him. Even from where she stood, Pippin thought she could see the brightness of his eyes.

"Aodh," Camille murmured.

Pippin's attention snapped to her. "What did you call him?"

"Aodh." Camille repeated. It sounded like a cross between 'ay' and 'uh'. No consonant. It sounded like nothing more than a grunt.

"Aodh," Pippin said under her breath, emphasizing the 'uh' sound. And then she heard it. Made the connection. Aodh had to be an old Gaelic form of Hugh. That single syllable with just the vowel sound was somehow more fitting for the otherworldly man than the anglicized version, Hugh.

In a sudden burst of energy, Camille grabbed ahold of the trike and shook it with all her might. Hattie lost her grip and careened backward, falling onto the street, her cigarette flying. Pippin and Jamie both leaped in to hold Rizzo in place.

Pippin heard Lil holler. Looked over her shoulder to see Lil taking the porch steps two at a time, racing down the walkway to them, her gauzy skirt whipping behind her. "What's happening?!" she yelled.

"Help Hattie," Pippin called to her.

Hattie was sprawled on the ground, legs wide, but sitting upright. She spotted her unlit cigarette on the street. Reached for it. "I'm peachy, darlin'," she said, waving Lil away, then she reached into the front of her shirt and pulled her cell phone out. A few seconds later, she was speaking directly to Lieutenant Jacobs. After she hung up, she gave a satisfied grin to Camille. "The jig's up. The law is on its way."

"Oooo! Oooo!" The high-pitched howl came from the porch of the inn. The five of them—Pippin, Jamie, Hazel, Hattie, and Camille—spun their heads toward the wailing. Bernadette Foley stood there staring at them, palms pressed against the sides of her face, her mouth wide and contorted. She looked like Edvard Munch's Scream painting, come to life. Hazel reacted, leaving the group behind, and scurrying up to meet Bernadette, who was halfway down the stairs. She dropped one hand from her face, now extending it in front of her, pointing in their direction. "Youuuuu," she yowled. "Take me! Take me to my Connell."

Camille—Bernadette's angel of death, just glared.

"I BET she has the Venatore tattoo as a tramp stamp," Lil said, watching Lieutenant Jacobs maneuver Camille Gallagher into the back of his county issued SUV.

Hugh—or Aodh—was long gone, vanished in the same ethereal way he'd materialized. Another one of his minions had been stopped in their tracks. He'd pretended, in an obscure way, to be Pippin's ally—born from the same bloodline—but she knew now that he was playing a game. They might share an ancestor, but they were on opposite sides of this battle. Hugh wanted the treasure Titus had stolen from Dagda, and he was willing to kill or sacrifice others to get it.

Pippin and Grey only wanted to break the curse.

Lieutenant Jacobs flipped a u-turn and drove slowly down Rum Runner's Lane toward Main Street, Camille restrained in the backseat. A layer of fog had rolled in, foreboding and sinister, and overhead, a murder of crows gathered. Glided. Circled.

As the lieutenant's taillights were swallowed by the fog, Jamie held Pippin's hand. Squeezed it tight. His bolstering energy flowed into her. She looked at him, then back toward the place Hugh had just stood, and she felt, deep down—suddenly knew with every cell of her body—that the battle was just beginning.

The End

Dear Reader,

I hope you enjoyed this installment of The Book Magic Mysteries. Reviews help other readers discover great books. They really do matter! If you are inclined to leave a review, I'd appreciate it. You can do so HERE.

Pre-Order the next Book Magic Mystery, Murder and an Irish Legend!

Turn the page for a recipe from Sea Captain's Inn!

. . .

READ The Secret on Rum Runner's Lane, a Book Magic Mini Mystery Prequel (Cassie's Story). Keep turning to read an excerpt.

FINALLY, join my newsletter for updates, character profiles, recipes, and more!

BLUEBERRY STRATA, A RECIPE FROM SEA CAPTAIN'S INN

This is the easiest breakfast dish around. You prep it the night before, let it chill overnight, then pop it in the oven in the morning. Voilà!

Ingredients:

- 1 loaf of French bread (stale is okay!), broken into small rough pieces
- 12 ounces cream chest, softened (lite or Neufchatel is fine), cut into small chunks
- 1 1/2 - 2 cups fresh or frozen blueberries
- 8 eggs
- 1/4 cup maple syrup
- 1 cup milk
- 1 cup half & half
- 1 tsp cinnamon
- 1/2 tsp nutmeg

1. *Coat a 9x13 inch pan with butter or cooking spray, or use a piece of parchment paper.*

2. *Spread the chunks of bread in the pan.*
3. *Layer the small chunks of cream cheese and the blueberries on top of the bread.*
4. *In a bowl, mix together the eggs, syrup, milk and half & half, as well as the cinnamon and nutmeg.*
5. *Pour the egg/milk mixture over the bread. Press the bread down to make sure it is all saturated.*
6. *Cover and refrigerate overnight.*
7. *In the morning, bring the pan to room temperature. Meanwhile preheat the oven to 350°.*
8. *Bake for 30 minutes, covered with foil.*
9. *Remove the foil and bake for an additional 30 minutes.*
10. *Allow to rest for a few minutes before serving with a side of warm maple syrup.*

Note: You can make this in individual ramekins instead of as a large single dish.

Enjoy this tasty breakfast dish!

READ CHAPTER ONE OF MURDER AND AN IRISH CURSE

Pippin Lane Hawthorne read books, but not always in the same manner that others did.

Most people started at the beginning and read through to the end. They read the stories of fictional people leading their fictional lives. Pippin did that, too. Most people absorbed the setting and the characters and the plot. Those things didn't matter to Pippin. Her relationship with books went much deeper. They communicated with her on an entirely different level. The words, the lines, the passages all conveyed meaning separate from the story itself. It was as if she were taking in the soul of the book. The pages communicated something far more abstract. Less tangible in terms of comprehension. What the words actually said, and what they told her were two entirely different things.

Pippin's twin brother (older by just 73 seconds) had planted the seed in her mind that how she interpreted the words a book showed her was based on her own schema. Her own experiences—and lack thereof. Her understanding was one hundred percent subjective. She construed the meaning behind the words. She could never know with complete certainty that any of the insight she gleaned was correct.

Such was the life of a novice bibliomancer.

There were so many things about her divination she didn't know. In any given situation, would *any* book communicate something, or did it have to be a specific book? When it had come to solving her father's murder, a resurfaced memory had led her to *The Odyssey*. When she'd needed to gain a deeper understanding of the two-thousand-year-old curse that had been lain at the feet of the Lane family, she'd turned to *The Secret Garden*, which had been her mother's favorite book. In other instances, the books that had helped her felt purely coincidental. *Treasure Island. The Tale of Two Cities. Captain Blood.* She had no familial connection to any of these titles—that she knew of, anyway—but they had given her direction, nonetheless.

She knew what she and Grey and Lily had to do. They needed to find the item Titus stole from Dagda and return it to him. It sounded so simple, but now she'd come to believe it was actually impossible. And that impossibility wore at Pippin's resolve, causing it to ebb and flow. After all, how does one find an unknown item that has been lost to history and return it to a deity that, until recently, she thought was purely mythical? Often, the challenges they faced seemed insurmountable. At other times she was bound and determined to finish what her father had started, no matter the difficulties. She built up her hope because of the research Leo done and the discoveries he'd made.

The cousins wanted nothing more than to break the curse once and for all. But they had already tried. Leo had tried. Cassie had tried. Presumably most, if not all, the members of the Lane family had tried to break the curse at one time or another, to no avail. These failures were another thing that ate away at her resolve and determination. Right now, this moment was one of resignation. She'd done everything she could think of to break the curse on her family. The men were swallowed by the sea. The women died in childbirth. Nothing she had done had stopped anything. Of course, she wasn't sure how she'd actually know unless they tested the curse, putting themselves in danger. Sending Grey out to sea, or one of them getting pregnant, but still... None of them were *willing* to sacrifice themselves or the others to see if the curse was broken or still going strong.

They had no reason to believe anything had changed. Which left Pippin feeling dejected and lost. She didn't know what else to do.

The inn was running smoothly. She'd taken only a few guests leading up to the holidays and at the moment, the last three were tucked into their rooms for the night. Hazel Hood, a traveling innkeeper who had been like her personal Mary Poppins—appearing just when Pippin needed her most—had jumped headlong into a whirlwind relationship with the curmudgeonly Doctor James Wilkenson. She hadn't originally intended to stay on Devil's Cove indefinitely, but the good doctor had changed her plans. Hazel had moved from the little room just off the kitchen at the inn to a small apartment above the Doc's practice. She worked five days a week at the inn, had helped Pippin get procedures in place, and now, more than six months later, the inn ran like a well-oiled machine. At this point, Pippin didn't think she could manage without Hazel.

Breakfast for the next morning was prepped, everything was locked up tight, and Pippin and Sailor, her honey-colored Vizsla, had walked on the beach—well, Pippin had walked while Sailor had chased the gulls. Now, with Sailor by her side, Pippin retreated to her bedroom. It had been Leo's study when she was little. She had taken it over to free up more rooms for guests.

She walked straight to the built-in bookshelf and found the hidden lever that only a select few knew about. She pressed it and a section opened with a quiet click. "Let's go," she said. Sailor couldn't hear her, but Pippin spoke anyway, patting the side of her leg as a visual cue. Sailor's tail whipped back and forth. She followed Pippin into the secret passageway, waiting by her side while Pippin closed the door, trotting up the stairs after her.

The stairs led to a small room...her father's secret hideaway. This was where he'd kept his research and the books most meaningful to him. Clues about the curse and how to break it. If she had any hope of success, she felt sure it was through something her father had left behind.

Sailor went straight to her bed, turned around until she positioned herself just so, and settled into sleep. Pippin was far from ready for bed. She started for the bookshelves that lined part of the back wall but stopped short when she spotted a book on the floor. She looked around, as if someone had put it there and was now hiding, but of course that was impossible. The small study had a desk, two chairs, the built-in shelves, and a little occasional table. There was no place to hide.

The book, though, hadn't been there the last time she was up here. On the cover was the profile of a rabbit, the sky in the distance like a painting streaked brown, gold, and amber. *Watership Down*, by Richard Adams. Pippin vaguely remembered a cartoon movie version of the story, but if she'd seen it as a child, she didn't remember. She crouched to pick it up, the question of how it had ended up on the floor circling in her mind. Books didn't just magically fly off the shelves. Usually.

She turned the well-worn paperback over in her hands. There had to be a reason it was just lying there for her to find. She could figure out how it got there later...if there was even an explanation. For now, though, she went with her gut, which told her it was important. She sat at the desk and placed the spine on the blotter. "What do you have to tell me?" she asked quietly, as if the book itself had ears and could hear and respond to her question. She didn't know how her bibliomancy worked. She just knew that it did.

She let go of the front and back covers, letting them fall open. Pages fluttered briefly, and then they settled. Instantly, the words of a single paragraph darkened. Undulated. Lifted and seemed to hover just above the page. She blinked, as if her eyes were playing tricks on her, but no, the words were still there, waiting for her to read them.

> *"Bigwig was right when he said he wasn't like a rabbit at all," said Holly. "He was a fighting animal—fierce as a rat or a dog. He fought because he actually felt safer fighting than running. He was brave, all right. But it wasn't natural; and that's why it was bound to finish him in the end. He was trying to do something that Frith never meant any rabbit to do. I believe he'd have hunted like the elil if he could."*

Pippin read the passage over. And then again. Grey, in a moment of skepticism, had told her that any message was impossible to interpret because she was the one who assigned meaning to it, and that meaning came from her experiences and her knowledge. He was right, but at the same time, he was wrong. She—and whoever was with her when she used her divination—did interpret the messages from the books. But sometimes they were perfectly clear and didn't need analysis or mystical deciphering.

Like now.

She was like this character Bigwig. She was an animal, fighting for the safety of her family. She fought because it was safer than not fighting. Safer than running. Because Cassie had already proved that running didn't work. Pippin's mother had left Cape Misery on the Oregon coast, ending up on the Outer Banks of North Carolina. She'd traded one ocean for another, but she hadn't been able to hide from the curse. It had still taken her.

And, of course, there were all the Lanes who had come before. Artemis, who they thought had changed his name from O'Dulany to Lane on the passage over from Ireland. The curse had taken his wife—Pippin's great-great-grandmother, Siobhan—during the crossing. The Pacific Ocean had taken Artemis. The fact of the matter was that the curse could not be outrun.

She went back to the lines from the book. Like the Bigwig character, Pippin was brave. And as Holly said about Bigwig in the paragraph, Pippin's battle also wasn't natural. She was at war with Tuatha dé Danann. They were Ireland's race of mythological deities...only they were *real*. They were real and because of them, the entire Lane family was forever doomed. No, not forever.

God, her head ached. She woke Sailor and they left the Burrow. In the bedroom, they both settled in their beds. Sailor stretched and made a mewling sound. She envied her dog. Sailor had nothing to worry about. She was fed, walked, played with, and loved. It was an easy existence. Or at least it was now. When the dog had been on her own, scrounging for food and trying just to survive, life hadn't been so carefree. Once Pippin got the dog to trust her, things had changed. They had each other. And Pippin had Grey, Daisy and Ruby, Lily, Hattie Juniper Pickle, Cyrus McAdams, and Jamie. She had a community of people around her now. Even with all her support, would the battle to break the curse finish her, as Bigwig's unnatural fight was bound to finish him?

"I guess that remains to be seen," Pippin muttered. Eventually, she drifted off to sleep.

Keep Reading

ACKNOWLEDGMENTS

Much thanks to my amazing readers, those who are part of the review club, and to Barbara Marquart and Susan Slovinsky. I really appreciate each and every one of you!

ABOUT THE AUTHOR

Melissa Bourbon is the national bestselling author of more than 30 mystery books, including the Pippin Lane Hawthorne (Book Magic) novels, the Lola Cruz PI series, the Harlow Cassidy (Magical Dressmaking) Mystery series, the Bread Shop Mysteries, written as Winnie Archer.

She is a former middle school English teacher who gave up the classroom in order to live in her imagination full time. Melissa, a California native who has lived in Texas and Colorado, now calls the southeast home.

A former secondary English/Language Arts teacher and Creative Writing teacher with Southern Methodist University's CAPE program and the Osher Lifelong Learning Institution with North Carolina State University, she has applied her love of teaching to the creation of WriterSpark Academy, an online school for aspiring and new writers seeking to hone their craft.

When she is not writing or igniting her WriterSpark through teaching, she hikes, practices yoga, cooks, and cuddles with her precious rescue pups, Bean, the pug, Dobby, the chug, and Pippin, the pint-sized super mutt. With her five kids scattered throughout the country, she and her husband are enjoying the empty nest.Learn more about Melissa at her website, www.melissabourbon.com, on Facebook @MelissaBourbon/Winnie ArcherBooks, on Instagram and TikTok @bookishly_cozy, and learn about about WriterSpark at www.writersparkacademy.com.

VISIT Melissa's website at http://www.melissabourbon.com

JOIN her online book club at https://www.facebook.com/groups/BookWarriors/

JOIN her book review club at https://facebook.com/melissaanddianesreviewclub

ALSO BY MELISSA BOURBON

Book Magic Mysteries

The Secret on Rum Runner's Lane

Murder in Devil's Cove

Murder at Sea Captain's Inn

Murder Through an Open Door

Murder and an Irish Curse

Lola Cruz, PI Novels

Living the Vida Lola

Hasta la Vista, Lola!

Bare-Naked Lola

What Lola Wants

Drop Dead, Lola

Harlow Cassidy (Magical Dressmaking) Mysteries

Pleating for Mercy

A Fitting End

Deadly Patterns

A Custom-Fit Crime

A Killing Notion

A Seamless Murder

Bread Shop Mysteries, *written as Winnie Archer*

Kneaded to Death

Crust No One

The Walking Bread

Flour in the Attic

Dough or Die

Death Gone a-Rye

A Murder Yule Regret

Bread Over Troubled Water

Mystery/Suspense

Silent Obsession

Silent Echoes

Deadly Legends Boxed Set

Paranormal Romance

Storiebook Charm

Made in United States
Orlando, FL
03 August 2023

35744177R00193